Also by Leif Davidsen

THE SARDINE DECEPTION

The Russian Singer

RANDOM HOUSE NEW YORK

The
Russian
Singer

LEIF DAVIDSEN

Translated from the Danish by

Jørgen Schiøtt

Library of Congress Cataloging-in-Publication Data
Davidsen, Leif.
[Russiske sangerinde. English]
The Russian singer/by Leif Davidsen.
    p.   cm.
Translation of: Den russiske sangerinde.
ISBN 0-394-58502-X
I. Title.
PT8176.14.A8R813   1991   839.8'1374—dc20   90-8828

Manufactured in the United States of America
98765432
First American Edition

Book design by Lilly Langotsky

This book is fiction, but it would be absurd to maintain that it is not based on my experiences through four years in Moscow as a correspondent of the Danish Broadcasting Company. However, any resemblance to persons living or dead is unintended and accidental. It is dedicated to Ulla for her invaluable help.

Part One

WINTER

Contempt of the law, fraud, corruption, and
encouragement to servility and flattery have had a
fatal effect on the morals of the society . . . the
spread of alcohol and drugs and the increase of
crime have become indicative of the decay.

MIKHAIL GORBACHEV, JANUARY 1987

1

Never take things for granted, especially not at night, when you are lonesome and alone. It was the second night of the new year. Soon I would be forty, and I was trying to take stock of my life. I had to decide if it were still worth fighting to save my marriage to Susanne.

As often before, I was looking down upon the scarred asphalt of the Sadovaya, where the frozen mixture of ice, gravel, and snow looked like a bandage that should have been changed a long time ago. The Sadovaya is the ring road that surrounds the center of Moscow like a cigar band. It means the Garden Road, but like almost everything else in the city, the beautiful name covered an unpleasant reality. The Soviet Union is a society that distinguishes itself by describing lies as truths and staring them straight in the face before turning its back on them, pretending that they do not exist.

It was a white and icy night. The frosty air was so brittle that sounds crackled before reaching one's ear. A petrified night, when chimney smoke and exhaust from the few cars danced in the blurred light like luring elves in a bog. A deep-frozen night, when the dark stillness of Moscow grew even quieter, so that all lonely and unhappy people did not know what to do with themselves; when the choice seemed to be between the bottle and suicide. It was early January, and the cold cut deeper than the thermometer showed, because it had come from the depths of Siberia surprisingly and suddenly after days of thaw and slush and false promises of impending spring.

Like many times before, I stood by the window smoking my pipe and looking out over the lifeless city, seemingly abandoned by people. I looked out at yellow façades and blackish blue windows. The scaly, dark yellow color of the dilapidated buildings was mottled with black splotches. Sharp icicles hung like fangs along the roofs. The telephone rang. I answered it, and life was never the same again: it spoke of death and mutilation.

The guard at the embassy was calling, with panic in his young voice.

"They have killed Sonia! And another one, too! They say she's dead! What am I to do?" he screamed in my ear.

"Pull yourself together and tell me what you know."

"But they say she's dead, and they won't touch anything until someone from the embassy gets there, and what am I going to tell them at home in the ministry?"

"Peter, get a hold of yourself, goddamnit! This instant!"

I cut him off in the most authoritative tone of voice that I could muster. There were three guards at the embassy in Moscow, serving in a twenty-four-hour watch rotation. They had had fourteen months of intensive Russian during military service and were then enlisted to answer telephones, watch the telex and the entrance, interpret and translate, and issue visas to the Russians who had been permitted to travel to Denmark. They were all quite young, about twenty years old, and their cocksureness was only superficial.

While the guard was catching his breath, I thought about

Sonia for a moment. She was one of the secretaries and had come to join us from a post in Madrid six months earlier. She was red-haired and very sexy, if you liked the vampy type.

My pipe had gone out, and I put it down on the bookshelf while I heard the short, hard puffs of his breathing calm down little by little. Below on the Sadovaya a truck rattled by, probably carrying black-market merchandise at the hour of the wolf. I thought about what it might be, mainly to clear my brain and make room for the information that he was about to give me, which would require decisions, action, and activity. Cement for a Party boss who wanted to build a small summer house for himself, a private dacha? Food for a private market transported in a state-owned truck against good payment? Or maybe rare goods like fruits from the south, beef of good quality, caviar, or hard-to-get spare parts for Lada cars? Or, hottest on the black market right now, video machines and tapes? The apparent calm of Moscow covers all the human vices and crimes.

"OK, Peter. Now tell me, or do you want me to come by?"

"No," he said more calmly. "You have to go to her apartment on Kutusovsky."

"Tell me what happened."

"They called from the Ministry of Foreign Affairs a couple of minutes ago. They said that they had received a call from the police. They've found Sonia dead in her apartment, and because she's a diplomat, they won't do anything till someone from the Danish embassy gets there."

"You said 'murdered' a moment ago?"

"That's what they said . . . killed, they said in Russian."

"Did the person you talked with identify himself?"

"Yes. Vladimir Basov. You know him, don't you?"

"Yes," I answered. I was very relieved. Basov was professional, experienced, and not particularly square for a representative of the Soviet Union. I found it hard to believe that Sonia could have been murdered—diplomats are rarely murdered in

6

Moscow—but I feared a suicide, which unfortunately is something not entirely unknown in Moscow diplomatic circles, particularly among unemployed wives. But who the hell was the other person, then? That is, if there really was another.

"Have you gotten hold of CW?" I asked. CW was our ambassador, a man who ran the embassy in an uncomplicated and nonauthoritarian manner with a minimum of clichés, formalities, and bureaucracy, much to my delight and to the deep annoyance of our ministerial counselor.

"CW doesn't answer."

"You know that he must have gone to bed not long ago, and he always takes a sleeping pill."

"Of course, that's right. What do you want me to do?" The voice was pleading, but he was breathing more normally.

"First you call back the Soviet Ministry of Foreign Affairs and tell them that I'm on my way. Then you send a telex to Copenhagen about what we know so far, and that I'm looking into the matter. But don't make too much of the murder business. Just write 'found dead,' and that I'm investigating the matter. Report to follow immediately. Then you go to the residence and wake up CW and tell him that I've gone to the apartment and will come by the embassy to report afterward. And you'd better get hold of Castesen as well and tell him to come," I added rather reluctantly.

I knew that Peter was bright enough, and that he would do as he was told without thinking too much about it. CW would take a long time to wake up, but coffee and cigarettes would make him effective. I had no great respect for his professional knowledge of the country that he happened to be in, but he was an experienced old hand with a well-developed political instinct for survival, and he possessed the most important virtue in diplomacy, which is the ability to tread water. Castesen was our dear ministerial counselor and the second in command at the embassy. He was the most important reason that I was strongly considering asking for a transfer.

"I'll take care of it all, don't worry," Peter said. "I sure am glad I got hold of you. You weren't in bed yet?"

There were a number of questions that I would have liked to ask him, but I didn't want to upset him more for now. He was necessary to keep the lines of communication open. We still needed him in case a Dane called from Outer Siberia having lost his passport, or if the big bang were to come on this particular, freezing January night. As his last action here on earth, he would have the honor of telling Copenhagen that the missiles were on their way; but before his message arrived, there would already be no one left alive to receive it. Still, he would have done his duty.

"Now just do as I've told you," I said, and hung up.

In the courtyard the cold stung my cheeks and nose, but worse, it thrust up underneath my coat and cut deeply into my thighs like knives. The cars stood like white sculptures in the dimly lit and fenced-in rectangle that served as a courtyard for this Moscow ghetto, where foreigners were kept segregated from good Soviet citizens.

Through the gateway I could see the guard shake himself in his small, brown sentry box. He appeared to be sleeping, but when I opened the door of the car with a crunching sound, he stepped out of his box and stared at me with an expression of amazement beneath the gray fur cap. He stood for a moment to make sure that I really had the intention of leaving, then he went back into the sentry box to phone his control center. He probably warned them that yet another foreigner was now loose in the streets of Moscow—better lock up impressionable minds.

Normally the surveillance did not bother me. It was almost a part of the everyday street scene. Local color, like the over-sized banners with visionary slogans announcing the imminent victory of communism.

The Volvo growled like a wounded animal, but then first one cylinder started, then the next, and I backed out with the steam of the exhaust like a whirling cloak around the rattling car, making the sentry disappear for a moment, until I managed to swing the rear end out, shifted into first, and rolled down the tire ruts in the deep snow of the hill. The guard's piercing eyes followed me through the small windows from which he watched over his little part of Moscow's world.

I made a U-turn and speeded up as I reached the ring road itself. There was very little traffic, and the hard mixture of gravel and ice was no problem for the snow tires. For the quarter of an hour that it took to drive out to the ghetto where Sonia lived—had lived—I tried to remember what I actually knew about her. It was not a whole lot.

She was sweet. She was sexy. Aggressive. Good at her job. Red-haired. Medium height. Great figure. Unmarried, like all the secretaries. Moscow was her third post. Late twenties, I imagined. That was all.

But what was she like as a person? I had to admit that I had no idea. She did her job. We would chat at work, but each of us lived our own private life. What were her dreams? Her opinions outside of the service? Did she have any particular political inclinations? A father and a mother—other family? Whom should we contact? It would be in her papers. But who was she really? Not just a functionary, looking at the world from her desk at one of our many Danish embassies. One afternoon she had made a pass at me, I suddenly remembered. I had come into her office with a letter for her to type, and she had deliberately turned her beautiful, oval face up toward me and pressed her breast against my shirtsleeve. I had pulled back my arm. One of my few principles: no sex with the personnel—especially not subordinates.

I placed myself in the left lane close to the one in the middle that was reserved for the shiny, black official vehicles. Most of the transparent cages in every intersection, which contained a policeman during the day, were empty now, so no watchful eyes followed me through the black winter night. As usual, the dim street lighting and the lack of glittering advertisements and illuminated shop windows made Moscow appear like a city in a constant energy crisis, and the few cars that I met either had the yellow license plates of journalists and businessmen or the red ones of diplomats. The gloominess of the night was accentuated by the fact that all the cars used only their parking lights. Every now and then a yellow, run-down Volga taxi clattered by with cakes of dirt on the sides, and windows that were iced over because of the inadequate ventilation system.

If it were really a case of murder, and if there were one more person involved, like Peter had said, we were in for trouble.

Instead of thinking about the tragedy of this death itself, I caught myself worrying about the possibility that the other party might be a Russian man. That would complicate the matter considerably—as if it were not complicated enough that a love affair had now ended in double murder. Or maybe double suicide?

Only accredited diplomats like myself have the right and the damned duty to associate with Soviet citizens officially and privately. For security reasons, the secretaries, the cook, and other such employees must not consort privately with Soviet citizens. They are not even allowed to go out alone, but only in the company of other NATO personnel or in friendly company, NATO says. They deal with classified material, often material involving allies, and if we discover that they are breaking the rule and meeting Ivan or others privately, we send them home immediately. That once cost the Danish embassy the best cook in the city. We found out that he practiced his art for a little Russian girlfriend, a student. He was given a couple of days to pack his suitcase. The suspicion that things he had overheard might have been whispered on the pillow was sufficient. The affair gave cause for endless regret at various official dinners for the whole winter. With some luck, the story could still be useful with a languishing dinner partner.

"So, little Sonia," I mumbled to myself. "What have you

been whispering? Sweet pillow talk in the ear of a little lover from Dzherzhinsky-plosyet?"

I passed the American embassy. Two policemen stood in front of the main entrance, stamping their feet against the frozen ground, and their breath moved along as they turned their faces to me. Signaling right, I turned onto Kalinin Prospect and continued along Kutusovsky, where the most important Soviet leaders' apartments are situated. It is also the city's largest ghetto for foreigners.

I had to drive past the complex. It is one of the many inexplicable absurdities of Moscow that you are rarely allowed to make a left turn, so I continued past the block and made a U-turn farther down the prospect, in order to drive back in the direction I had just come from. I finally made a right, turning past dark shop windows into the complex itself. RUSSIAN SOUVENIRS, read the sign above the shop. Not far away were empty vegetable boxes in a mess next to a heap of frozen and spoiled potatoes. Nobody had bothered to clear them away. Probably they had lain there for four days already, waiting for the work brigade whose job it was to remove frozen, rotting potatoes and smashed old boxes. It was unthinkable, of course, that anyone who was not paid to do so would take it into his head to clean up. I was in a gloomy and depressed mood, and all associations seemed to turn negative.

Two policemen stood in the middle of the gateway. Their faces were white as sheets, and not just because of the cold: they were very nervous, I could see. One of them walked up to the car. I rolled down the window just enough so that I could talk with the man and hand him my diplomatic card through the narrow opening.

He took it without a word and studied it carefully in the feeble light. The complex was big. Six hundred families from almost every country in the world lived there, rich Westerners with dollars as well as people from the Third World who were rich in rubles, but poor all the same. Correspondents, diplomats, businesspeople. The only thing they had in common was their status as foreigners. The courtyard was one big mess. Cars had been parked at random, and in between them there were large heaps of snow with sooty surfaces, as if they had been thrown there by some negligent giant. Several cars had almost disappeared underneath a cover of snow and ice. They had been stripped of all their insides and stood drooping on collapsed tires.

The policeman handed the card, in its thin plastic cover, back through the opening and saluted. He screwed up his eyes in his chalk-white face underneath the gray cap with the red badge in the middle.

Sonia's place was in the second block on the right, where the Danish embassy had rented a few apartments. Still, I parked the car in the first spot I found in the rows, backing in between two peeling Ladas, disregarding the fact that the ground was sloping a little. It would be difficult to get the heavy, rear-wheel-driven car out again on the slippery surface.

When I left the car, the cold again cut like knives. The only sound I could hear came from a single car outside on the prospect. The lights were on in several apartments, which could either be offices or private residences. Journalists and cops work around the clock. And diplomats, I thought. There were no sirens, no blinking blue lights, no flashing photographers or inquisitive television people.

But there was someone, of course. When I approached the block, I first saw two patrol cars. MILITSY, it said on their sides: state police. There was a man sitting in each of them. There was also one of the red-and-white ambulances that look like big box vans meant for the transportation of laundry or other goods; and, although they were even more discreetly parked, I also noticed two black Volga cars with curtains in the rear windows.

Yet another policeman stood in the door of Sonia's stairway. He saluted and asked for my documents. I stamped my feet while he scrutinized my Russian ID card. The cold had caught hold of my thighs so firmly that they were already quite numb. The policeman looked as if he not only was indifferent to the cutting cold, but even enjoyed it in the particularly bizarre way that some Russians seem to exult at the wonderful severity and hardness of their winter when the temperature really drops. One more salute and I entered.

There were two guards by the elevator, but they let me pass without asking for identification. The one thing in particular that gave me a strange and uncanny feeling was the silence. No sound came from the apartments. The policemen just looked at me without a word. So the noise seemed almost obscenely loud when I closed the heavy lattice door of the elevator and then the interior doors, and, creaking and hissing, it began its ascent. Down in the stairway the dirty green color of the walls was broken only by the long row of mailboxes streaked with gray. They had come loose on one side and hung askew, as if they might fall down any moment. They had hung like that for the three years that I had frequented the building.

There were four men standing outside Sonia's door, which was slightly ajar. Three of them wore uniforms, while the fourth was dressed in a light-colored, full-length lambskin coat of clearly Western cut. That was Basov. Having spent a lot of time abroad, he possessed that great status symbol: Western clothes and even a pair of elegant hand-sewn boots. They all wore the most Russian of all the accessories of the Moscow winter: the *shapka,* the ubiquitous fur cap. They looked at me as if I were bringing the message that all their privileges in the system would be taken away from them.

They were big shots. Two captains and a colonel. All three dressed in the quality uniforms of the state police, gray coats with shiny buttons and stars in their caps. They nodded at me when I stepped out of the elevator, but none of them, not even Basov, reached out his hand to greet me. So in order not to give them too much of the initiative, I took the diplomatic offensive right away.

"I see, gentlemen, that you have been inside already in spite of the diplomatic status of the apartment," I said.

"Your Russian will make it easier." It was the colonel who spoke, a stout man with a heavy face, sad and red-veined. A battleground of vodka bottles. It was probably a face that had been shaped by a hobby which consisted of drilling holes in the ice and spending entire Sundays fishing as an excuse for taking a pull or two at the bottle to keep the cold at bay.

"You have no right to force your way into a diplomatic preserve alone."

Basov stepped forward. His short, compact body radiated friendliness, and his face was one big broad smile. He was the most un-Russian of all the Russians I knew in Moscow. He reminded me most of all of a successful lawyer somewhere in the Midwest of the United States. He had served at the Soviet embassy in Washington and had only recently been down-graded to the Scandinavian department of the Soviet Ministry of Foreign Affairs. Why, I did not know. The Ministry of Foreign Affairs was, like other Soviet institutions, paralyzed and petrified under what was now the third dying leader isolated in the Kremlin. The resulting insecurity expressed itself in an unbearable mixture of inferiority complex and persecution mania, combined with completely unrealistic arrogance and megalomania. But Basov handled the situation better than most. His years in the United States had infused him with a good portion of robust American humor.

"Hello Jack! Nice to see you! How are you doing?" Like that. As if we were not standing in front of a door behind which, they said, a member of the staff of the Royal Danish Embassy lay dead, but had run into each other like so many times before at some reception and were now going to pump each other politely, so that we could both go home and draft a small, appropriate report to show how fantastically well-informed and analytical we were. However, it did take a little of the ugliness out of the atmosphere, although the three men in uniform still looked as if they did not quite know how to take my defiance. They were not used to having their authority questioned.

"Basov, you at any rate know the rules!" We had discarded formal address between us at a bibulous lunch some months earlier. Strictly speaking, it was against the rules of both systems, but we got along well together and both belonged to a newer generation in the service.

"It was an emergency. Only the guard who gave the alarm has been inside. And only for a moment. You'll see why for yourself."

"But why did he have to go in there in the first place?"

"The smell, Jack."

It was heavy, warm, and rotten, like beef that has lain for too long on a hot day at the private market, where farmers sell the products from their small allotments. At first I had not perceived it as unpleasant, but now I did. It was nasty. It not only burned in your nostrils, it smothered and stunned your nose; it was nauseating. We were all sweating in our heavy coats.

"May I see your identification?" I said instead.

Without a word the colonel reached out his hand and let me have a glimpse of the red ID card that belongs either to the Office of Public Prosecution or the officers of the KGB. I had not thought for a minute that he belonged to the police of the Ministry of the Interior. Of course, they called the KGB right away when a foreigner was involved. He was a representative of the Second Directorate, which spent a great deal of its plentiful resources on watching over the doings of foreigners in the Socialist fatherland. Basov was also groping for his card underneath his coat. The two other uniforms did not stir:

subordinates have no identity when their superiors do the talking.

"That's not necessary, Vladimir Alexandrovich," I said, and Basov smiled.

"Then maybe we could get to the point?" It was the colonel with the dissipated face. He took one step forward, so that he stood in front of Basov. He wanted to make clear that he was the one in command.

I said nothing. He held my gaze, waiting for me to give in. He would be a good poker player.

"I'm waiting," I then said, reluctantly. He straightened himself a little, pushing forward his chest in the heavy gray military coat with the silvery buttons. He smelled faintly of garlic. But there was no alcohol on his breath, and his gray eyes were quite clear.

"On behalf of the Office of Public Prosecution of Moscow we request permission to officially investigate apartment number forty-five, Kutusovsky Prospect seven."

I waited, and he took out a sheet of paper from a small black briefcase that he carried over his shoulder next to his service pistol.

"The purpose of the investigation is to elucidate under what circumstances two not yet identified persons have died, following information carried out shortly after midnight by the person living above the apartment, on the basis that the informer felt strongly inconvenienced by the smell from the aforesaid apartment."

He paused. Then I cut in.

"If you insist on being formal then state the names, dates, and times instead."

He really was a good poker player. He didn't bat an eye, but held my gaze like before.

"We are wasting time," I said. "Let's just get into the god-damned apartment."

"Does that mean that we have your permission and consequently the permission of the Danish embassy to undertake such an investigation?"

"Yes! And now let's get inside." I was going to push past him, but he didn't budge. The two captains discreetly moved over in front of the entrance, from where the rotten smell came.

"Would you be kind enough to sign here?" the colonel said, handing me the paper. I should have known. Of course, they had to have it in writing. Soviet rule is based on the military and on heaps of paper. The purpose of most of the paper is to avert blame. Nobody in the Soviet Union voluntarily takes on responsibility. I groped for a pen inside my coat, and just when I was about to sign, it occured to me that maybe I'd better read what I was signing. It was more or less what he had read, but with the names of the various people who had been involved so far. There were four identical copies, and I initialed all four.

"The whole name, please," the colonel said. I signed my full name on one of the four sheets. That had to be enough. I pocketed the pen again. He stood for a moment, then he raised an eyebrow, and Basov produced his pen. Mine had been an ordinary blue one which had cost about fifty cents. Basov's was an expensive Parker.

Basov signed with his full name.

"And now maybe we can get inside!" I said.

The colonel looked at me. "When you see what's awaiting you, you'll regret your impatience," he said in a tone of sinister prophecy.

2

Colonel Gavrilin led the way. He was right, of course; but not quite. The colonel could not know that I had spent my military service in the medical corps and had earned extra money at a hospital. I had seen corpses before—but not corpses that stank.

The smell was the worst part. The hall was overheated, but looked normal. The central heating was turned on at full blast, and the windows were hermetically closed. In the living room a television set connected to a video machine was droning, white dots dancing across the screen. The video was on, too, with its green button lit. A lamp had been turned over, but was still burning. The room was furnished with a dining table and four chairs, a sofa and a coffee table, two old upholstered armchairs, and a carpet of indeterminate brownish colors that had once included red. That was the living room, but it was not where the dead women were.

They lay in the bathroom and in the bedroom.

Sonia had taken the last bath of her life. Her red hair clung to her face, just above the surface of the water. The outline of

her body could be only vaguely distinguished. The blood that
had left her body from her cut wrists was discolored brown by
now, in the cold water. Her forehead was bruised, as if she had
changed her mind at the very last minute and tried to move,
to stop an irreversible process. Her eyes were closed, strangely
enough. She was milky white in the slimy water, which had
run into the tub for her last bath a long time before: the light
of the electric water heater was off indicating that the water in
the container had had time to again become scalding hot.

The other woman lay on her stomach on the double bed, her
white buns like small hills on the black sheets. The eiderdown
lay on the floor together with a leather whip. Her hair, brownish and long and covering her face, was parted in the back,
revealing a narrow leather string that had been tightened
around her neck. It had cut deeply into her skin. On her back
were four small birthmarks placed so symmetrically right
above the small of the back that it looked as if they had been
tattooed. Her toenails were painted red. From beneath a lock
of her hair a large open eye was staring, as if in a suspended
scream. I did not know whether I should construe the scream
as an expression of fear. I had read, of course, that orgasm can
be felt more intensely if the large carotid artery is pressed, that
is, if one is close to being strangled. I had also read that it could
end in tragedy. It was an old-fashioned bed, large and wide
with real posts. The woman's wrists and ankles were tied to the
posts with leather strings, but the knots were loose, almost like
bow knots, and could easily have been untied. On the floor lay
something that appeared to be her clothes. It was probably
against all the rules, but I picked up a blouse. It was made of
thin, blue cotton, but easily covered up her obscenely exposed
sex between her widely spread legs.

The colonel had been right. I regretted my impatience.

The captains had remained in the hall, growing even paler
in the heavy, hideous smell. The colonel, Basov, and I walked
around together. First we found the woman in the bedroom.

And then Sonia in the liver-colored water. Then Basov left us, and I could hear him throw up in the toilet next to the small kitchen with the old gas cooker and the mixed-gray cabinets containing the essentials.

I knew the apartment very well. It was badly in need of repair and new furniture, but the Ministry of Foreign Affairs had to economize, and the apartments of the secretaries in Moscow were not on top of anybody's list. It had been a year since the last time I had been there. Castesen and I had looked it over together, and he had written in his report that the apartment was in such good condition that there was no need for repairs. I suddenly remembered, while we were contemplating Sonia in the bathtub, that in the same report Castesen had called attention to the fact that his own apartment, on the other hand, needed a new bathroom. Which it got, of course. "Gentlemen don't take showers," Castesen had said, without the slightest touch of irony, when he had tried to explain to me why he wanted to tear down a rather new shower cubicle in order to make room for a new and bigger bathtub.

Sonia should have had a shower cubicle.

"May I?" the colonel calmly asked. He stood by the telephone. I nodded, and with almost meticulous movements that did not suit his coarse hands, with the bitten and dirty fingernails, he took out a handkerchief and lifted the receiver. Then he checked himself and put it down again without dialing the number.

"Officer, come here!" he shouted. The colonel was a hard old devil, but the officer was not. He was quite pale, and sweat was dripping from his fur cap, which he had not taken off. I stood with mine in my hand. The colonel had kept his on, too, but there was not one drop of sweat on his red-veined face. His eyes were quite cold. He stood with his legs far apart, shifting his weight first forward and then backward without being able to find a comfortable position.

"The Criminal Investigation Department. The entire investigative team. Right away," he commanded. The officer turned on his heels without a word and left the room, with a relief that was visible even from behind. The colonel took off his fur cap, but did not wipe his forehead. I did, and unbuttoned my coat. Basov entered. His face was white, and his wispy hair fell down over one eye. He had unbuttoned his fine imported coat, and there were stains on his pin-striped suit. Basov was muscular and compact and apparently tried to compensate for his lack of height by building up his muscles. He had a narrow waist and heavy, strong shoulders with short, thick arms that ended in a pair of much-too-small hands.

"Let's watch some television," I said in English.

"OK," the colonel said, "but use a cloth." He had spoken English as well. I raised my head and looked straight at him, but his face did not change its expression and his gaze remained empty. Over the droning growl of the television monitor I could hear Basov's heavy, lisping breath.

In this Kleenex era gentlemen no longer carry handker-chiefs, at any rate not when the gentleman is me. Apparently the colonel knew that. Without a word he handed me his.

I pressed PLAY, the video looped in the tape, and the image flickered through. Next to the television there was a pile of videotapes; about five or six. They seemed to have been used. There were also videotapes next to the video itself, but they were still wrapped in their plastic seals. A couple of seconds later the image appeared clearly on the screen.

"*Bossemoi*, my God," the colonel exclaimed between his clenched teeth. It gave me a perverse pleasure that he not only reacted, but even invoked the Lord. That becomes an atheist. Basov reacted more profanely and let out a long, fluent Russian oath, brilliantly suited to the television program.

It was pure, unadulterated pornography in clear colors and natural sound. The participants were three women and two men, and what they were engaged in was yet another attempt to create something new on the master and slave theme. All five performers appeared to have access to a well-equipped shop selling the bizarre paraphernalia that enter into sadomaso-chistic relationships. There was everything: whips, masks, chains, and steel-spiked vests, besides a good deal of erected organs and exposed sexes submitted to various kinds of torture. My taste is considerably more down-to-earth, and at my age pornography has become something only moderately interest-ing that can no longer shock, only surprise.

The colonel and Basov did not feel that way. Now they were both sweating, and their faces were filled with a mixture of abhorrence and fascination, lust and disgust.

All that I could think of was that the Danish embassy in Moscow was facing its most difficult task ever, if this situation was to be solved without resulting in unnecessary tensions in Danish-Soviet relations. With their usual ingenuity the Rus-sians would use the scandal for pressure in every area from bilateral trade to defense politics.

I pressed STOP, and could practically hear the air whistle out of their lungs. Their inhalation of the hot, saturated air of the apartment was just as audible when I fast-forwarded and again pressed PLAY. More hardcore pornography, but something of an anticlimax, I should think. It was quite normal. One man, one woman, one water bed. But still, the acrobatic positions that they switched between with lightning speed were impres-sive. Basov and the colonel stepped closer and began to breathe faster. Actually, the girl was beautiful and the man well-equipped, but they both had that completely blank and disin-terested expression on their faces that makes me think most pornography is about as exciting as the telephone directory.

I let them watch. It gave me time to think and look ahead instead of wasting time on futile considerations about the hor-ror of the whole situation. I was a cynical devil, that's what Susanne always said. She herself was so emotional that she could become furious whenever I offered rational solutions to problems that, deep down inside, she did not believe could be solved in a rational manner.

I think that everything in this life must begin with an analysis of the situation, and on the basis of that analysis you calculate, decide, and take action. That clear statement once caused Susanne to throw a potted plant at me, with the remark that I probably hadn't included that in my fancy fucking analysis.

And yet . . . While the representatives of Soviet rule amused themselves watching a male organ disappear miraculously deep down the throat of a heavily made-up girl not much older than fifteen, I tried to figure out what the situation was.

As I walked about in the apartment, I thought that what I saw was simple: sadomasochism that had been taken one step too far and ended in murder. Sonia had got a little too involved in the sex game and had strangled her friend. Conscience-stricken, she had then committed suicide.

I went back into the bathroom. They had really got into it. I remembered that Sonia had a bruise on her forehead, but I just wanted to check. It was warm in the bathroom, but still there were ice ferns on the small window. Beautiful, cool figures like an abstract painting. I could hear a toilet being flushed, and the water hissing in the pipe. From the living room I could still hear the grunting sounds from the television, and a woman screaming in simulated excitement.

I went out in the kitchen.

There was a pot on the electric cooker. It contained the dried-up leftovers of something that looked like a stew. There were some pieces of stiffened, hairy meat and sliced carrots, just about what one could expect during the winter in Moscow. It was what there was. In the sink three plates had been stacked negligently with knives and forks placed casually on top. Why three? There were two empty champagne bottles and an empty vodka bottle. Next to them stood a quarter-full whisky bottle. It was my brand. Ballantine. So why not? I took a pull. It tasted quite normal, so I took another one. It burned my insides and felt good. Suddenly I began to shake all over, and in spite of the ice ferns I saw a head in the kitchen window, pale as death with black holes in place of eyes, and I felt the sweat run down my sides from the armpits. I took one more pull and stopped shaking.

"If you want to break the law and destroy evidence, at least let me be your accomplice."

"Goddamnit, Basov! You could have killed me!"

Basov grinned.

"*Davai!*" he said, reaching out his arm. His eyes were wild and cheery at the same time.

I handed him the bottle. He sarcastically raised it. Being Russian, he *would* propose a toast even in a macabre situation like this, I thought angrily. But he simply put the bottle to his mouth and took a long swig. He held out the bottle to me inquiringly. I shook my head. He took another swig.

"What the hell are you doing?"

The colonel stood in the doorway, his heavy body filling the narrow entrance. His red face stood out sharply against the muddy-gray kitchen cabinets and the cheap tile floor. Being loose, the tiles shook as he stepped forward and pulled the bottle out of Basov's hand. Basov looked like a schoolboy who had been flogged, even though he was compact as a boxer.

"Shit, so what!" the colonel said, and took a long pull himself. To make our alliance complete, we each took one more, and the colonel finished the bottle in one gulp. It's against every Russian's nature to recork the bottle once it has been opened.

I felt better by now, but I was still sweating. I took off my coat and held it over my arm.

We stood in silence. No one seemed to have anything to say. None of us felt like being in the bedroom near the body and the pornography, or in the bathroom, where Sonia lay, with cut wrists and bruised forehead, staring into the ceiling through the lids of her closed eyes.

Fortunately, we were soon rescued by the arrival of the team from the Criminal Investigation Department. With un-Russian efficiency, indicating that perhaps the capital of socialism had more deaths requiring investigation than appeared from *Pravda*'s coverage, they began their investigation. The Soviet Union had not published any criminal statistics for years.

I made the fingerprint experts begin with the telephone and then called the embassy.

The ambassador himself answered the call.

"How bad is it?" he simply asked. He was wide awake.

"Worse than you can imagine."

I heard him breathe into the receiver. I could almost hear the unuttered questions that I knew he would never ask over an open phone.

"OK. Come when you can. Is there anything I can do in the meantime?"

"I'm staying here for now to check possible papers. But you might send a guard. He should be able to take it . . . once Sonia is out of here."

Around me there was hectic, but professional and very efficient, activity. Photographs were taken. A physician had first examined the girl on the bed and then gone into the bathroom. Technicians had begun to go over the living room. Their leader was a man of about fifty with small, almost black eyes and fingers that were yellow from nicotine.

I kept wishing that they would open the windows. The smell and the heat became even more oppressive now that there were so many of us in the living room. Outside in the hall I could see the ambulance personnel with stretchers and white sheets to cover the bodies. It was so final. So clear that this was serious and that it was the end for Sonia.

"Is there anything else I should do?" The ambassador sounded impatient, as if he were repeating the question for the third time. If that were the case, then I hadn't heard him the first two times.

"You might say a prayer for Sonia's soul. She's going to need it," I said.

"I'll do that," he answered dryly. CW still had his Christian faith. Mine evaporated when I began to take an interest in the world around me.

The investigation continued methodically. There was not much for me to do, so I sat down on a chair and looked at all the confused activity, which apparently proceeded according to a certain system. Every now and then I was handed a paper. I checked that it did not contain any classified information. It never did, not once. Sonia might have had many secrets, but being a traitor to her country did not appear to have been one of them. I felt just as filthy as the whole situation. It somehow got a little better after they had wrapped Sonia in a body bag and taken her away. The other woman was left lying on the bed after the physician had examined her, but they did, after all, cover her with a grayish sheet. Basov sat down by my side. We sat without saying anything.

The first thing that the colonel had done was to find the other woman's internal passport. That meant she was a Soviet citizen. The internal passport has to be carried by all Soviet citizens. It states what nationality or ethnic group a person is, Russian, Jewish, Estonian, and so on, where he works and, most importantly, where he has his residence permit, his *propiska*. You cannot settle down anywhere you want.

The colonel had not shown me the red passport, but had given it to a young chap in civilian clothes who had been sweating from eagerness, without knowing what to do with himself for a long time. He left with the passport. That had been a couple of hours ago, and now the result stood in the doorway. A too-heavily made-up young girl in a cheap coat of imitation fur, high heels, with a sullen and morose, but also pretty, face underneath a knitted cap. Fast work.

The colonel stared at her in that arrogant way that only Soviet officials can look at their subjects. A mixture of contempt and indifference with a twist of sexual interest. She was attractive, even if she was wearing much too much makeup for my taste. Painted as if she came straight from the stage. A face like a mask, expressing practically no emotion. Suddenly I admired her for that. Many Soviet girls would have looked frightened out of their wits face to face with the colonel, not to mention the apartment—and in a police state even innocent people often feel guilty in the presence of the authorities. She immediately had a head start.

"What do you want with me?" she asked. Her voice was pleasant, and I detected a slight accent in her Russian. It sounded a little like mine, and yet it was different. Baltic, I guessed.

She took off her thick, knitted cap. Her hair was blond. She also unbuttoned her coat. Underneath it she wore a long, tight-fitting dress, which shone like cheap, imitation silk. She wore typical knee-length, dark Russian boots, the kind that could be seen on women's legs everywhere this winter, as if they were in the army and had had them handed out by some disinterested sergeant. She probably had her shoes in her handbag, which was big enough to hold a quick buy in case hard-to-get articles should turn up. Shoes were always brought along. Boots were necessary if you wanted to survive in eight months of slush or on rugged, frost-buckled sidewalks and streets.

"What do you want with me?" she again asked.

The colonel looked at her for a long time. He held her red internal passport in his hand and then slowly read. "Lilli Ivanova Smuul: What kind of goddamned name is that?"

She did not bat an eyelash.

"It is mine," she said simply.

"Are you from the Baltic republics?" The colonel could not quite get over the fact that she did not seem more frightened.

"I was born in Estonia."

"Yes, it says in your passport that you are registered as Estonian."

She just nodded.

"Your sister had another last name, but you have the same middle name." It sounded like an accusation rather than like a question.

"My sister kept our father's name. I took my mother's," she said flatly.

"And why?"

"That's my own private decision," she said, again with only the faintest suggestion of emotion in her voice. Bravo, I thought. Don't let the asshole intimidate you! And he gave it up, too. Maybe because I was present. Estonians and Russians do not exactly have the reputation of loving each other.

"Are you registered at the following address together with your sister, Vera?" He read an address that I did not catch. Moscow is surrounded by an endless zone of suburbs, one concrete high-rise after the other.

She nodded.

"Then come here!" The colonel barked out the order. That became too much for Basov, after all. He gently took the young girl by the arm and led her over to the dead woman, who was still covered by the sheet.

"I'm afraid it isn't particularly pleasant, Comrade Smuul," Basov said, using the formal form of address among Soviet citizens.

The colonel smiled a little contemptuously. I had a headache. A dull pain in the back of my neck. The whisky was burning in my throat. It was very warm in the small apartment. The colonel took one long step ahead of Basov, reaching the bed with the grayish sheet before him. Quickly, he pulled the sheet back so far that both the distorted face with the leather string and the half-exposed breasts of the twisted body were revealed. I could tell that once again Basov felt deeply uncomfortable. He was cursing inside, I felt, probably cursing the usual arrogance of the KGB. But the girl stayed composed. A faint shiver by the mouth, a short audible inhalation, but the painted mask stayed impassive. All that I could see was that the color drained away beneath the thick layer of powder.

She nodded a couple of times.

"Yes, that's Vera."

The colonel still held the sheet pulled back. "You are sure?"

"Yes. I'm sure."

"Damn you!" I said in English, pulling the sheet out of the colonel's hand and covering her up. For a second he looked surprised, then angry, but he ended with a slightly amazed expression. He then motioned the two ambulance people who stood waiting with the dark blue body bag.

"You can go ahead and take it away now!" he said. The authority must always have the last say.

"As for you, Citizen Lilli Ivanova Smuul, you are hereby summoned to appear for interrogation tomorrow."

She just nodded, standing as if in another world, but seemed relieved that apparently she was allowed to leave.

Suddenly I had the feeling that I had seen her before, but could not remember where. Her eyes were green. They were the only part of her frozen face that appeared to be alive. Her beautiful lips were pressed together.

"When was the last time you saw your sister?" the colonel asked.

She had good nerves. She just turned her head a little toward the colonel. Her skin was white and transparent on the neck where the makeup ended.

"More than two weeks ago. I've already told that to your assistant." She nodded in the direction of the young man in the stiff suit, whom the colonel had sent off with the dead girl's internal passport.

"And now you're telling *me*! You're registered at your sister's address. Where was she for so long?"

"She went her own way. You know that better than I."

"Where did she take her foreign . . . " the colonel hesitated and threw a glance in my direction before he continued, ". . . foreign business connections?"

"That I don't know."

"Home to you, maybe?" he went on, switching to the informal form of address to show his contempt. "Is that what you're saying, citizen? So that you could share the loot? Possession of foreign currency is a serious crime."

I was beginning to admire her. She didn't let herself be intimidated.

"You know very well that's not true. The police have been to see us before."

Basov whispered something into the colonel's ear. The girl looked over at me. Her face was expressionless, and the green eyes held mine for only a second, then she looked away again.

"You are an honest citizen, Comrade Smuul, so I understand." The colonel said it without irony and then continued in a gentler voice, "You don't know where Vera has been?"

"No, I never did. But we had an agreement. No business connections in our house. I did not want that."

"Then where did she go?"

"I never asked."

"But you were family, after all. People normally confide in their family."

"Certain things are better left unsaid."

The colonel was shifting his weight on the balls of his feet. Basov cleared his throat. I think he was trying to get the colonel to stop this interrogation in front of a foreigner. The girl also seemed to think that dirty laundry should not be aired in front of capitalists.

"Comrade Kovsun will inform you when and where I wish to speak with you tomorrow." The colonel pointed at the young man in civilian clothes.

"Very well." She turned to leave.

"Comrade Smuul?" She stopped. "You don't seem particularly surprised. Or unhappy!"

It was a question that I, too, had asked myself. Yet Russians rarely display their emotions in public; only when they say good-bye to each other at railroad stations.

"I expected it to end like this with the life she was leading. And even though we were sisters, we didn't share the same outlook on life." I don't know if a Western criminal investigator would have accepted the psychology of such an answer. But it made perfect sense in Russian.

"Then you may go," the colonel said, almost softly.

"Where can your sister have met a Danish girl named Sonia?" I asked. "Do you know anything about that?"

Everybody looked at me with amazement, but I didn't care.

She turned her face to me. Again I was looking straight into her green, strong eyes.

"Jack Andersen, the Danish embassy," I said with a small, ironical bow. She just looked at me, then at the colonel, who nodded.

"My sister spent much time at hotel bars frequented by foreigners."

"But I don't think Sonia did."

"Do you think it or do you know it?"

"Your sister never mentioned Sonia?"

"No."

"Under another name, like a nationality?" This time I held the green eyes as long as I could, until she turned them away. I was getting interested in knowing what was behind the mask.

"Last time I talked with Vera, she didn't say anything, but

one month ago she was very excited. She said that she had met someone, and that her fortune was made."

"What did you say then?"

"I said nothing."

"Isn't that a rather strange reaction, Madame?"

For the first time I received a suggestion of a smile when she heard the old-fashioned, prerevolutionary form of address.

"Not when you got that story at such regular intervals that you stopped believing in it. Dreams don't put food on the table."

"But they nourish the soul better than water."

This time the smile even reached the green eyes. It appeared and disappeared as fast as the shutter of a camera.

"My compliments on your Russian."

"But no Sonia?" I insisted. She shook her head. She would like to leave, I could see. Basov came to her assistance.

"You may leave, Comrade. The representative of the Danish embassy will be fully informed of the results of the investigation."

The colonel looked as if he didn't think that was such a good idea, but he made no comment on Basov's interference.

The girl left, holding her head high and throwing her hair back lightly as she disappeared through the door together with the young officer. In one hand she held her cap, in the other the big handbag. She didn't look back.

The technicians continued their work. Basov offered me a cigarette, and we sat smoking until the guard from the embassy arrived and took over. The bodies were gone, so he took it calmly. He was sufficiently well trained not to ask questions that I would not have answered anyway, in the presence of so many representatives of the Soviet authorities.

In the courtyard, the frost immediately pierced my limbs. Among ghostly white cars the exhalations whirled from cold military faces. Everywhere there was discreet activity. It was getting on for morning, although the darkness was total. I could hear the traffic increase outside on the prospect. My own car started without any problem in the cold, as if it had retained some warmth, but it didn't move. The rear wheels spun around, screeching against the slippery surface. I tried a couple of times. Two policemen were watching with stony, inscrutable faces. They had no intention of helping.

I got out of the car and tried to budge the heavy Volvo. It didn't work. The exhaust was burning in my nose. Then I felt a light pressure on my elbow through the heavy winter parka. There she stood, green eyes. Wrapped from top to toe with her scarf covering the lower part of her face.

"Do you know how to drive?" I asked.

She looked at me, as if the question were quite superfluous. It wasn't. In Moscow women rarely drive cars. They drive trolley buses and streetcars, but not private cars.

She could not reach the pedals, so I leaned forward over her in order to get to the seat release mechanism underneath the front seat. She smelled nice in the cold air. She depressed the clutch and put it into first.

"OK," she said with Western intonation.

I went behind the car. There was a bank of frozen mud, ice, and snow that I could use for support, and while the policemen contemplated us with great interest, I pushed with my feet against the bank. The tires screeched for a short second, then the car shot forward, but she managed to wrench the steering wheel around and place the car with the front pointing in the right direction. She shifted into neutral and applied the hand brake before getting out.

"Thank you," I said. "Can I give you a lift?"

"No, thank you," she said. "I can easily find a taxi here." Her voice sounded muffled, but pleasant through the scarf that was wrapped several times around the lower part of her face.

"It isn't as easy as all that. It would be no trouble at all," I continued in Russian.

She shook her head. Suddenly I didn't feel like saying good-bye to her. Her strange green eyes shone in the darkness of the courtyard.

She formally reached out her gloved hand.

"Good-bye," she said.

She began to walk away.

"If I want to speak with you later . . . ?" My voice sounded almost desperate. I don't know why.

She turned halfway around.

"You can find me in Prague," she said, surprisingly. I was so tired that it took me a moment to realize what she meant. She wasn't talking about the city, of course, but the restaurant. She was already some distance away, so I almost had to shout: "It's a big place!"

Her voice sounded distinctly through the air: "I'm sure you'll find me if it's necessary."

"How?"

Then she said clearly in English, "I am the singer in the band."

3

Council of war at the embassy.

Heavy and compact in his dressing gown, CW looked very much like an actor in a Noël Coward play. Castesen was impeccably dressed as always, but with a silk scarf around his emaciated bird's neck instead of the habitual necktie. The man had shaved. I could not stand him, and that was mutual. He was everything that I could never become. I was a proletarian who had left my proper place in society to hobnob with gentlemen on the polished floors of the diplomatic service. Castesen's family had served the king and Denmark for centuries, ever since the time of Frederick VI. My father had been an English sailor, my mother a charwoman, or, as it is called today, a cleaning lady; or, even fancier, a sanitation employee. (The old lady would have choked completely on her filter cigarette if ever she'd heard of that notion.)

We were drinking coffee and whisky. CW's head was drooping, but he was listening. Castesen was leaning back in his chair with his long, sinewy legs crossed, smoking French cigarettes. He looked angry, and he was letting out sighs and roars of outrage as I told them what I knew about the accident, and the fact that the Soviet girl was obviously a prostitute.

"Did they say that directly?" Castesen interrupted. His polished voice had the fine touch of inherited arrogance emblematic of our moribund upper classes.

"The word doesn't really exist in Russian. Prostitution doesn't exist officially. But it's tolerated, and yes, that's what they meant. If you would make an effort and learn just a little bit of Russian, you would understand—maybe," I said.

"In my experience French has always been a language with which one can get pretty far," he said condescendingly.

He knew very well that I don't speak French.

CW looked tired. He raised one heavy shoulder and drew himself up in the chair, shifting the weight of his belly, the impressive size of which was a product of many dinners and official receptions. "Go on, Jack." And so I did. I told them that the case was in competent hands, that Basov was all right, and that he had promised me a preliminary report in the morning. I would have full access to the investigation material. I said that in my opinion the suicide itself was not so damaging to Danish interests in the future, and that the pornographic cassettes were much more serious in this connection. Pornography is illegal. A representative of the Danish state appeared to have been involved in black-market transactions with pornographic videotapes. That was serious, I thought.

"OK," CW said, pouring himself another whisky. I had one, too. Castesen declined.

"Damage control?" CW said, and lit his cigar. His large and comfortable office in one of the most attractive embassies in the city was shrouded in blue fog. "Any suggestions?" our boss continued. "Or should we begin with an estimate of how bad it is?"

Castesen twitched in his chair. His lean and neatly bearded face was ashen. He looked older than his almost fifty years.

Maybe he just couldn't take getting up in the middle of the night; or maybe part of the reason was that, according to rumors in the department, his name would be high on the list in connection with the filling of an ambassador's post in Paris that had recently become vacant. No doubt Castesen would do anything to get that post. A smoldering scandal might create a climate that would make the conservative foreign service and the politicians refrain from a possibly controversial situation. But for now, Castesen was the favorite. He had served in all the right places; and he had persistently circulated a rumor in the department that he had accepted Moscow reluctantly, but was willing to do his bit in a difficult place. It was quite understandable that the man was nervous.

Castesen cleared his throat and said, "First of all, we hush up the whole thing. Second, we go to the protocol and express our regret about the pornographic cassettes. We describe Sonia as a mental case. Someone who, in spite of our careful screening, has turned out to be rotten fruit. We sweep the dirt under the carpet, and say that of course the embassy has not been involved."

"So Sonia must take the rap, and to hell with her," I said.

"Does she deserve any better? Are you now going to play the knight all of a sudden?" Castesen said. He lit another French cigarette.

"That's all very well," CW said. "Right. Castesen will go to the protocol tomorrow. I'll go there later, when we have more official material. Tomorrow Castesen will plant a little seed that Sonia was enticed. That it was a trap . . ."

Castesen looked nervous. He was extremely security conscious. Hardly said his name on an open line; hardly talked of what he'd eaten for dinner in a room that might be bugged. I had to admit that in Moscow his suspicions were often confirmed.

"For that matter, it might very well be the case," CW added, and looked up at the ceiling in a significant way.

"They certainly got hold of the sister very fast," I said. "As if they had both the dead girl and her sister in their files already."

"Aren't they all there?" CW paused for a second. "I mean, I suppose it's part of the cost of the business."

"More or less," I said. "Some are official. Others are part-timers, so to speak."

Castesen was jumpy. He cleared his throat again, before speaking with his dry, pleasant voice which grated in my ears all the same. He was cracking his knuckles. He really wasn't feeling so well, I could see.

"Jack, you saw no compromising papers . . . ?" He let the sentence linger in the air.

"Only compromising positions," I said.

Castesen looked imploringly at CW.

"Jack, Castesen does have a point." CW used the English expression. His language had not gone unaffected by the many years abroad.

"There was nothing, but what she may have passed on or told her lesbian lover on the pillow God only knows. She did, after all, have a certain level of clearance."

CW puffed at his cigar, sending the fat, blue smoke up into the ceiling. He would have had a hard time in the United States, where smokers are considered more harmful to society than Communists.

"I think we'll have to go over that aspect in the Submarine," he said after a while. The Submarine is a soundproof room at the British embassy, checked at regular intervals for bugging devices. We borrowed it when we wanted to discuss classified material, something that we could never be sure of doing in private in our own offices.

"Yes. And let's stop here," Castesen said. Because of me, I guessed. He found me careless, both in the way I dressed and in my attitude toward security questions. Castesen often wondered how I had ever managed to get clearance, not to mention the fact that the service had accepted me. He saw it as one example among many of a decline in morals.

"It may result in an external investigation, of course," CW said. He continued, "*Enfin.* To conclude! Jack will stay in touch with Basov tomorrow. Castesen, you'll go to the ministry to pour oil on troubled waters and arrange a meeting that I'll take as soon as we have the reports from the medical investigator and the police. And we should all check our drawers and try to get a general idea of what she had access to. I believe I can say that much at an open meeting. I'll send a telex home right away. I'll phrase it softly, but make it clear that there's no immediate cause to suspect her of having crossed. But of course we'll change a couple of procedures and codes. That's how it'll have to stand for now."

Castesen leaned forward, resting his long, blue-blazered arms on his bony knees. "We won't be popular with the allies. And I have a coordination meeting tomorrow. Well, actually we're talking about today."

"Of course, it might just be sex," CW said with disgust. I imagined that he had simply suppressed the fact that Sonia had been found with someone of her own sex. That was the kind of thing the existence of which an old-fashioned type like CW would normally rather forget.

"Then maybe we can try to get a couple of hours of sleep," Castesen said, and began to get up.

"There's just one more thing," I said. Castesen sank back in the chair with an audible sigh.

I continued, "Which one of us, CW, is going to write the telex for the ministry to take to the Danish police?"

"Why on earth should we involve the Danish police?" Castesen said.

"Because Sonia has parents. They live in Funen. And she has a younger brother who studies in Aarhus. Somebody has to tell these people that a person they probably loved is dead . . . regardless of what she may be guilty of."

For once Castesen didn't answer.

"I'll take care of it," CW said.

"Then that'll be all, I suppose," Castesen said, as if he were presiding over the meeting.

"CW," I said, "if you make it absolutely clear that it's a case of suicide, that ought to take care of the problem with the press."

"The press isn't involved at all," Castesen said. He abhorred all journalists who didn't work for either *Le Monde* or *The Times* of London.

"No, not if it's a case of suicide. But if some of the Danish newspapers get wind of the pornography part, they'll probably want to write a line or two about it."

"It won't get out. We all agree on making it clear that we're dealing with a case of suicide," CW said.

I wasn't so sure. The ministry at home was as full of holes as a sieve, and many of the journalists in Copenhagen had good sources, both among the officials and those politicians who had access to the information of the ministry.

"Jack, when it gets to that point, you'll deal with the practicalities of sending the body home, won't you? After all, she must have a Christian funeral," CW said.

Castesen left first. I couldn't quite make up my mind if it was worth going home. It was almost six o'clock, but I felt like going home to take a shower. CW saw me out. In spite of the fact that he was wearing only his dressing gown and pajamas, he accompanied me all the way outside. It had begun to snow. Tiny, hard grains of frost glittering in the dim light. Two policemen were guarding the Danish embassy, one at either end. They were looking at us. My face felt frost-bitten immediately, but CW seemed unaffected.

"One hell of a night," he said, rather dreamily. "A couple of years before my retirement. I could have done without that."

I didn't answer. Then he took me by the arm in a sort of fatherly way.

"I got the feeling that something was bothering you."

He was perceptive enough.

"There's a couple of details, but probably the technical investigation will clarify those," I said.

"That's right, son," he said intimately. I was a little surprised. CW kept his distance with people, particularly with staff members.

"Why did Sonia have a wound on her forehead, and why were there three plates? Why this odd number?"

"It's cold. I'd better go inside," he merely said.

"I'll be back in a couple of hours," I said. "Good night."

"Good night," CW said into the drifting snow. "Oh, Jack, if you have the time, you might ask around a little about Sonia among the staff at the embassy, and with the local employees, too. You have a good way with people."

The local employees were our Soviet personnel.

"All right."

"But discreetly, Jack. Discreetly."

He then shut the door with a slam, and I was alone in the drifting snow and the cold. I was tired and felt old, so I hurried into the car. I turned on the hot-air fan and kept it on all the way home, but I never really got to feel warm.

As I locked myself into the apartment, I could hear the phone ring in that shrill hysterical way that meant it was the Soviet trunk exchange calling. I dropped my coat on the floor and took the call, although I would actually have preferred not to. My whole body was aching. It was Susanne, calling from Copenhagen, where it was about four o'clock in the morning. She seemed half drunk and in a really bad mood, and in the background I could hear the sounds from a noisy and intoxicated party.

"Where the hell have you been?" she shouted. "This is the fourth time I got through!"

"How are you, Susanne?"

"I'm arriving tomorrow. Come and get me at the airport."

"If I can. Otherwise I'll send the chauffeur."

"You'll be there yourself, I tell you. And where have you been?"

"I can't discuss that on an open line."

"What kind of asshole excuse is that!" Her voice sounded muffled, and I knew that she had to be rather drunk to be swearing like that.

"Sonia is dead."

"The new one . . . the redhead?"

"Yes, she's killed herself."

"Well, that's not so uncommon in Moscow, is it? That's still not a reason for not coming to pick up your wife at the airport." She sounded a little more sober.

"I can't promise to do that, Susanne. I can't say more, but I'll send Sascha, OK?"

"You can go to hell . . . stop it, Tomas . . . I'm tired of you. No, not you, Tomas."

"Good-bye, Susanne," I said.

"Good-bye, asshole. It's over. I'm only coming to pack my things."

"Let's talk about it tomorrow," I said, but I was talking only to the great murmur of the cable that drew the thin wire between Moscow and Copenhagen. I stood holding the receiver for several minutes with a sinking and burning feeling in my stomach, until the Soviet trunk exchange operator cut in and asked if the conversation was over.

"Yes. It's over," I said, and hung up.

4

I was back at the embassy by ten o'clock. Not surprisingly, the atmosphere was rather subdued. CW had informed everybody when they came to work at nine. No details, of course. Just that Sonia was dead. Later I was told that CW had used the expression, "had decided to part with this present life by her own hand." Like I said, CW was a man of faith. They still exist. I hadn't managed to get any sleep, but had broken through the tiredness and reached a false feeling of being fresh. A long hot shower, a razor shave, coffee, and fried eggs helped. I enjoyed making my own breakfast.

Our housekeeper, a Russian woman in her fifties, arrived just before I left for work. She greeted me coolly, as usual. She didn't approve of the fact that I couldn't manage my wife. I didn't care. I asked her to make pancakes for dinner that evening: blinis, Russian pancakes. I was going to buy some fresh caviar and open a bottle of champagne. Then we would have to try to have a sensible talk for the last time, Susanne and I.

The Danish embassy is a yellow building, old but pleasant-looking, situated on a small road behind the Soviet Ministry of

Foreign Affairs. Originally built of wood, it now had a coat of plaster. Superstitious people say that the many rooms are haunted—it was built on top of a plague cemetery. The embassy has a large garden, and rumor has it that they pitted the mass murderer Beria somewhere by its far corner.

The snowplow had been there. Along the road were large compressed banks of ice. People were constantly on the point of falling over holes and knotty brownish black lumps of ice that were never completely cleared away from the sidewalk. It was bitterly cold again, and the clouds hung low and menacing over the city. The capital was weighed down by a massive and immovable cover of smog, and everyone seemed furiously depressed and hung over after the New Year celebrations. The faces were as empty as the shelves of the shops.

On my way to work I drove past freezing, stamping policemen in heavy gray uniform coats and square-toed boots. The fabric of their uniforms was of somewhat better quality than what most of the hurrying pedestrians had wrapped around themselves. I had a sensation of death's heads and extinct souls. The windows and bodies of the cars were covered with thick layers of dirt. The pace was immovably slow. The whole frozen, petrified, and ugly morning was an image of a society in stagnation and decay. A society that had come to a standstill in its third leadership crisis. At the Kremlin was yet another old man, who could hardly walk, spoke with difficulty, and could show himself to his people for only brief moments of time. Chernenko had been an incomprehensible disappointment to most people. The last push over the brink of a precipice. With him all ideals, the few that were left, had been definitively replaced by the deepest cynicism and disillusion. Those who had the opportunity to do so lined their own pockets. The people bowed their necks and accepted their hard lot like so many times before in history. I don't know of any other nation that bears its suffering as patiently and willingly as the Russian people.

So I was not in such a great mood, either, when I arrived and unlocked the door to my office.

I only had time to open *Pravda* before there was a knock on my door. It was CW in an immaculate dark suit with vest and watch chain. Freshly shaven with rosy cheeks, he appeared to be in his element. He placed his big form on the sofa.

"The desk says that we must handle it on our own for now, but they'll brief the minister today, and then we will see."

I said nothing. I kept staring at the pages of *Pravda*—at letters that suddenly seemed unintelligible, although I had studied and loved the Russian language for fifteen years.

CW sighed. He looked pale somewhere behind the freshly shaved and incredibly youthful face. Only his discolored, tobacco-stained teeth revealed his real age: almost sixty-six. He looked like the well-paid president of a medium-sized and solid provincial bank.

"So it's business as usual," he said. "Castesen goes to the foreign ministry at noon as we decided. I've informed everybody, and in Copenhagen they assure me that we'll get a replacement soon. They want the situation neutralized as quickly as possible. And that's probably going to be the minister's attitude as well. There seems to be a general consensus that both we and the Russians must be interested in a fast solution."

It didn't make much sense. But I knew what he meant. Like me, he was bothered by the many pornographic videocassettes. But what worried both of us most was the possibility of a leakage of classified information; not only Danish, but also the information that we receive from our partners in NATO. I didn't answer. I looked out through the ice ferns at the frozen garden, buried and benumbed under several feet of snow. It was a large old garden, one of the most positive private aspects of being stationed in Moscow, that was brought into splendid bloom every summer by Mrs. W. CW's wife, whom we always referred to as Mrs. W, shared the pleasures of the garden with all the employees, high as well as low. Like her husband, she was a lovable person, and she was now finally in a position where she could relax, as CW's career was drawing to a close. She could see an end to the trivial diplomatic dinners and the responsibility for formal receptions. She had done her job. CW had reached his goal.

"I'm planning to have a little talk with Carl," I said.

"Is that wise?"

"Strictly private. She might be in the computer."

"Do you have her name?"

"I'll have it later, I'm sure."

CW got up. He hesitated for a moment. His belly pressed against all the buttons of his suit.

"Do what you think is best. You know that I trust your judgement one hundred percent." In the doorway he said, "But it's my clear impression that the minister wants the situation normalized as quickly as possible. 'Business as usual' is what the desk wrote."

I thought about his warning for a while. But then I called the American embassy anyway and asked for Carl Sorensen, who, in spite of his name, was at least fourth-generation American.

We talked for a while about this and that, and when we had finished cursing the Russian winter, I asked if he had ten minutes for a drink later in the day.

"I'm a little overbooked today," he said.

"It's important," I said. We were good friends. As close as you can get when everyone you meet has either just arrived or is about to leave.

"Yes, I hear that you're having a minor problem," he said.

"Nothing we can't control."

"Can you call again around five?" he then said. He knew better than to ask on an open line.

"Of course," I said, thinking that this was it as far as the airport was concerned. I would have to deal with Susanne's anger later. If your private life is down the drain anyway, you may as well seek comfort in something you can control. Work, for example.

I looked at a couple of visa applications. I was consul, and besides being of assistance to Danish citizens, it also implied that I issued visas to Soviet citizens who wanted to visit Denmark. I checked them against the names of known KGB agents that we had in our own files, and I used the extensive computer system of our allies to ensure that an active or dormant agent didn't get an entry permit under the cover of cultural exchange programs or union visits.

We were only three diplomats at the embassy, so we all had to help each other. Every week I sent a newsletter home to the ministry, a report in which I gave an evaluation of the situation. Rather like writing an article. I enjoyed it, even though I only wrote it for one man: the man at the Soviet desk, that is, the Soviet department. If I were very lucky and did a good job, the minister might also read the report. I wrote very well, and I had good sources after three years, but on this day that was of no use to me.

"What the hell," I muttered to myself. "He himself told me to do it. He only said that I should be discreet."

I began with the Danish staff. First the guards. One was asleep, and another had relieved me at Sonia's apartment, so there was only John left to supervise the television monitors that show anyone who approaches the main entrance of the embassy and other strategic corners of the place.

I was glad that it was John. I definitely didn't like him. He smelled like a man who, living in Moscow and thinking he had to make do with Russian soap, chose not to use any soap at all.

He was sullen and bad-tempered and took every order as a personal insult. He dressed like a perpetual student who had gone to the dogs, and he spent his day discussing the differences between four Danish Marxist parties, although he was himself extremely right wing. These were all legitimate prejudices that I harbored against him, but on top of that he was lousy at his job. He handled the practical tasks all right, so we couldn't touch him, but he was extremely rude to both the Russians and the Danes who for one reason or another sought the assistance or needed the services of the embassy.

John was sitting with his legs up on the table, drinking coffee. He was about twenty-one years old, had a close-cropped beard and a couple of pimples on his forehead. He looked rather pale.

"How about offering me a cup of coffee?" I asked. He removed his legs from the table and found a mug for me. We then sat in silence for a while, sipping coffee. I looked at him over the rim of my mug. He wore contact lenses.

"Did you know her?" I asked.

"What do you mean?" He jumped as if I had pricked him with a needle. "What the hell do you mean?"

I said nothing. Just looked at him.

"The others are going to tell you anyway," he continued. "I've been with her once. But it was a long time ago. Right after she arrived here." He poured coffee, but his hand shook so much that he spilled some. He cursed loudly.

"There's nothing illegal or wrong about that," I said. "So why are you getting so upset?"

"She was a goddamned whore," he said. "I'm telling you, the things she wanted me to do to her. Not for me, man." He looked at me indignantly, as if I had accused him of having sex with minors. What he said interested me. Before his colleague had relieved me, all the paraphernalia had been removed from Sonia's apartment.

"Where were you together?" I asked.

"Why are you asking me about all this stuff? CW said that the bitch committed suicide. Why are you dragging me into it?"

"I'm not. I only asked where you were when you were together. I'm not asking for obscene details."

He tried to laugh, and his coffee almost splashed over.

"There aren't any. Details, I mean. She was goddamn sexy, I tell you. An incredible body. But when she got started with all her filth, that was it for me. It shrunk and became no bigger than this."

He was waving his little finger.

"And then what?"

He nodded and rocked back and forth on his chair.

"Well, then . . ." he said, and paused. "Then she smacked me one and took her clothes and left. All that fucking red hair, I guess!"

"Where were you together?"

"Is this going any further, are you writing a report or something?"

"No, it's quite private."

"It was here," he then said, looking embarrassed and aggressive at the same time. "Nothing ever happens here at night anyway, and I could hear both the telex and the phone."

I didn't like this at all. I didn't like the idea of Sonia snooping about at the embassy in the middle of the night.

"How often did this go on?" I asked, making my voice sound hard and commanding.

"Only that one time," he said. He was holding his coffee mug so hard that I was afraid it might break in his hand. He was starting to sweat, too, but I actually believed him. Men don't usually like to admit having had to give up halfway. His wounded ego had probably been an effective antidote against Sonia's charms.

"What about Niels and Peter?"

He shook his head.

"She made passes at them, I think. But they had girlfriends at home and weren't interested."

Suddenly his face changed expression. Nervousness and shame gave way to grievance. He looked very young. It struck me how young he really was. When I was twenty-one myself, I had thought that I was very grown-up, but undoubtedly I had been just as immature.

"Now I think I know what it is you're aiming at," he said. "You think I let Sonia nose around in here at night. Nope, I tell you. Do you think I'm crazy? I ran after her and let her out as soon as she had gotten her clothes on. And it was only that one time. I swear!"

"OK," I said. "I promised you that this would stay between you and me. How much time do you have left?"

"Two months."

"I advise you not to apply for an extension or to try to get employment in the ministry later on. For then this conversation will no longer be private."

"You really are an asshole!" he said. "I ought to smack you some."

"I don't think you're quite big enough for that, my little John," I said.

"Well, don't be too damned sure. You'll come home someday, too," he said.

I turned around demonstratively and locked the door.

"Go right ahead," I said.

"Don't be too fucking sure."

Then I grabbed him by the collar of his shirt and pushed him up against the wall. I leaned up against him and pressed lightly against his throat, but put most pressure on his body, squeezing him with my shoulder till he began to breathe with difficulty. He resisted a little, but he had no strength.

"What did you tell the others?" I asked with my face close to his. His eyes were wide open with fear. I knew his type. He was full of hot air and would like to have a knife at his belt, but he was afraid of physical pain.

"What the hell do you mean?"

"Did you say you couldn't get it up with Sonia . . . ?"

"Hell, no."

"Then what did you say?" I put a little more pressure on his neck, and he began to gasp.

"What do you think? I said I'd fucked her, of course. What else should I have said?"

"And she didn't walk about on her own?"

"No . . . Jack . . . let me go. I swear . . . I saw her out. All she wanted to do was to whip me. That's not me, man. I'm afraid of everything that hurts."

I let go of him. He collapsed on the floor. I didn't like what I had just done, but if he had given Sonia the opportunity to snoop around an entire night on her own, we would be in a serious situation. Then I would have had to report him. Then we would have had investigators from military intelligence, police intelligence, and the ministry, and my next post would be Ulan Bator or somewhere almost equally bad: the press department of the Ministry of Foreign Affairs.

He was quite crushed when I left. Either the pool of applicants for the auxiliary posts at our missions was very limited, I thought, or else those who selected them were blind.

The rest would almost have to be an anticlimax. There were so few of us that it was easy to do an overview. Besides CW, Castesen, and myself, there was our accountant, who was on Christmas vacation. He had been gone for a long time. Then there was Sonia's colleague, Jette—and the three guards. That was the Royal Danish Embassy in Moscow. We also had a trade division that was located somewhere else in the city. It consisted of a trade counselor, an attaché, and a secretary. I would have to get to them later. If I wanted to play the detective, there weren't very many fellow countrymen to investigate. Under the aging Kremlin leadership, Moscow had become a low-priority station. Nothing happened here. The Soviet Union was an armed giant with feet of clay. I was there because I was interested in the country, but there weren't many people like me in the service. Most of the others thought of being there as a kind of punishment. A temporary station in their career.

First I went back and called Peter, the guard whom I trusted the most. I woke him up. He was sleepy, but he was just as competent as I expected him to be. He confirmed John's story; both that Sonia had tried her luck with him, but in vain, and that John had really gone for it. He had just about fucked the beautiful Sonia day and night. Peter was an acute fellow, so I asked him if he thought Sonia might have looked into the papers a little too deeply.

"She was too dumb for that. She had nothing but sex on the brain, but she was great fun and good at her job," Peter said.

I barged into Jette's office without knocking, making her start as if she had a bad conscience. I did it on purpose, hoping to catch her in the act, and I succeeded beyond my expectations. She almost managed to hide the bottle, but not quite. It was peeking out from behind a picture.

"You shithead!" she screamed. "And to think that I've tried to get you in bed."

"Hi, honey!" I said.

She really looked shaken, so I let her collect herself a little. She had shared the office with Sonia, who apparently had been hiding more beneath the surface than she had revealed, at least to me.

"We both need a drink," I said. "I'll go and get some glasses."

Everybody knew that she had a problem with alcohol, to put

it mildly. But a lot of people do, and there was nothing wrong with her work. Five minutes later we were drinking whisky together.

"Yeah, Jack, she was something, all right," Jette said. She was a big girl. She must have been quite gorgeous once, but by now you could read all the empty bottles in her face, and it was getting difficult for her to keep her ample curves confined to their proper places. She was close to forty, and in a desperate sort of way there was something indomitable about her. She was easily provoked to laughter. No one knew why she drank.

"In what way, something?"

"She was a bitch."

"She was a good secretary," I interrupted.

"The best," she admitted magnanimously. "But that didn't keep her from being a bitch."

"Why didn't you like her?"

She laughed loudly.

"But Jack! I liked her very much. Why do you think I need a drink this morning? We got along very well together. She was great fun. But she was a bitch the way she always had to try to get laid. I don't know why. But so what? I drink. Sonia used sex. What's your secret, Jack? What do you do to make life bearable?"

"Work," I said, and raised my glass.

"And then you have your darling Susanne, right?" she said teasingly. "Where is she, by the way?"

"She arrives today."

"Time for the great reconciliation?"

"More like the opposite."

"Then there's still a chance for you and me?" She again laughed her coarse mannish laughter. "You should see yourself, Jack. You don't have to be scared. I'm not on the prowl. I've given up. I'm satisfied with a marine every now and then."

She laughed again to hide her insecurity and despair. Why is everybody so damned lonely?

"Maybe Sonia was into marines, too—or was she more interested in girls, maybe?"

Jette leaned forward. "Why do you say that?"

"Wasn't she?"

"Sonia a lesbian? Well, why not? She never tried anything with me. She was the center of attention at all the parties this winter, when we singles got together. You know, ten Finnish nannies, fifteen horny American marines, and then Sonia and little me."

Her hand shook a little as she raised the glass to her lips. She spilled a drop on her gray blouse and shook her head irritatedly.

"Did she have a steady boyfriend or girlfriend?"

"Why do you want her to be into women, Jackie boy? She was into men. Ask the Americans. I don't know what she did to them, they looked shaken the next morning. But they came back for more."

"Do I detect a bit of jealousy?"

"Jack, you're an idiot! Do I really look that horrible this morning?" She smiled and her ravaged face lit up. "Jack, when I deck myself out with rouge and tuck in my tummy, I have enough offers. And I'm not particularly complicated or demanding. Look at the positive side of life in this dump: there are young American soldiers in great physical condition, and other bachelors as well, who aren't allowed to go out with the natives, for then they're punished and sent home, so they have to come to us old girls instead. They're bumpkins, but what the hell? I'm not finicky. Wham-bam-thank-you-ma'am is good enough for me. And if once in a while I'm so lucky that there's a pair of arms to hold me in the morning, well, then life's not so bad at all . . . oh, damn."

She started to cry. She covered her face with both hands and stifled her sobbing, but her shoulders were shaking. I went over to her and put my arms around her and held her for a while. She sniffled. I poured her another small whisky that she downed immediately.

She shook her head as if to get her thoughts back in place. Then she said, "Do you realize that more people commit suicide around Christmas than at any other time of the year? It's supposed to be so damned merry. The families are together, and the rest of us feel more alone. Then it makes no difference how many people you're surrounded by."

"But you haven't."

"Not directly. I'm doing it the agreeable way." She was pointing at the whisky bottle.

"Why do you think Sonia did it?"

"I don't know. I can't understand it. She wasn't the type, even though she was unhappy, all right. She chased men so that you'd think they were the key to life—and if you'll permit my saying so, they aren't." She was still sniffling.

I kept my mouth shut.

She continued, "Sonia once said to me, 'I don't know why I bother, but once everything is completely broken into pieces, there's nothing you can do about it, you just go on and on.' I don't know what the hell she was talking about. Probably something in her childhood. It almost always is, anyway."

"She never mentioned to you that she was thinking of killing herself?"

"My dear Jack, that's not exactly what we girls talk about in the office. I hardly knew her. She was a bitch, but she was nice. She was fun to go out with. She was good looking, so we met a lot of interesting men, many of them young, and I always got my share." She was about to start crying again.

I kissed her on the forehead.

"*Davai*," I said, and emptied my glass.

"You're OK, Jack, but go away now. I have work to do."

"You're not so bad yourself."

"Sure, we're a couple of lovely people," she said. "But instead of disturbing a working girl, why don't you look over your shoulder and have a chat with your colleague?"

I had already opened the door to leave, but now I stopped and closed it again.

"What do you mean?" I asked.

"I'm a nice girl, of course, and don't want to spread gossip about a married man, but still, Sonia had certainly turned the head of one of the big shots around here."

"What are you saying? You can't possibly mean CW?"

"*Nyet,* you fool. Mrs. W would never allow that. Besides, he's not interested."

"Castesen?" I said with amazement.

"Well, since she never got into your pants, at least not as far as I'm informed, there aren't that many left. Castesen could neither keep his eyes nor his hands off her, from the moment Sonia stepped through the door for the first time. You see nothing, of course, because you always walk around with your head in the clouds . . . but the man was lost. From day one."

5

I didn't barge into the office of our ministerial counselor, but knocked on the door like a good boy. Castesen was leaning over his tidy desk, upon which heaps of pressing matters were arranged in small neat squares as meticulously as the way he dressed, writing with a fountain pen. It moved across the paper with flowing ease. The ministerial counselor made it clear to me that he was a busy man. With a nod and a barely audible "Moment" he offered me a seat while he finished a sentence. I sat beneath the photographs of the royal highnesses, who were staring at each other in profile, and contemplated him. He looked terrible, although he was impeccably dressed as always. He had dressed for his meeting at the Soviet foreign ministry and was wearing a dark blue three-piece suit. Serious clothes for serious people. As far as that was concerned, Castesen and Gromyko shared the same outlook on things. Actually, Castesen was only meeting with the vice-chief of the Scandinavia division; CW would meet the chief when we got around to the more serious talks. Castesen looked pale, but he seemed less tense than the night before.

Anyway, he always looked as if he were carrying nothing less than the burdens of the entire nation on his shoulders, surrounded by incompetent morons. One thing that could not be said against Castesen was that he took things too lightly. I didn't envy him his heritage, either. Imagine having to live up to several generations of forefathers in the service of the king and being able to study famous ancestors at the National Museum. I could just imagine how he had grown up with a continuous refrain from a chorus of unproductive aunts who had never done a day's worth of honest work: "Henrik dear, you really have to pull yourself together. A Castesen would never have behaved like that under the old king."

Castesen continued writing for another five minutes. The pen wore the initials HVC, which stood for Henrik von Castesen, but the little "von" appeared only on his card and wasn't for everyday use. His greatest problem was that his father had been one of the most respected and intelligent ambassadors of his generation. I had met him shortly before his early death. A handsome man who, precisely because he knew his own worth, was polite and friendly with everyone he met. The exact opposite of his son. But maybe he had been a monster at home. What do I know? I only remember my own father as a brutal, drunken shadow in my early childhood, before my mother banished the English drunkard to drifting perpetually about the seven seas, from one waterfront dive to the next, where he may still be drinking and whoring himself unconsciously through life.

"Could you make it brief, Jack? I'm busy!"

I gave a start. I had been looking at him without focusing, lost in my own world, and he had been nothing but a vague shadow with a fountain pen, bent over some task. Now he was looking at me nonchalantly without putting down the pen, a sign that he hadn't finished but would like to get a smaller, not very pressing, quickly settled matter out of the way.

"What do you think of the situation?"

He discreetly raised one eyebrow, put down the mono-grammed fountain pen, and folded his narrow reading glasses.

"I find it serious, but not disastrous. It's waves, not a storm."

"That's one way of putting it, of course," I said.

He was fidgeting with his glasses, opening and closing them. There were small folds in the skin of his ostrichlike neck, which was a grayish color, wrinkled and rather loose. He apparently couldn't take staying up all night. He lit a cigarette with a gold lighter—everything about him was perfect ("We only have one life, so we may as well live with quality," I remembered him once saying)—and held out the blue pack, offering me one. I shook my head.

"How did you see Sonia?" I asked.

"As far as I know there were no complaints about her work."

"That wasn't exactly what I was thinking of."

He inhaled deeply and blew out the smoke. He didn't seem to like the taste. He put the cigarette out in the ashtray with a disgusted expression and resumed his activity with his glasses.

"Then what were you thinking of, Jack?" he said.

"Well, she was rather good looking."

Castesen laughed, a short sharp laughter.

"If you like the type, but I don't suppose that you're disturb-ing me before an important meeting in order to discuss women?"

"I hear that you were rather taken with her . . ." I let the sentence linger in the air. My voice had been quite neutral. He sat staring at me calmly. No blushing, no confession. No anger, for that matter. He lit another cigarette. Apparently he had forgotten that the last one tasted badly. He looked me straight in the eyes.

"Have you been listening to gossip, Jack? Have you had breakfast with gossipmongers?"

"I only asked if you thought she was good looking."

"Jack, my friend," he said, still in his silky voice that had been trained by long negotiations and lots of empty phrases at countless so-called necessary diplomatic gatherings. "The difference between you and me is simple. I have style, background, and breeding." He drew out the last word. "You have education and a little polish, but you are what you were born: a proletarian. And now do me a favor and get out."

"Did you fuck her, Castesen?" Once you have been branded as a proletarian, you may as well behave like one. Some red spots appeared in Castesen's gray cheeks. He was getting angry.

"That's enough. You have no right to pry into my private life. And by asking a question like that you demonstrate once again your complete lack of breeding and tact. But that's not surprising, of course." As before, he angrily put out his cigarette and immediately lit another.

"I'm not concerned with morals, Castesen . . ."

"Stay away from my private life."

Castesen had been married for seventeen years. Whether happily or not, I don't know, but it functioned well. She looked after him; he looked after his job. She arranged the diplomatic dinners that he demanded, would speak for him with furious loyalty if anyone dared utter the slightest criticism, and declared herself totally in agreement with her husband about the fact that boarding school in England was the best thing for their children of fourteen and sixteen. "I miss them, of course, but Henrik says that it's an investment in the future. And then, it would be wrong to think of the money or of myself," she often said to complete strangers at receptions, after the third gin and tonic. On the surface they were a successful couple, the ideal diplomatic match. If Castesen had affairs, he was discreet about it.

"It isn't private, Castesen," I said calmly.

"Who has asked you to snoop?"

"It's not private, Castesen, when Sonia has been having sexual relations with a Soviet citizen. And definitely not if the Soviet citizen was operative. If you've been involved with Sonia, too, then what do you think your chances are for getting that ambassador's post? Then maybe, and I stress maybe, there would be certain complications of a security-related nature." I was being really nasty. And probably envious, too.

Now he laughed again, and this time more relieved.

"Oh, it's a vendetta that you're on. I've always sensed your hostility. Actually I've seen it as rather childish. It's a product of your own insecurity and lack of independence. You ought to change careers, Jack. Join the police. I can just see you as a dumb, flat-footed cop asking moronic questions."

I got angry, of course, but before I could say anything, he threw a telex at me. It fluttered to the floor like a winged bird, so I had to get up from my chair and bend over to pick it up. I read it and put it down on the desk in front of him.

"Congratulations," I said.

"Thank you," he said. It had just arrived, I could see. A single line from the ministry back home: "Congratulations. The post is yours. It will be Warsaw. It will be announced officially later today. Carsten."

"Have you told CW?"

"Not yet," he said, with his small, self-satisfied smile. As for Carsten, I knew him very well. One of Castesen's devoted partisans, who had tagged his own dawning career to the great Castesen name in the assumption that it would pay off in the form of future promotions.

I looked out at the garden. Down by the garages one of our Soviet chauffeurs was scraping ice off a car. His name was Shura. He had two children and a wife who was a teacher. He was crazy about soccer and thought that Elkjaer was one of the best forwards in the world. I knew idiotic stuff like that, while Castesen concentrated on the essentials. I could hear the grating sound in the silence of the office in spite of the double windows. They weren't completely tight. There were threads of ice along the edges.

"Probably he'll call us all together, so that we can drink to your success," I said ironically.

"But you'd rather not do that?"

"That's not what I'm thinking of. It might cause certain difficulties if it got out."

"I know exactly what you're thinking of, Jack," he snapped. "But it's absurd. Even if your idiotic allegations were true, and I'm definitely not saying that they are, my attitude to security and professional secrecy is well known. It's certainly not lax. If once in a while you'd pull yourself together and read up on the profession, you'd know that I've written a widely read classified report on security systems at the embassies. It's read even in Langley, I'm informed."

"I have read it."

"But of course you disagree with its premises and its conclusions."

"That would be difficult. Like everything else about you, it stays within the realm of the predictable. You don't cross anyone. You think a certain right-wing conservatism is non-controversial. If you stay on that track, you figure that you won't offend anybody. And you're probably right," I said.

"Ideological nonsense!" he said. "Others would call it common sense. This whole conversation is meaningless. Your slander campaign against me has run out of ammunition before it even got started."

"Then you may as well tell me if you actually managed to get such a sexy young girl in spite of your mature age." Always appeal to men's vanity, then you can get them to do anything, Susanne used to say.

Castesen looked complacent and arrogant. He felt that he had won. "That's one question to which you'll never have the answer. The girl is dead. Considering the way she behaved, I'll be the last to deplore it," he said. "And now get lost!"

I went back to my own office and tried to think and to get some of my everyday tasks over with. I again looked at Sonia's personal record. Nothing out of the ordinary. A stable career after passing the trilingual secretary's exam. Fine papers. Good references from her two previous stations, London and Madrid.

I called Peter. He hadn't gone back to bed. I asked him to drop by before going to work: I had a small, unconventional task for him. He caught on immediately. I spent the next hour in my office working with routine matters. I tried not to think of Susanne, who would get furious when I didn't turn up at the airport. Then Basov called. They had completed the on-scene investigations and would like to seal the apartment for a couple of days, until all the official papers were finished. He wanted to know if that was OK with the embassy.

"It's OK, Vladimir," I said. "A couple of days, you say; so I take it that the police don't consider this a very complicated case?"

"You'll receive a preliminary report, Jack. Let's wait till then. But I can tell you this much: they see it as an accident and a suicide. That aspect of the case can be closed rather quickly."

He asked me to be at the ministry at 4 P.M.

I knew very well what he meant by "that aspect of the case." The more problematic part, of course, concerned the pornographic videocassettes and the Soviet girl. The videos would probably be an issue. If Sonia had had those tendencies as part of her personal baggage, there weren't any problems; but if the cassettes had been intended for the black market, then it was serious. There had been quite a few. Hopefully it had just been Sonia's and her girlfriend's way of getting in the mood. Or Sonia's male lovers' way—apparently she had been bisexual.

Peter arrived a moment later. Long and lanky, he walked into my office. He was tall, blond, and of a happy disposition. I liked him very much. He didn't have the slightest desire to become a diplomat, something I considered a very positive quality in him. He wanted to become a journalist or, as he said, a reporter. He had chosen the intensive Russian education program of the military and a term in Moscow as a shortcut to the language. A couple of days before Christmas he had told me that he had been accepted by a school of journalism in the fall. His term at the embassy had coincided with the deterioration of my relationship with Susanne. As it grew progressively worse and Susanne traveled to Denmark more and more often, I had spent an increasing amount of time with Peter. We both liked to go out running in the summer and to ski in the woods around Moscow in the winter. We were very comfortable together. And sometimes I caught myself thinking of him as the grown-up son that I would never have. I trusted him.

He was wearing blue jeans and white sneakers and a home-knitted sweater. He looked very Western, but I knew that he could also dress in a way that made it possible for him to pass for a Soviet citizen. His Russian would give him away, but if he made an effort, he might pass for a Baltic.

"Hi!" he said, and flopped onto my sofa, placing his legs on top of the pile of newspapers and magazines on the table. He planted his heel right in the eye of a milkmaid who was explaining how rich her life became when she milked more cows than prescribed by the plan. "Oops!" he said, when he saw my expression. I really didn't care, but you have to set the limit somewhere. This was my livelihood, and my reputation was strained enough already.

"Have you recovered from last night, Peter?" I said gently.

He got his legs off the table and drew himself up on the sofa. His fair cheeks had turned slightly red.

"I'm sorry I carried on like that," he said. I could see that he remembered his agitation on the phone.

"That was just human."

"But you stayed calm. Like a rock," he said. "Can I have a cup of coffee?" He reached for the thermos and poured some into a paper cup.

"That comes with age," I said, and watched with envy as he dropped two pieces of sugar into his coffee. Discreetly, I placed my hand by my belt. There was not doubt about it. I was watching my food intake and still my stomach pressed against the belt more and more.

"Yes, aren't you getting a little fat?" Peter said with a grin. He was an observant guy. I couldn't help but laugh along with him.

"It's old age, Peter. I'm getting there."

"Give me a break. You're not old. Remember Tine? The girl who visited me in October. She said that you had that kind of tough look that covers wild emotions and that you walked like a coiled spring. She thought that you were simply it. Kind of a Danish version of Paul Newman."

Like an idiot, I swallowed all this, until Peter said: "But she also said that she's mainly into old men."

"Will you shut up. . . . is she your girlfriend?"

"Not exactly. I'm free-lance."

"But not with Sonia."

"No. She wasn't my type. I'm more turned on by the tall and lean ones. And she was too aggressive. Besides, I usually stick to the old rule that says: work is one thing and fornication another."

"That's not quite how it goes, but I get the idea," I said.

"It's not that I'm a saint or anything. It just causes too many problems when you want to get out of it again." He looked quite serious. Peter had an air about him, an easygoing manner that gave him few problems with the opposite sex.

"Do you have a lot of contact with John?" I asked a little nervously, for Peter wasn't the type who would squeal on colleagues or be disloyal.

"Not really."

"Why not?"

"We don't have much in common. John dreams of a career in the department. He wants to become a bureaucrat like you. Why did you become a diplomat, anyway? It doesn't seem to be you at all."

"To avoid becoming a schoolteacher of Russian and social science," I said.

"That's not true."

"Why not? Besides, I like my job, and I'm good at it."

"I would die after one year. John doesn't want to have anything to do with the Russians or to experience Moscow, so I go my own way. And I want to become a journalist. John thinks about as highly of journalists as of concentration camp guards."

"Do you realize that you walk about on your own so much that it has attracted attention? It's almost in conflict with the terms of your contract."

"Castesen said that to me four months ago."

"And what did you say?"

Peter looked at me innocently. "I said that as an educated man I thought he'd appreciate the fact that I was trying to improve myself by going to museums and concerts."

I laughed.

"Actually, he didn't believe me," Peter continued, looking quite dejected, but then his face lit up again. "Too bad. I just went on. And when he got on my case again a couple of months ago, I told him he could send me home if that was what he wanted. I wasn't going to work in his rotten ministry anyway. I wanted to be a free man." He proclaimed the last words loudly, like a trumpet.

"And you've never been approached ever so slightly by people who want to know a little about what we do?"

He looked quite disappointed. "No. But it would have made a good story."

"OK, Pete!" I said briskly. "How about a small free-lance assignment? It consists of two parts. It's between you and me, and you report directly to me, OK?"

"Great!" He leaned forward. I was taking a chance with him. I had known him for eight months. I knew that he was intelligent and that he could keep his mouth shut when he was supposed to—but what I was doing was undoubtedly illegal.

I asked him to pry about the city. He might check out the hotel bars in Moscow that were frequented by foreigners. I asked him to talk a little with the marines who guard the American embassy and with whom I knew that he and other singles in Moscow had many parties. I also asked him, when he traveled home to Denmark at the end of the week with the diplomatic bag, to quite privately contact an old friend of mine who worked for the military intelligence service. He was to personally hand him a letter from me and get an answer, also by hand, which he would deliver to me personally here in Moscow. Was that clear enough?

"Clear as ink," Peter said. "It'll be fun, only I don't understand why you bother to go through all that trouble just because a little bombshell has killed herself."

"Just do as I tell you."

"Great, man! Exactly like in a spy novel!"

6

The meeting was being held in the foreign ministry at Smolensk Square, only a few steps from the embassy. I had chosen to walk in spite of the freezing cold. It cleared my head. The foreign ministry is a skyscraper built by Stalin, in the gingerbread style that was his particular version of Gothic pompousness. The cars on the ring road running past the ministry were moving at a snail's pace. Farther down the road two black Volgas had run into each other. *Sipki,* read a sign in the rear window of one of them, in red letters painted on a piece of cardboard. It meant snow tires. The Volga that had run into the rear of the car with studded tires had no sign. The two chauffeurs stood talking and smoking while they waited for the police, oblivious to the traffic that was jamming up around them. The last thing I saw, before I entered through the massive portal into the warmth of the building, was a policeman slowly walking in the direction of the scene of the accident. He looked quite shapeless in his heavy, black coat and large winter overboots, with a white truncheon dangling lightly from the wrist of his thick glove.

The colonel was in uniform. Either he had several of the kind or an extremely tidy wife or servant. It was impeccably pressed. His cap lay on the table in front of him. On his chest were a number of decorations. He was freshly shaven. Only his tired, bloodshot eyes revealed that probably he hadn't slept for forty-eight hours. On the dark mahogany table lay a pile of papers in a red folder: Sonia's death.

Basov looked like something the cat had dragged in. His clothes were wrinkled, and his athletic figure stooped. But he was the only one who gave me a friendly smile as I stepped into the office. It was bare and functional. Like most official offices it was done in shades of brown. On the wall was a formal picture of Lenin.

There were two other persons present on the fourteenth floor. A little farther down alongside the table sat the middle-aged man with the narrow face, dark eyes, and nicotine-stained fingers who had arrived the night before and appeared to head the technical investigation. A woman sat in a corner with a notepad on her lap.

Basov offered tea. We talked about everyday matters while a woman brought in glasses in gray metal holders. Politically, the most important issue that winter was the possibility of resuming the dialogue between the superpowers. Chernenko had decided to send his foreign minister, Gromyko, to Geneva to meet with his American colleague.

"And how is the general secretary? He's in good health, I hope," I said.

The faces of both Colonel Gavrilin and Basov took on that haunted, painful expression that was so easily provoked when they were reminded of the fact that the superpower now had its third leader in as many years, one who was incapable of appearing in public because of illness and old age.

"Comrade Chernenko carries out his duties," Gavrilin said.

"And there are very competent people around him," Basov added. "It's almost possible to speak of a second general secretary at this point," he continued. The colonel looked at him warningly, but Basov remained unconcerned.

"I see," I merely said.

"Comrade Mikhail Sergeivich is said to head several of the meetings of the Politburo with great competence when Chernenko is detained," Basov said, surprisingly. His words weren't wasted on me. Gorbachev, whom we were all observing carefully and considered the man of the future if he could hold his own against the old guard around Chernenko, was Comrade Mikhail Sergeivich. And the leader of the super-power was referred to simply as Chernenko without titles. That was interesting. It was an important piece in the puzzle, and it would be part of my next report home. This was the kind of thing that turned me on, and for a moment I felt quite cheerful, but the colonel brought me back to the present.

"Maybe we could get started?" he said brusquely. Basov didn't look subdued, but smiled rather triumphantly. He had taken advantage of the situation to plant a seed, hoping that I would spread it to the world. Then it would return to Moscow and become a pawn in the brutal power struggle that was taking place in the Kremlin.

The colonel opened the red folder. His large, broad peasant hands carefully held the many sheets of paper. They were standard Russian, grayish and stiff, and densely covered with writing. I saw several stamps on the pages as he monotonously read aloud the entire heap. On his nose he wore a pair of narrow reading glasses that looked much too small for his large, ruddy face. When he had finished reading, he took off the glasses and closed the folder with a meticulous little click. I finished my tea. It had gotten cold. I had taken quick notes along the way.

Everybody had done a good and very professional piece of work, I said, and I may have sounded somewhat arrogant, for Gavrilin reacted vehemently.

"Don't you try to patronize me!"

"I didn't intend to."

"I'll try not to speak to you like a childish Intourist guide. I see the problems, the slovenliness, the moral decay as clearly as you do." He raised his voice. "But the filth doesn't reach us. We're still the sword and the shield of the Party, and the day will come when we'll have our way against the helpless, incompetent drunkards who are throwing dirt on communism. Comrade Andropov's much-too-early death slowed down a development, stifled it, but that won't last forever."

Basov was moving uneasily in his chair. He had turned quite pale. He didn't like that a representative of the KGB was openly threatening to overthrow the government. Every Russian Communist harbors a deep fear: the ghost of Beria. Stalin's chief of police had hundreds of thousands of Party members sent to their deaths. Since then, the Communist Party had always sought to keep the security apparatus on a short leash.

"Do you have any questions?" Basov said in order to bring the conversation back on a safe track.

"I would like to have a copy of the investigation documents," I said.

Basov looked at Gavrilin, who didn't react.

"It doesn't have to be now," I said. I knew that copying machines weren't so easy to get to, even in the Ministry of Foreign Affairs. They were locked away like everything else in the Soviet Union, for fear that the word might be spread through uncontrolled channels. Basov would need the written permission of a superior to use a machine.

He looked relieved.

"You have to understand that we've worked right up till now, and there hasn't been time to copy. But if you'll send a chauffeur tomorrow morning, the documents will be ready."

"All right. Let me just run over my notes so I can write a preliminary report to my ambassador."

I looked at what I had jotted down. It was clear enough. The name of the Soviet woman was Vera Ivanova Petrov. Age twenty-seven. She had died from strangulation between 9:30 and 9:45 P.M. on December 30. There were no other signs of physical violence, apart from some scratch marks on her back. Under Sonia's nails the medico-legal experts had found traces of blood, the same type as Vera's. Sonia had died an hour later. The cause of death was loss of blood due to the severing of the arteries of her wrists with a razor blade. The razor blade had been found in the bathtub. The only indication of violence was a blood effusion on her forehead. According to the experts it had been caused either by a fall or by a blow with a blunt object. The police report stated that the effusion had been caused by a fall, where Sonia's face had hit the edge of the tub. Maybe she had tried to get up. Had she changed her mind?

There were meticulous descriptions of the stomach contents. I noticed that both women had had a high alcohol percentage in their blood. There were lists of what had been found in the apartment. What was most remarkable, apart from the sexual accessories, was the large amount of cash: almost twenty thousand rubles and three thousand dollars.

The neighbors, a Bulgarian diplomat and an American journalist, had been interrogated. The American had reported that he hadn't noticed anything out of the ordinary. Several parties had already been in progress on December 30; and on New Year's Eve most of the apartments had been lit and full of noisy guests till the small hours of the morning. He hadn't known Sonia, only to say hello to. The super had made a statement. He was the one who had been fetched by the Bulgarian diplomat when the smell began to reach his apartment. The super had then got hold of the policemen who guarded the block. In their statement it said that Sonia had returned home in her car at 4:32 P.M. on December 30. The car was a dark blue Golf and easy to recognize because of the red diplomatic license plates and the number 010, which is Denmark's identification number: D 010 867. She had had a female passenger in the car, but the policemen hadn't examined the individual's papers. They were certain that neither Sonia nor her visitor had left the building again. The front door showed no signs of violence.

That was the reason, of course, that the policemen had been so nervous when I arrived that night. It was their responsibility that a Soviet citizen had been smuggled into the building. It's generally assumed that all foreigners' apartments are routinely bugged. Apparently that hadn't been the case with Sonia's apartment that night; but if it had, it would under no circumstances appear in a report for us. I was convinced that Gavrilin had checked the apartment rather carefully before they had called me. Or Basov, for that matter.

Thirteen videocassettes with hard-core pornography, and ten blank ones, had been found. There were a number of fingerprints other than those of the two dead women. They were being analyzed in the central fingerprints register.

"Well, then, I guess that's all there is to say about it," I said.

Colonel Gavrilin looked straight at me. "As far as the two women are concerned, that's it for the Soviet authorities. We have no suspicion of a criminal act involving anyone other than the two dead women. A sex game went too far, and the other woman took her own life. Her bizarre sexual taste in itself seems to indicate a deviant mind." He paused for a moment. "As for the criminal violation of a long line of clauses, Comrade Basov informs me that diplomatic immunity makes it impossible to interrogate the staff of the Danish embassy. But pornography is illegal in the Soviet Union. And I don't suppose I have to remind you of our Exchange Control Act."

Those pornographic cassettes were going to cost the Danish state a lot politically. They were going to hover like a sinister shadow over all bilateral negotiations for a long time into the future. I caught myself cursing Sonia and all her filth.

"However," the colonel continued, "we clearly intend to

pursue the case as far as Soviet citizens are concerned, since they aren't above the law like that. We want to get to the bottom of the whole smutty affair. It would help us in our investigation if the staff of the Danish embassy would agree to have their fingerprints taken . . ."

"That's out of the question," I said angrily.

"Only to help us identify the fingerprints in the apartment. Afterward, the fingerprints would be destroyed, of course."

"It's completely out of the question. And even your suggesting it is a breach of diplomatic practice," I said. "Basov, perhaps you could inform Colonel Gavrilin of the Vienna Convention?"

"That's not necessary," the colonel said in a voice that cut like metal. "I'm not a diplomat, but a policeman. And when I'm faced with a crime, I want to solve it. It's as simple as that. And I'm telling you, Mr. Andersen . . . if I find that others at your embassy are involved, then I'll arrest those individuals."

"Basov!" I said. "This is outrageous. I'm not going to put up with being threatened, directly or indirectly!"

The colonel pushed back his chair. He didn't shake my hand, but merely said, "Thank you for now. Maybe we'll see each other again. Good-bye." He then gathered up the documents of the case in the red folder and walked past Lenin, who was staring down from the wall. The thin man with the narrow lips got up and quietly followed.

I could hear the hissing, wintery sound of the cars down on Smolensk Square. I looked out of the window at two large rectangular buildings with dull lights in the windows. They were hotels, completely alike: Beograd One and Beograd Two. The cars were moving through the intersection in a dense, asymmetrical stream. The two black Volgas that had run into each other had been removed.

"I think we'd better arrange a meeting between the ambassador and Kamarassov," I said to Basov.

"Yes, my friend. There's a good deal for them to discuss in confidence."

I thought about the case as I walked to the American embassy. I was hoping that Carl would have five minutes. I had never got around to calling him. Down the ring road among muffled-up Muscovites pushing their way with their shopping nets, and under the road through a gray pedestrian tunnel filled with dirt and ice. An old woman wrapped in layers of coats and shawls was muttering to herself in a distracted manner. Every once in a while she begged money from the passersby, who pretended not to see her. On the other side of the ring road there was a long line reaching around the corner of the block. From the backboard of a blue truck two men were unloading boxes with potatoes, throwing them hard on the ground. Two women with several layers of clothing underneath their white smocks were setting up scales. There was no movement in the line: people stood as if frozen to the ground, waiting. I regretted not having taken the car, after all. It was bitterly cold, and it was beginning to snow; small hard grains of frost whipping through the darkness. The city was almost black. The cars had only their parking lights on, the streetlights were dim, and only a feeble glow emanated from the shop windows.

The usual policemen were posted in front of the American embassy, a large, yellow, boxy building on the ring road. Behind it, the United States were building a new embassy complex, but the construction work proceeded slowly. Because of my fur cap, the policemen took me for a Soviet citizen, in spite of my expensive coat. The two men, both dressed in black and armed with pistols, moved closer together and blocked the entrance. It's against all international agreements that the Soviet Union prevents its own citizens from having free access to foreign embassies in this way. I tried staring hard at them, but they didn't budge, so I laboriously fished out my identity card. They made great show of examining it before they saluted and let me continue into the warm embassy.

Inside, a black U.S. Marine stood behind a glass wall. I told him who I was and asked permission to use the phone that hung on the wall.

"Hello Jack! How are you?" Carl said a moment later on the telephone. "Meet me in Uncle Sam, and we'll have a cup of coffee."

It was nice and warm in Uncle Sam. Just as warm as it was icy cold outside in the embassy courtyard, where you had to run the gauntlet between broken bricks and large compressed blocks of ice and heaps of snow. Uncle Sam is the cafeteria of the embassy, a small piece of America in Moscow, with advertising posters for Budweiser and California wines. Only American diplomats and journalists could pay there, with small punch cards that only they could buy, so I sat down by a table and waited for Carl. In a corner a group of correspondents sat drinking beer and exchanging rumors. It was the usual stuff about Chernenko, who was dying, and Sakharov, who was either dying or on his way to the West. I nodded at a couple of them whom I knew vaguely, but they didn't invite me over. I sat for five minutes and got the warmth back in my body. It spread with a buzzing sensation from the torso to the fingers, which turned quite red. Then I called home from the telephone in the cafeteria. I let it ring a couple of times while I looked out into the kitchen. The Russian staff was frying hamburgers and french fries. I felt hungry. I hadn't had any lunch. I hoped that Carl would treat me to a burger. It was irritating to be in a place and not be able to buy anything, in spite of having money. It struck me that Russians probably felt like that all the time when they looked at the shops where only people with hard currencies could shop. When they saw the merchandise that they themselves would never have access to. I knew of no society where privileges and tickets of admission to every aspect of life were meted out to such a degree, dividing the population into haves and have-nots. A new, man-made class system where the rules that determined rank and precedence were as complicated and impenetrable as at the court of a medieval prince.

There was no answer, so I called the embassy. I got John. I asked him to send a car to the American embassy. He said that he would do so if he could get hold of the chauffeur.

"CW wants you to come over for a drink in about an hour," he continued neutrally. "CW wants to say a few words to Castesen, and feels that we should all be there to congratulate him, in spite of the tragedy. That's what he said."

"OK. I'll be there."

He paused for a second before he said, "Your wife is already here. She just arrived."

I said nothing.

"You want me to put you through?" he asked.

"No. Just send the car," I said, and hung up.

A matron in a white smock, who had been there for as long as anyone could remember, banged a steaming burger with onions and cheese and French fries down on the counter. My teeth were watering. She was wearing a white chef's cap with wisps of hair sticking out from underneath its edge. The staff was the one thing that constantly called to mind that this was not the United States, but Moscow. "Cheeseburger!" she bellowed into a small mike, her voice resounding harshly in the loudspeaker above my head.

"Are you hungry, old boy?" Carl Sorensen was standing right next to me. He wore a crew cut and was a couple of years younger than I. His face was attractive in a neutral, general sort of way, the most characteristic features being a very white smile and a nose that looked as if it had once been broken.

"Very."

"My treat. Cheeseburger, OK?" he said in his flat, Midwestern accent.

We sat down by a table in a corner. I tore a scrap of paper out of my notebook and wrote: Vera Ivanova Petrov, 27, Muscovite, probably a prostitute, died December 30. I pushed the slip across the table to him.

He threw one glance at it and put it in the pocket of his jacket.

"I'll see what I can do."

"Consider it a favor."

"OK, you owe me one. Is it bad?"

"I don't think so, but there's no harm in checking."

"True, old pal. But I promise nothing."

"Good enough," I said.

He looked at me with concern. "Are you in shape, Jack? You look a little green about the gills. How about a couple of rounds one of these days?"

"If you aren't scared," I said.

He laughed. "That's just a word."

"OK, let's talk on the phone tomorrow. Susanne is here."

"Say hello to your beautiful wife. Am I going to have the honor of seeing her this time?"

"I don't know, Carl. I think she's come to say good-bye, and this time she means it." Carl had followed the decline of my marriage rather closely.

"You're a fool if you let go of such a great wife."

"Maybe she's the one who's letting go of me."

Carl looked at me. His eyes were very blue and narrow. He shook a cigarette out of the pack and then handed the pack to me. I took one, too. It was an unfiltered Camel. Carl was one of the few Americans I knew who still smoked. We had been friends for more than two years now, and had spent several weekends together at Savidova on the Volga River, where, behind barbed wire, the Russians had built a vacation colony for us. Susanne and Carl got along well together. I remembered long sunny Saturdays filled with wine and laughter, and Susanne creeping into my bed naked at night, smelling of wine and toothpaste and cool perfume. She had been tanned as usual, but in the soft darkness the white outlines from her bathing suit gleamed around her breasts and her sex. She had been soft and warm from the sun, and the wine and a happy day had made her want me. I got depressed at the thought that that time would never come back.

"It's a man's job to hold on to a woman. Keep her warm in bed, Jack, then she'll stay with you," Carl said without any trace of irony in his voice.

"That's a lot of baloney."

He looked a little offended, but then he shrugged and said: "What do I know of marriage? I've never left my hat on the same peg long enough for any woman to get me up the aisle."

"You can still make it."

He shook his head, either to say that he couldn't or maybe to say that he couldn't imagine throwing himself into such a risky business.

"Is beer OK?" he said. "I think the general has the food ready." The matron in Uncle Sam had been there so long and had probably caught so much gossip that everyone assumed she would have advanced at least to the rank of general in the KGB. Officially her English vocabulary was limited to "yes," "no," "OK," and "cheeseburger."

Carl got up to fetch the food. He walked lightly, like the boxer he had once been. I followed my favorite spy with my eyes. His official function was that of third cultural attaché, but he didn't spend much time at the Bolshoi. He was thoroughly professional and my friend. I felt at ease in the warm cafeteria. The atmosphere was light and friendly and around us people spoke English. Moscow felt far away. It wasn't the worst place in Moscow to postpone my meeting with Susanne.

7

Susanne sat on the sofa at CW's residence with a drink in her hand. I walked over to her through the small group of Danish and foreign colleagues that CW had managed to drum up. He was very much into formalities of this kind and made a point of celebrating important dates: the queen's birthday, Constitution Day—and Castesen's promotion to ambassador. It would have been more appropriate if we'd all worn black armbands.

Susanne smiled and offered her cheek for me to kiss, which I did, dutifully. She smelled of gin and Chanel No. 5. Her eyes were slightly bloodshot, but she still looked good with her oval face and luxuriant hair. Her figure was getting a little too lush, though. Soon she'd have to watch it. But that was probably me driving her to drink.

Jette sat next to her on the sofa. She was smiling secretively as if she knew everything about us and moved over to make room for me next to my wife.

"How was the flight?" I asked.

"I thought you were going to ask me how I am," Susanne said.

"How are you, Susanne?"

"You know what he really wants to ask me, Jette?" Susanne said, leaning over me so that her breast pressed against my arm. "He would like to ask if I've remembered to buy all the newspapers in Kastrup. Isn't that right, Jack?"

"I think I'll go and get a drink," I said.

CW had gathered about thirty people at short notice. Most of them stood with drinks in small groups, talking with blank expressions on their faces. Lena, the Russian maid, was carrying a tray of glasses around. I smiled at her when she came up to me and indicated with her finger where my special drink was placed: Scotch on the rocks.

"How's your son doing?" I asked her. Her son was in Afghanistan.

"I had a letter from him yesterday. He's doing well. He writes that he's bored."

"At least that's better than if it gets too exciting."

"They probably tell him what to write," she said, and moved on.

There was another maid, also dressed in black. That one I didn't know. Lena's usual colleague had been sick for a while. The new one was offering snacks on a tray. I spotted Mrs. W, who was having a conversation with the wife of the British ambassador, but at the same time making sure, with her trained and tired eyes, that the trays were carried around in the right order, and that everyone had enough to drink. She knew it all by heart. I looked over at Susanne, who was talking with Jette. My Swedish colleague had taken my seat. Susanne looked up at me, smiling ironically before turning her eyes away.

Castesen stood with CW, beaming like a sun, although it was obvious that they both needed sleep. The dark blue suits couldn't hide the exhaustion. I crossed the room to join them, saying hello to people right and left, but without making the effort to stop and make conversation. It was a small celebration, so everyone discreetly avoided talking about what was really on their minds: Sonia's sudden end.

There were beautiful old paintings on the walls. A grand piano dominated the high-ceilinged rooms. The clean parqueted floors shone warmly. The voices sounded like a distant murmur between the light-colored walls. Outside, behind the closed French doors, the garden lay dark and cold. I moved around in diplomatic eights exchanging remarks with colleagues and acquaintances, slowly approaching the spot where Susanne was sitting. But she was gone. I turned around and stood face to face with Marie Castesen. She was a few years younger than me, a small, thin woman with long hair that she wore down her back like a sixteen-year-old schoolgirl. She and Castesen had met when she was very young and had had children early. She was from some provincial town, but had assumed an accent as if she had grown up in one of the rich, northern suburbs of Copenhagen. It never sounded quite convincing, though. Her voice cut into my headache. "A sad day, isn't it, Jack?"

"I wouldn't exactly call it merry."

"No, I can imagine how it must affect you."

"No more than everyone else, I guess. But what's happened can't be changed, of course."

She let the ice cubes roll around at the bottom of her glass. Her face was ravaged, but she didn't try to conceal the damage with makeup. Her eyes were aggressive. "But he has earned it. He deserves to get that post. In spite of everything you've done to prevent it."

I had been thinking that she was talking about Sonia. Now I realized that it was Castesen's promotion that was supposed to gall me.

With a broad grin I said, "Marie, congratulations on your husband. It's too bad for you that it turned out not to be Paris." I raised my glass.

"Poland is a sensitive and extremely important area," she said in her affected voice. She loved everything French, she often said. So did Castesen. Marie had never found it worth her while to learn Russian. She took French lessons in Moscow. She always tried to make it clear to everyone what an exciting life she led as the wife of a diplomat, and one of her ways of doing so was by sprinkling foreign words into her Danish: an elevator, for example, became a lift. She drew in her horns, though, when CW gave her an icy glance one time she leaned up against him and called him "Mon Vieux."

"You're right, Warsaw probably isn't so bad at all," I said. She looked at me suspiciously. It always made her nervous when I was friendly.

"What do you mean by that?" she asked.

"Do you know the story about the Soviet officer and the French officer?" She shook her head and took a sip of ice-cube water from the bottom of her glass, while she swept the room with a long glance to find Lena with the fresh drinks.

"They were going on a trip. The Soviet officer was going to Paris. And the French officer was going to Moscow. They both took the train. Then they met in Warsaw and both thought that they had reached their destination."

She just looked at me with a small smile, so I took a deep pull of my drink, and then Lena appeared and saved us both.

"You don't like me. You don't like me, because I've gotten somewhere, and particularly because Henrik is everything that you can never be," she said.

"I've already been told that once today," I said.

"Why are you always out to get Henrik?" she asked.

"Am I?"

"Yes," she said so loudly that she checked herself and lowered her voice. "You do everything in your power to oppose him. You don't think he's qualified. And he says that you're spreading gossip about him."

"I don't give a damn about Castesen," I said.

She smiled contemptuously. Now she'd caught me. I could not reason, all I could do was be rude.

"You're a vulgar person, Jack. Just as vulgar as your idiotic name."

"But you're an angel on earth."

"At least I know how to behave. I don't see the necessity of being an inverted snob, trying to imitate the most vulgar part of the population. I know how hard Henrik has worked for that promotion. I know how much it means to him and to his family. And I know that he deserves it. He should have had Paris. He's far better qualified than the incompetent to whom they gave Paris."

"Amen," I said.

"Why are you so hostile, Jack?" Her voice sounded friendlier.

"That's the way of the lower classes."

"Do you really think that anyone in the eighties is seriously concerned with such a thing as class . . ." She didn't finish the sentence.

"Castesen is fond of talking of natural breeding."

"That has nothing to do with where a person was born."

"We ought to be thankful for that, you and I," I said. "We come from the same mews, and the smell sticks no matter what we do."

She smiled condescendingly. "Maybe you'll grow up some day."

"Not the way grown-ups behave."

"You're putting on an act, Jack. You're pretending to be different, as if you were just playing your way through life without ambitions. You're trying to give the rest of us the impression that you don't want anything, yet you're one of the most ambitious men that I know. You don't use your elbows. You use large, sharp knives, and most of them you're hiding up your sleeves."

"What did you think of Sonia?" I said.

"She was a whore."

"Why? Because she went after your husband?"

"Jack, you're just jealous. Instead of making me angry, you make me feel sorry for you. You're like a little boy who's stuck in a lift."

I looked at her. She was looking at me with a haughty smile as if she had a secret. Finally she lowered her eyes and was about to turn on her heels when she checked herself and said in a low voice, "What Henrik does or doesn't do with other women is no concern of mine. As long as he respects me, and as long as I'm number one and his wife, he can do whatever he wants to do."

"Well, here's to Henrik," I said, and raised my glass, and strangely enough she raised hers as well. She belonged to a dying breed of women: no education, no independence, totally reliant on her husband financially. A life without Castesen would be a life in a one-bedroom apartment. It would mean no more furs, no more travels or receptions, no more respect. I knew her spoiled, snobbish children: they were definitely not going to accept that their mother took on a badly paid unskilled job. They belonged to a new generation that cared only about money and status. Castesen would keep the children. Marie was trapped with her three years of Danish literature at the university a hundred years ago. I could understand her, the poor old girl. If I were her, I'd be willing to swallow a camel or two.

I drifted past the groups of people and through the tobacco smoke over to Castesen, who was holding court with the British ambassador and CW. Castesen was beaming like a child in an amusement park. His skin had almost taken on some color, other than the usual gray. When I approached the group, I heard Castesen tell the same story that I had just told Marie. Castesen had more success. Even though they had undoubtedly heard it before, they all laughed politely.

"Jack," Castesen said cordially, "I believe you know every-one here?" He nodded to each of the four people standing in a circle around him. I had been in Moscow for more than three years and knew everybody, so there was a moment of embar-rassed silence.

"Why, Jack is our senior here and has been here longer than anyone in this group, I believe. One of the most experienced and knowledgeable diplomats we have in Moscow," CW said angelically, but Castesen caught the gibe. CW was not going to put up with anything. If anyone were to be snubbed in his home, CW would be the one to do it. Castesen shifted his weight from one foot to the other and got the conversation back on track.

"You were saying, very correctly, Brian, that with Solidar-ity underground and the Communist Party Bonapartized, the situation in Warsaw is particularly explosive right now, which makes it an extremely interesting post at this point." That was the kind of nonsense that Castesen excelled at, but the British ambassador smiled his professional smile.

"Very interesting, to be sure."

"Yes, for in spite of its superpower status, you have to admit that Moscow is a place where the standstill is almost complete," Castesen said.

"Until Chernenko dies; then development will explode, and Moscow will be the cynosure of the world for many years to come," I said haughtily.

"Chernenko will probably last another couple of years, and afterward I think it's most likely that the Party will play it safe once again and choose somebody stable from the old guard," Castesen said.

I was bored, and my glass was empty again. I heard CW save the situation with a remark on the importance of Warsaw from a Danish point of view. Obviously we had a particular obliga-tion there toward our allies as far as surveillance was concerned. Then his voice disappeared, and I stood facing Susanne, who also held an empty glass in her hand.

This time she wasn't going to get away.

"Who is Tomas?" I said in a low voice.

"Get me a drink, honey," she said, and held her glass out to me.

"Damn it, Susanne!"

"He's my lover."

"I've understood that much."

"Are you jealous, Jack? That's not like you. We've both had our little flings, right?"

"But why so demonstrative this time?"

"Let's talk about it when we get home, but it's over, Jack!"

"It's been over before."

"I've found a job," she said.

"Congratulations. If my glass weren't empty, I'd drink to your happiness."

"Always the ironic Jack. Aren't you going to ask me where?"

"Where have you found a job?"

"That's none of your damned business," she said. That was how bad it was between us.

Jette came brushing up against us like a large, affectionate barnyard cat.

"A little marital showdown in the middle of Castesen's great night," she said. "Can I listen in? The second person's loss is the third person's gain, right?"

"Even your proverbs stink," I said.

She hushed me. "You're in a mean mood today, Jackie boy," she said.

I was perspiring all over and not feeling well. I was fed up with all the superficial blather that I had to listen to. I suddenly remembered the old man in *Cat on a Hot Tin Roof*—Big Daddy—when he says to Paul Newman, "Can you smell the mendacity?" The mendacity around me was so thick that you could cut it with a knife.

"That's just the way he is," Susanne said. "That's why I can't stand him anymore. But actually we were talking about how boring it is here in Moscow. I arrived only four hours ago, and it feels as if I've never been gone. All that the men talk about is politics, and all the women talk about is what they can't buy and when they'll get out. It's fucking unbearable."

"Then leave, Susanne. That's something we working girls can't do so easily," Jette said in her coarse, inebriated voice.

"That's exactly what I'm going to do," Susanne said.

Once again Lena saved the situation with her tray of drinks. She held it out with a small, ironic smile at the many problems of the masters, and we put on our nice faces as we reached for our drinks.

"I'm leaving in a short while," I said, and left them.

Susanne came along. We didn't say a word to each other on our way home. I drove carefully through the dark streets. I'd had far too much to drink, and shouldn't have been driving. I wasn't worried about the police, but feared for our own safety. The police would either not care or would accept a bribe of five rubles. The whole nation was in the process of drinking itself to death anyway, so one foreigner more or less didn't mean much, as long as he didn't run over a Soviet citizen. Which is what I almost did. It happened just as I was about to turn right and continue up our little road. A man who appeared to be dead drunk suddenly veered around and staggered across the sidewalk out onto the middle of the road. He nearly fell, but recovered his balance. However, the weight of his body had its own inertia, and in an accelerating, running movement, it pulled him across the road and into the snowbank on the other side. I jammed on the brakes, making the rear end of the car skid. I hadn't been going particularly fast, but still the car rotated a hundred and eighty degrees, coming to a stop just before it would have hit the man. He got up and stared at me with eyes that saw nothing. Then he swayed, keeled over once more, and stayed down this time.

I got the car back on the road and slowly drove the short distance home and into the courtyard. Miraculously, there was an empty space. The man would freeze to death if he were left lying there, but the policeman who guarded the building had seen the incident. He would probably call for a car to take the man to the detention hospital, or the "Get Sober" clinic, as those places were called. In the winter many drunkards froze to death.

I kept seeing his empty white face; but I was spent, I couldn't take on responsibility for him. Susanne was shaken, too. We took off our coats and sat down facing each other without a word. We had almost become sober, and neither of us felt like drinking more.

I made an omelette for us, which we ate in silence. Susanne made coffee, and then we sat down in front of each other again.

Then Susanne began to talk. She spoke softly and created a feeling of confidence and intimacy between us. She spoke logically, and she was right, so I didn't have to say anything. She said that we had to let go of each other. We hadn't had much together the last two years in any case. Moscow hadn't been the cause, but had precipitated a process that had already begun. She saw no reason to discuss the collapse of our marriage. Instead we should be happy about the good years we'd had together. We should also be glad that we didn't have any children. Then she looked up.

"I'm sorry, Jack. Maybe that would have made things different." I said nothing, but my head felt as if it was going to explode. It was my fault. I couldn't have children. We had tried for more than two years before Susanne made me see a doctor. I was sterile. Naturally, I had assumed that it was her.

She calmly told me that she had found a job at her old bank, and that the bank would pay for a computer course for her. She would move as soon as she had packed. She had found a lawyer and asked me to do likewise. She was hoping that it could all take place quietly and calmly, and that we could part as friends. Then she took a small sip of her coffee, and I remembered how she had drunk wine in the same neatly sipping way when we had made love a century ago in the small Italian mountain village that we had called our own.

"Where are you going to live?" I asked.

"I was hoping you wouldn't ask."

"But I do ask."

"I'm moving in with Tomas."

"Out of the frying pan into the fire."

"I've known him for a while." She groped for her lighter and found it. She tried exasperatedly to light it several times before she succeeded. Down on the Sadovaya the screeching brakes of a truck could be heard over the dense muffled sound of traffic on snow and ice.

"It's none of my business. But who is he? Do I know him?" I asked stupidly, but I felt like knowing who was going to take over my woman.

"You don't know him. He's a student . . ."

"A perpetual student?" I said.

"He's only twenty-four," she said.

"Oh, come on, Susanne. Are you robbing cradles now? He's more than ten years younger than you." I had raised my voice.

"I know my age, thank you. And I knew that you would react like that. That's why I didn't want to say anything." She angrily put out her cigarette.

"Goddamnit, Susanne."

"Can't you try to be a little more articulate? Why don't you take a look at your own prejudices. If you found a girl of twenty-five, everyone would find it natural. When a woman does it, she's made fun of. I thought you were more sophisticated than that, Jack."

"Do you have to move in with him?"

"He says that he loves me."

"What about you?"

"He makes me happy. I don't drink all the time, like when I'm with you. I enjoy being worshiped." She leaned forward and looked me straight in the eyes. She didn't raise her voice, but stressed every word. "I enjoy being desired. I enjoy sex with him, Jack. Going to bed with you had become like fucking with a machine. And yes, I think I love him. At any rate, I'm very much *in love* with him. That's wonderful, Jack. I haven't tried that for many years, maybe never. Are you satisfied? Do you have to drag everything down?" She yelled out the last sentence.

"There's always a lot to be said for young potent meat, isn't there?" I shouted. I could feel the alcohol again, and it was making me aggressive. I knew that I had to watch it. I had never hit her, but now I was getting close. The whole day and many other days of my life were like a coiled spring in my stomach. Reality was falling apart.

"Let's stop now, Jack," she said softly. "I didn't mean to hurt you."

"I don't need any goddamn pity."

"Jack," she said pleadingly.

I took the coffee cup and threw it against the wall, shattering it with a hollow sound. That was enough. The tension began to dissolve inside me, but I must have looked very angry and frightening. Susanne had pulled all the way back on the sofa. She looked more afraid than I'd ever seen her before, so frightened that she made me afraid of myself. There was nothing more to say. It was over. Susanne severed the tie between us completely in the end. She held her hands over her stomach and said: "Jack . . . don't hit me. I'm pregnant."

8

I hit harder than I meant to, working my straight left into his side, but he was still quick, and, catching me as I relaxed my guard, he cut my cheek. We were both panting like overweight circus clowns as we freed ourselves from the clinch. I was too aggressive. My blood was up, so I persisted and tried a fast, calculated combination before I almost lost control of myself. I drove him back with one blow after the other, using the weight of my body without restraint. We were both wheezing and spitting through our gum shields. His eyes were small and narrow, but not afraid, and of course he took advantage of my lack of self-control. He did the only right thing to protect himself and caught me with a right-handed counter cross that made my head ring. With a bump I sat down on the foot-worn wooden floor.

"We'll stop here, I think," Carl said somewhere in the distance. Slowly, his angry face looming over me came into focus.

I nodded, but remained sitting as I took off my gloves. He turned on his heels and went to the corner for his towel. He found mine, too, and threw it at me on the floor. Still sitting,

I began to wipe off the sweat. Carl looked at me with calm eyes. His body was glistening with perspiration. He took off the black boxing helmet, revealing a red mark on his cheek. His crew-cut hair stood straight up in the air. The skin shone through a bald spot that was beginning on top, but his body was still firm, with only a suggestion of "handles" above the hips. I pulled off my helmet, too, and threw it across the floor.

Carl walked over to me and leaned forward, extending his hand. I smiled and let him pull me up. I felt a little foolish.

"Did it do you any good?" he said. "Did you get it out of your system?"

"Did you have to hit that hard?"

"Damn it, you were smelling blood. You were back in the ring, man. You were going for a knockout." His voice sounded neutral, but I could see the anger somewhere right behind his calm eyes. A red spot was beginning to form under his left rib cage.

"I'm sorry," I said.

"Oh, forget it. But who the hell was I a stand-in for?"

"Moscow in general," I said.

"A big adversary," he said.

"And myself, to some extent," I continued.

"An even bigger one, but let's stop this cracker-barrel philosophizing nonsense and get in the shower. I have something for you."

I trudged after him.

Carl Sorensen and I shared a passion for boxing. That was how we'd come to know each other. I had gotten as far as a regional championship. Carl was an old college champion. I was a natural light heavyweight, while he was one class below, but he was a lot faster and in better shape than I, so we were rather equal when we took three or four rounds in the dusty room underneath the American embassy. We tried to recapture our lost youth by taking a good long run, half an hour with the sand bag and the punching ball, and finally a friendly fight during which we tried not to hit each other too hard in the face. It was a great arrangement, one we both enjoyed. Susanne derisively called it boyish nonsense.

But Susanne was gone. And so was Sonia. She had been shipped to Denmark in her zinc coffin, and two weeks after her death it felt at the embassy as if she had never existed. I had almost forgotten about her myself in the routine of the day-to-day, but still her presence hung over everything like a shadow.

We stood under the hot shower next to each other. Women undoubtedly have a special sense of solidarity between them, but men, too, can have an intimacy together when they have shared a physical effort and shower together afterward: Locker-room boastfulness when you're young; a relaxed common understanding when you've grown older.

"Is she gone?" Carl asked over the gurgling sound of the water in the drain on the floor.

"Five days ago."

"She'll probably be back."

"Not this time. She's moving in with another guy."

"So I guess he was the one I had to be a punching ball for," Carl said. "Is he as good looking as me?" he continued with his crooked grin. His cheek had begun to swell where I had hit him. I cautiously placed a finger on my own cheek, which felt sore and swollen as well. At least I wouldn't have to listen to Susanne's derisive comments when I got home. She had always found it ridiculous that a grown man came home looking like someone who'd been in a fight. It had happened once before, when Carl had miscalculated; he had hit me too hard and split my eyebrow. Otherwise there was rarely anything showing when we two old men tried to remember forgotten skills and pleasures.

"At any rate, he's ten years younger than you," I said after a while.

Carl whistled.

"I see," he said. "No wonder you hit so hard today. Now I understand much better why he needs a good beating."

"We're the ones who are old-fashioned."

"Maybe, my friend. Maybe. But that doesn't make it hurt less."

"You had something for me?"

Carl sent me a sidelong glance. He suddenly looked businesslike, although we remained standing under the warm water. It was a nice sensation to feel the warmth on my physically exhausted body; and besides, the sound of the water worked as a screen against possible bugging. I looked down my own body. "Handles" on the hips, a beginning belly, chest hair that was turning gray, changing skin color, and veins that were becoming more conspicuous. Old age was on the march, and it was always most noticeable when we stood naked in the shower.

"I don't have much, but your little Russian prostitute is not a professional as far as we know. She probably reported to the local KGB thug at the hotels in order for him to leave her alone, but we have nothing on her to make us believe that she was a professional."

"But still you had a file on her?"

"Yes, we have a little on her. She was also involved in some black-market business. Beriozka checks, currency transactions. But they all are. They can hardly avoid that if they hang out at hotel bars."

"In other words, not exactly a persecuted innocent?"

"All right, but this is a favor and only between you and me," he said over the sound of the streaming water. "We checked her out about a year ago. One of our marines fell for her charm, and the idiot brought her inside the embassy. He claimed that she had said that she was Finnish. Those guys never learn."

"But you took it seriously?"

"Seriously enough to risk a contact with one of our people in the system, but he came back with a negative. The marine swore that she was only interested in money and gifts from the dollar shop. Not information. He was nineteen, and she was apparently a very sophisticated lady in bed. We sent him home, but they reached the same conclusion in the States: it was sex, not treason."

"Is there more?"

"That's what I can tell you. And even that is too much. Sorry, old pal. But you know the rules."

"Thank you," I said. We began to lather up and rinsed off in silence. Just before we turned off the water, I asked, "Do you have anything on her sister?"

Carl hesitated with his hand on the faucet. "I didn't even know she had a sister. You're chasing a moonbeam, Jack. She was a prostitute. Like so many others here, she was hoping to meet an old businessman who could carry her out to freedom via the wedding palace."

"You're probably right," I said.

"Come, I'll treat you to a beer and a hamburger at Uncle Sam," he said.

"Sounds good."

He turned off the water and looked at me. His eyes were friendly and warm.

"You don't look good, Jack. You're not feeling quite well, I think. Why don't you come home with me afterward? It's been a long time since we last emptied a bottle of Scotch together and solved all the problems of the world."

I was grateful for his offer. It was an appealing thought: to get half drunk at his apartment and shoot the bull while listening to his old records of Dylan, The Grateful Dead, The Doors, Janis Joplin, and the other biggies from our youth; but Peter was due back from Denmark with the mail bag, and I had a dinner date at the Praga.

"It sounds good," I said. "But I'm going out."

"OK. But the door is always open."

"I know," I said.

He slapped me on the shoulder.

"Come on, let's have that hamburger and a cold beer," he said to take away the embarrassment that we both felt all of a sudden.

Monday was mail day at the Danish embassy, the day the courier arrived with the diplomatic bag from Copenhagen. Along with the diplomatic mail came private letters. We took turns making the trip. It had become a tradition that we gathered in the basement under the embassy, in a small dusty room where we drank beer and received our letters. Exaggerating a little, we called it "the bar." Actually, the guards bought a case of beer and some potato chips, that was all. Some of the Danish students used the evening as a recess from the difficult, complicated everyday life in Moscow. We strictly followed the rules, so they weren't permitted to send their mail through us, but of course there was no harm in offering them a beer.

Peter had made the trip to Denmark and back. I had not had time to talk with him yet, and he looked at me as if he couldn't wait. We were standing around a couple of chairs with our cans of beer, going over the letters that had arrived. There weren't any private letters for me, only one from a lawyer. Susanne's lawyer, I imagined, so I stuck it into my briefcase without opening it.

Jette's big frame appeared beside me. "Have you been in a fight?"

"I walked into a door."

"Well, forgive me for asking," she said. "I was only trying to be friendly."

Peter stood fidgeting impatiently behind her. His open face was eager like a child's before the gifts are unwrapped. Jette gave up and left to join a group of students who were discussing the food situation. They always complained, rightfully, about the fact that it was almost impossible to get something decent to eat. Peter handed me a white envelope with no sender's name or address, only my name written in block letters. I stuffed it into my inside pocket.

We went over to the window, a little removed from the others. The room was buzzing pleasantly. The students were sending longing glances toward John, who was broiling frankfurters in the back—they could hardly wait. Castesen rarely turned up: he was too high and mighty to mingle with the common people. CW would come by every now and then to chat with the students. In a sort of avuncular manner he would ask them about their life and health and entertain them with stories from the many countries that he had been stationed in. They looked upon him with indulgence, like a strange creature from another planet, but actually they rather liked him. Every Christmas Eve he invited them and other members of the small Danish colony to a Christmas party at the embassy. It was almost enough to bring tears to the young students' eyes when they saw the lit Christmas tree and smelled the roast pork.

"Any news?" Peter asked, obviously vexed that I didn't ask him the same question.

"The investigation has been closed. Sonia's body has been sent home. I've received all the papers from the Russians. An accident and a suicide. The case is closed."

"I did as you suggested and snooped around a bit," he said.

"Then what did you find?"

He took a pull at the green beer can.

"Not much, but enough. I talked with the marines, the journalists, and the girls at the National. Sonia was often bored. Then she hit the bars. She always went to the bar of the Australian embassy on Fridays. Sometimes she went with journalists and marines to the dollar bar of the National. They all knew her there. One night she met Vera. They began to go out together, and people say that they provided videocassettes for the black market. They made lots of money on that."

"I see," I merely said.

"Sonia had a reputation for being game for anything. They say she went out with Russians. You could easily have fired her."

The videocassettes explained the large amount of cash. VHS tapes brought in up to five hundred rubles on the black market. If there were pornographic recordings on them, they could fetch as much as two thousand rubles. But I knew that the black marketeers rarely sold a pornographic tape. Instead they arranged showings at home, charging between ten and twenty rubles for admission. I remembered once reading an article in a local newspaper about two brothers in Armenia who had received ten years of prison each for showing pornographic videotapes. In seven months they had earned half a million dollars. The police had confiscated diamonds, gold, and caviar from their apartment.

"So Sonia smuggled them into the country in the diplomatic bag?" I asked.

"It looks like it. It's a lot of money to refuse. They say that Vera had quite a hold on her."

Peter took another pull at his beer.

"Why don't you come with me to the Praga?" I asked. "You've earned it."

"I'd like to."

"Then you'll meet a Russian celebrity."

He looked at me.

"Demichev," I said.

"That fool."

"Yes, but a fool of some distinction," I said.

Before we left for the Praga, I went into my office. Everything was quiet at the embassy. All that I could hear was the muffled sound of American voices from the video in the guards' room. The guard on duty was watching a film to while away the long evening and night. I opened the white envelope with my paper knife. There was a single sheet of paper inside. It was typed, but with no sender, date, or anything else that might identify its provenance. But of course, it was from my friend in the military intelligence service. I sat staring at it for a while. It was a habit I had developed after the separation. I would be occupied with some small task, a report or a document that I had to finish. Then it would all slowly get out of focus, and my thoughts would disappear, as if through a tiny hole in my brain. I would completely forget what I had been doing, as though my brain were the memory of a computer and someone had pressed the delete button by mistake and removed the program and all the input. What was left was just empty darkness. I didn't understand why, because I didn't miss Susanne, not consciously at any rate. But I felt alone and often very lonely, even though I was surrounded by people all day long. I sat in this mental darkness for a while, and as usual, I couldn't remember what I had been thinking of. I tore myself out of the nothingness and angrily switched on both lamps over my desk. I lit a cigarette. Then there was a knock on the door. It was CW.

"May I?" he said, and stepped inside. He was dressed for some dinner party, in a dark three-piece suit.

"Do you want a cup of coffee? It's rather old. From this afternoon."

He didn't, but I poured myself a cup and placed the letter with the typed side facing down against the dark brown mahogany of the table. He cleared his throat. I looked at the books on my shelves. They were all about Soviet history, about present-day politics and international relations, disarmament and security matters. Susanne had been of the opinion that I and others like me ought to read philosophy and psychology, then maybe we wouldn't go on leading the world straight toward Armageddon. Like most upper-class children of her generation, she had never let go of her mild Danish version of naive faith in socialism and the fundamental goodness of human beings. CW cleared his throat once more.

"What is it, CW?" I asked.

"Jack, my boy. You know that I think very highly of you and of your professional qualifications."

"Get to the point, CW."

"Even though you're definitely a rough diamond."

I smiled at him. He looked seriously at me.

"We're going to the ministry tomorrow. I'd like you to come with me. Today Kamarassov has given me to understand that Sonia's case can now be considered closed. Unofficially, he has also indicated to me that there will be no bilateral complications. And as a sign of goodwill, everything seems to indicate that Aalborg Shipyard will get the order they've fought for so long to obtain."

He lit a cigarette.

"Why this un-Russian desire for reconciliation? Like the Americans say: What's in it for them?" I said.

"Nothing, it seems. Still, I've been instructed from back home that I can promise that the minister will use part of his speech at the next general assembly of the U.N. to at least mention a nuclear-free zone in the north. Chernenko would like to make that one of the token foreign policy issues of the year."

"That doesn't sound like much. What's behind this?"

He leaned toward me and whispered, "It's not for us to ask. The message from back home is clear enough. Let's sweep the whole filthy affair under the carpet. The Russians are more than willing to forget it. Thank God."

I got up and turned on the television in the corner. When the picture and the sound came through, I turned it up rather loud. Then I leaned over CW, who looked somewhat hunched up.

"Why are you bringing this up now? We could have discussed it during working hours."

"Jack, my boy. It's well known in the department—and even worse, outside as well—that you're asking questions, and that some of the questions are of such a nature that you appear to be blackening another man's reputation. It might damage your career."

"In other words, this is a warning," I said angrily.

He got up. He placed his hand on my shoulder.

"No. It's a favor. And it's also making amends. I told you to ask around. Now I'm asking you not to. I want you to do well. Someday, I would like to see you in my chair."

"OK."

With a sigh of relief he sat down again.

"Does that mean that you're going to cooperate?"

"I'm not a policeman, am I?"

"No, thank God. You'll become a good ambassador someday."

I smiled at him. "Do you know how one of your great colleagues in the past, an Englishman, described your job?" I asked.

CW said, "And when you've read the paper that you're hiding from me, then burn it."

I looked angry.

"Jack. That's why I'm telling you: Stop now. Sonia wasn't worth it. Life goes on. We have far more important tasks. She was just another secretary, and a bad sort to boot. Her interests can't possibly be more important than those of the society as a whole."

"I don't believe that she killed herself. And if she did, then someone forced her to do it," I said.

"You're not being logical," CW said. "Drop the case. There

are more important issues on which you may apply your un-questionable abilities at these complicated times." To show me the conversation was over, he moved toward the door.

"Don't you want to hear what your colleague thought of the profession?" I asked.

He opened the door a little and looked back at me before he quoted, "An ambassador is an honest man who is sent out to lie for his country."

"You're so clever," I said.

"It was Sir Henry Watton."

"I'm impressed."

"He served under one of the more interesting kings of England, James the First."

"Get lost, CW," I said.

"Like I said, a rough diamond . . . good evening, my boy."

He closed the door with a small click. I turned the sheet of paper around. It was just a couple of lines:

> Your speculations about subject A are of no consequence for the actual situation. Your allegations and insinuations about subject B are totally irresponsible and ill-founded. Drop it!

9

It was snowing again, but not very much. The air was acrid and heavy with gasoline and gases and fumes from the diesel engines of the trucks. The city crouched under gray, heavy clouds that made the skyscrapers along Kremlin Prospect disappear in frosty mist. The Praga restaurant is a large building not far from the old, pretty Arbat quarter, which Khrushchev ruined in part with big blocks of concrete, to the great sorrow of Muscovites. But they could do nothing. The Arbat proper was now being made into a pedestrian street. It was one big mess of construction work, dark and sinister. The Praga stands like an ancient, prerevolutionary ship in the middle of the destruction, with its pastel orange color among all the gray concrete. It consists of several restaurants and is a popular hangout for black marketeers, Western diplomats and correspondents, Soviet officials, and bureaucrats from the nearby Comecon headquarters. There is a worn elegance to the place, a sense of times past. However, one encounters the new kings of the Soviet state right away: the doormen, who ruthlessly screen those who want to get inside. Like everywhere else, position or money will ensure admission without any problems.

Demichev stood stamping his feet, waiting. We saw his long and lanky figure in the expensive lambskin coat and his narrow eyes beneath the large fur cap. His cigarette moved arrogantly up and down in the corner of his mouth. People recognized him, and he enjoyed that. He had been the angry young poet of the sixties and had never outgrown the part, although money and prestige had caused the anger to give way to an unfailing sense of the limitations imposed by the society. I put up with his self-centered showing off. He was fun to be with, and he introduced me to many interesting people in his Peredelkino dacha that was paid for by the state. We had become friends. I knew that he was hiding his despair behind a boisterous mask.

"Jackie boy!" he roared in his good English when he caught sight of me and Peter. "Let me get you past these nonentities and corrupt devils who guard the Praga like a nice Russian girl used to guard her virtue in the old days. Who's your young friend? Why didn't you bring a good-looking Danish girl instead? Where's that woman you wanted to show me? Is she beautiful and warm like the fire of my mother's stove? Come, let me have a good look at you. You look like shit."

"Hey Pyotr," I said, and looked into his lively, intense eyes. He was past fifty, but looked younger. He had a tan.

"Where did you get your tan?" I asked. Peter stayed in the background and looked at us with a little smile. I could almost feel how his computer brain was working and processing the first impressions. Demichev grabbed me by the upper arms and looked at me, then he embraced me and gave me a big kiss while still patting me exaggeratedly on the back.

"I've been in the United States to give poetry readings and present my new film. I took one week in the sun in Florida, and since then I've been working in Sochi. My film was a great success, and Jack is interested in playing the lead in my next one." He let go of me, making it possible for me to look at him with due admiration.

"That's great," I said.

"Is Jack going to play the lead in your next film?" Peter said ironically.

Theatrically, Demichev opened his arms wide and looked appealingly at the Russians who were following, out of the corners of their eyes, the masterful way he dealt with the English language and us foreigners.

"Young man, Jack isn't Jack. Jack's another Jack. Jack Nicholson, my good friend. I had lunch with him the other day."

"Don't know him," Peter said.

"That's enough, Peter," I said in Danish. "Behave yourself or I'll send you home to bed."

Demichev continued in Russian, addressing his audience as if from a stage, "This young man doesn't know the world's greatest actor, Jack Nicholson. There, you see. They know nothing in the West. They are *nyekulturnie*. They've lost culture for idiotic video shows and mindless entertainment. They don't read poetry. They don't see decent films, only American trash. Comrades, we have a lot to be proud of. Don't believe in our lies, but don't believe in theirs, either." He was swaying a little, and I realized that he had been drinking. I noticed that a couple of policemen were beginning to look askance at us.

"I'm cold," I said.

"Jackie boy, this isn't cold. I was in Siberia during the war. It was so cold that your piss froze before it hit the ground and grew like a big yellow mound in front of you."

"You're already in the middle of the dinner conversation, I can hear." The articulate voice belonged to Caroline Nilsson, who was the cultural attaché at the Swedish embassy. She had been in the city for only three months, but spoke Russian like a native: the beautiful, melodious Russian that is spoken in

Leningrad. Her grandmother had been Russian, and she had her grandmother's fine St. Petersburg accent.

Demichev stopped in the middle of yet another rattling sentence.

"Madame," he said, and kissed her gloved hand, staring into her face without restraint. Caroline was about forty years old and possessed the cool beauty of a Swedish summer day. She radiated pure luxury in her full-length fur coat and expensive fur cap. The Russians who were standing on line to get into the Praga stared at her openly.

I had met Caroline shortly after her arrival. She was a real career woman. Not that I have anything against that, being a real career man myself, but she was a little too calculating. She was perfect from the red nails to the straight nose and the skin that had been kept young looking with lotions and fresh air. She rarely drank, and made sure that her slender, healthy body stayed slender by doing aerobic exercise in summer and by skiing in winter. She knew all the right authors, had always seen the latest Russian plays on the smallest stages, and had read the most recent issue of *Novy Mir* almost before it was out. With a new expression that I'd heard on a trip back to Denmark, she was "at the cutting edge of events." She had arranged her life within such narrow confines that, at the reception where I had met her, she had coolly explained that she had let herself be sterilized to make sure that irrational biological urges didn't limit the course of her career.

She had two marriages behind her. Her husbands hadn't understood the way she prioritized her life, as she calmly explained. Caroline declared quite openly that her goal was to become ambassador. She would have to work hard for that—the Swedes are hardly any better than us as far as that is concerned. In all of Danish history there have been only two women ambassadors. So the chances weren't that great. Or, as Castesen would have put it: the risk was minimal.

She spoke warmly of the Russian poets' soul; of their zeal and strength in the face of an oppressive political system; of the sincerity and understanding that permeated their poetry. She had often referred to Demichev as yet another renegade and opportunist, but she had also expressed admiration for the poems of his youth and for some of his most recent works.

"Caroline Nilsson," she said, and let him keep her gloved hand in his for a moment before she discreetly, but firmly, freed herself. I could have done without the nonsense that followed, but Peter made no attempt to hide how much he was enjoying himself. He loved to watch so-called grown-up people make fools of themselves.

"It is rare," Demichev said. "It is rare," he repeated, with feeling. "It is rare that the beauty of a voice is in such perfect harmony with the beauty of the face. If you knew how often I have chased like a beggar through the night to find the face that matched a beautiful voice that I had heard on the telephone or on the radio. For hours and days the sound of the voice would haunt me, making it impossible to sleep, to make love, to think, or to create my poems. Months later I would meet the voice, and the woman who possessed it would have no beauty herself. It's a crime when a woman with a beautiful voice isn't equally beautiful herself. But it's a crime that you have not committed, Madame."

"How about saving the speeches for dinner, Pyotr," I said.

"Don't be so Western European, Jack," she said. So the cool Caroline wasn't entirely unsusceptible. Susanne had declared after one encounter with Demichev that if I ever brought her together with him again, she would first throw up all over that prize idiot and then demand a divorce.

Demichev looked at me with his tired eyes. Then he offered Caroline his arm and pulled her in the direction of the door. The doorman stopped him. To avoid a scene, I pushed my way in front of them, saying, "The Danish embassy." That was as good as "Open sesame!" Demichev chose to ignore it. He even kept his mouth shut while we got rid of our coats and until we were shown to the table reserved for us in "The Hall of Winter."

The Hall of Winter is the most prestigious restaurant, a luscious room with mirrors, large paintings of fat people eating, and an aquarium with green plants and fish. Waiters in white tie and tails, white tablecloths and nice silverware, and a menu that is two feet long. Sometimes you can actually order up to a third of the listed courses. We were shown to our table by a stiff headwaiter. The restaurant was packed. Vodka bottles and the green bottles of Soviet champagne grew like plants in spring on all the tables set with *zukursky*, the many small Russian appetizers of which caviar is the best known. The noise was infernal. A band of six musicians was pumping out the most popular pop song of that winter. On the dance floor Russians of all ages were writhing without restraint: fat ladies swinging other fat ladies; young women with heavy makeup dancing the Soviet version of rock'n'roll with their lovers. Garish neckties, beer bellies, and cheap shoes. It was only nine o'clock, but now was the time to have as much fun as possible—the restaurant closed at eleven-thirty.

It was impossible to have any kind of conversation. I had ordered various appetizers beforehand: pancakes with caviar, salmon and salty sturgeon, meat and salami, lettuce in mayonnaise, and there was even a small plate with sliced green cucumbers, a miracle in the winter in Moscow. Demichev managed to place himself next to Caroline. I sat down where I could see the bandstand. I was the host, but I left it to Demichev to order the warm dishes and the beverages. I noticed how a bill disappeared into the waiter's hand: we would get special treatment. It soon arrived: vodka, champagne, and brandy. Demichev was too much of a Russian not to order whole bottles. It reminded me of a secret report that I had once seen from an institute in Siberia. It said that forty million Soviet citizens were alcoholics, and that one child out of ten was born with injuries or defects caused by alcohol. It wasn't hard to believe.

The music stopped, and people walked back to their tables. The air was thick with tobacco smoke. The waiters rushed about. Some of them, that is. Just as many others stood by the door, watching the world come to an end with closed faces. The musicians didn't leave the stage. Now I saw why. Next to the stage with its music stands, drums, and microphones was a small tent, its entrance covered with a curtain. From behind this curtain the singer appeared. She wore a long, close-fitting dress that accentuated her breasts and narrow hips. For a Soviet girl, she had a very good figure, but still she had the slight suggestion of a pot belly that bad and heavy nutrition gives most girls in the Soviet Union. I thought she looked great. She walked to the stage and had some difficulty stepping up over its edge because of the narrow dress. I caught a glimpse of her thigh as the slit of the dress opened. The guitarist gave her a helping hand and smiled at her. She turned around. It was Lilli. Like last time, she wore heavy makeup, but it seemed less glaring in the stage light. She began to sing a Beatles song, "Can't Buy Me Love." She had a good voice, but sang without passion or interest, as if it were something to get done with. The sound system was turned up as loud as possible. I tried to keep looking at her, but the people on the dance floor got in the way. She appeared every now and then between the sweating faces, like a doll in a shooting gallery. I felt an incredible urge to talk with her.

Demichev was leaning over Caroline, attempting to have some degree of a conversation. He held his filter cigarette in an affected manner, making it stand out like a bizarre growth between his fingers. Caroline sat listening, with her beautiful, cool face, her red lips slightly parted. She was wearing a gray, businesslike pants suit. Demichev was completely absorbed, but I suddenly realized that he was looking over at me. I had been so preoccupied with watching Lilli that I hadn't noticed his attempts to catch my attention. It was only when Peter nudged my side with his elbow that I became aware of Demichev's raised glass.

"To women!" he shouted, and emptied his full glass in one gulp.

"To women!" I said, and emptied mine as well. Caroline took just a sip of her vodka.

"You have eyes for Lilli?" Demichev shouted. "You have eyes for the beautiful Russian singer?" he continued. "You want me to introduce you?"

"I've already met her."

"But do you know her like I know her?" he said in a tone of voice that made me jealous, even though it made no sense at all.

"I thought her sister was more your type," I said loudly.

He roared with laughter and screwed up one eye against the smoke from his cigarette.

"How about both at once? Wouldn't that be something? Do you want me to tell her that you're interested?"

"Shut up, Pyotr," I said.

Caroline looked at us with a little smile. She sensed the hostility in the air: the smell of males marking their territories. Peter was smiling broadly as he downed a slice of bread with a thick layer of caviar.

"Why don't you bring her along next Saturday?" Demichev shouted over the music. "I still haven't managed to persuade my beautiful table partner to come. But eventually I will, I'm sure. Do you want me to ask Lilli for you?"

"Who says I want to bring her?"

"I'm a poet. I feel that you want her to come. In here." He placed his hand on his heart with an exaggerated movement.

"Her sister is dead," I said. "Vera was found strangled."

He said nothing, but took the vodka bottle and filled all our glasses to the rim. Then he raised his own. "Here's to the man with the scythe, may he harvest somewhere else," he recited.

"You're too goddamned Russian," I said.

"That's why I've stayed here. I can't live anywhere else. But don't think I haven't thought of it. *Davai.*" He emptied his glass in one long pull. Peter and I did likewise. Then he asked Caroline to join him on the dance floor. He danced with exaggerated movements, she with precise little turns of her hips and controlled movements of her arms. They were like night and day, but they both had rhythm. The dance floor was seething, and the smoke gathered and separated in the multicolored spotlights that were meant to create a discotheque atmosphere, like in the West in the seventies. Lilli was now singing one of the popular, Italian songs of that winter, about love and longing. It was just as banal as Demichev trying to draw Caroline closer to him on the dance floor, while she tried to maintain a dancing-school distance. After pecking at my food for a while, I gave up and lit a cigarette. When the music stopped, it was as if the silence made time stand still for a moment, but then the voices rose toward the mosaics of the ceiling like a curtain of sound. Demichev led Caroline back to the table and threw himself voraciously on the food, chewing and champing noisily and drinking and spilling and talking nonstop. I don't remember much of what he said, but it was mainly about his own genius.

Caroline seemed at the same time fascinated and repelled by him. She didn't protest when Demichev exclaimed, "I'm a peasant boy from Siberia, just a plain *Sibiryak*. I've never learned good manners." She listened attentively when he gave a witty and detailed account of all the obstacles and problems that his new film script had to overcome, and we all laughed when he did a cheerful imitation of a cultural bureaucrat changing the commas in an author's manuscript. When he started over on the story of his childhood in Siberia during the war, I got up and walked across the room to the small tent next to the stage.

Lilli sat inside together with the other members of the band. They appeared to be drinking tea and brandy.

"*Priviet,*" I said. "How are you?"

She looked up at me. She didn't seem surprised, but stared at me attentively with the inquisitive gaze of a small child examining a grown-up it doesn't know.

"Hello, Jack Andersen," she said formally. "The guests aren't really allowed in here, but would you like a cup of tea or a drink?"

I took a seat. A heavy man with a beard made room for me by the small table and poured tea into a glass in a small metal holder. He gave me a glass of brandy as well. Nobody spoke as I plopped two pieces of sugar into the tea and slowly stirred. Through the curtain we could hear the buzzing voices from the restaurant outside. Someone shouted. There was an argument, but it died down just as quickly as it had begun.

The man with the beard got up.

"We'll do a couple of numbers. Just drink your tea, Lilli," he said in a friendly voice. They treated her like a fragile piece of porcelain; like someone they had to look after. They looked at the foreigner suspiciously as they edged their way along the table and went outside to do their job.

"Once I dreamed of becoming a musician," I said when I heard them strike the first chords. Lilli smiled. She had a small, pretty face. It was a pity that she marred it with all that makeup. Her eyes were green and clear.

"It's hard work, and it's not well paid," she said.

We sat for a while.

"What about Vera?" I asked.

"What about her? We buried her, and that's that."

"I would still like to be a musician. I see myself as a real rock'n'roll star," I said.

She smiled so much that her eyes became narrow slits.

"That's something else. You should hear me sing in private sometime with my friends. When we do it just for the fun of it and play our own songs, not those songs they tell us to do here."

"I would like that very much, Lilli," I said. I was fidgeting with my tea glass. I hadn't touched the brandy. She lit a cigarette. Her nails were painted, but she had bitten them. Her hands were delicate and small.

"Why is your name Jack—and then Andersen?" She had difficulty pronouncing Andersen correctly in Russian. She had switched to the familiar form of address. It wasn't unusual among young Russians, but it gave me a feeling of new intimacy between us. We were sitting in a small tent by ourselves, cut off from the music and the voices outside. The sound level had risen again.

"Why is my name Jack? You mean an English first name and a Danish last name?"

She nodded and looked at me with her green, beautiful eyes.

"That's because I'm a mixture," I said. "My mother was Danish, and my father was English."

"You're saying was. Are they dead?"

"Yes, my mother is dead. Maybe my father is still alive. I don't know. He's a sailor. One day, when I was still a child, he left and never returned. I guess I was thirteen years old. It took me an awfully long time to get over that, strangely enough, because he was a rotten father."

"Then you're like me," she said.

"Your parents are dead?"

"My father is. But you're a mixture like I am. My father was Russian. My mother is Estonian. So I don't belong anywhere."

"Maybe you're just a Soviet citizen?" I said.

She shrugged. "Maybe. If such a thing exists. In my passport it says that I'm Estonian."

"And in Vera's it said that she was Russian."

She laughed. "There, you see. Nothing makes any sense."

We were silent for a moment.

"I have to work," she said.

"I wanted to ask if you would dance with me," I said.

"I'm not allowed to," she said. In some idiotic way I felt glad that she had answered like that instead of saying that she didn't want to.

"We're going to the National afterward. Do you want to join us?"

"No. That I don't want to do."

"Would you go to a party with me next Saturday? It's at Demichev's. In Peredelkino. You know him, I understand."

I looked probingly into the green eyes, but they revealed nothing.

"I noticed that you were with Pyotr. Actually I noticed you right away. I've been looking for you every night since that night, you know."

"Because you thought I wanted to ask you about Vera?"

"Maybe. But perhaps also because I felt that you wanted to talk with me."

"I thought that Russians would rather not have any contact with someone like me," I said.

"In that respect I'm more Estonian. I grew up in Tallinn. That's not Russia, but a part of Europe. We're just so unfortunate to be on the wrong side of the border."

She got up.

"I really have to work now," she said. "The plan must be met." Her breasts were pressing against her dress, and the skin of her upper arms was glowing warmly. I could see a part of her neck where the makeup ended: her skin was clear and white. She had little curls all over her head, which gave her a boyish look. In the back her hair was cut very short, leaving the neck clean and delicate. She wore heavy, tinkling earrings.

"How about Saturday?" I said, with something close to desperation in my voice.

"I thought that you were married, Jack," she said as she stood before me. "You're wearing a ring."

So I was. I had forgotten all about it. After eight years of marriage, putting it on and taking it off had become a habit, something that I did without thinking.

"My wife has left me," I said.

"That was stupid of her," she said, leaning forward and kissing me on the cheek. I reached out my arms to feel the soft skin of her naked upper arms, but she pulled back.

"What time is that party at Pyotr's?" she asked.

"Two o'clock in the afternoon," I said.

"You might try to be at the Mayakovsky metro station at one-thirty," she said.

"That's right, you know Pyotr, of course," I said.

She laughed, and her green eyes shone in the half-light. "Not as well as he would like to."

That made me childishly happy, but the feeling of warmth in my guts didn't last for very long.

"I was married to one of his young poet friends."

"Was?"

"He killed himself. You should stay away from me, Jack. I bring nothing but misfortune to others. I think my mother is a witch, and that she has passed something of that on to me."

She was quite serious. I wasn't surprised. In this godless, atheist society there existed a superstition so strong that even top political leaders sought the advice of wise women and quacks.

"I'll take the chance," I said.

Demichev had become more drunk while I had been away.

"Did you get laid in there, Jack?" he shouted across the table, where food and drinks lay like a battlefield. My cutlet lay cold and greasy on its plate. Champagne had been splashed all over the cucumbers, and the edges of the pancakes were turning upward. Demichev had used the sliced meat as an ashtray. The noise was deafening, and the level of drunkenness in the restaurant had reached new heights.

"Come, I would like to talk with you," I said loudly enough for Demichev to hear through the music. Caroline was flushed and her perfect hair slightly rumpled. Peter was on the dance floor with a middle-aged Russian woman. It was obvious that she had asked him to dance, not the other way around. The habitual aloofness and reserve of the Russians disappear completely when the music is playing and they're out to have a good time.

Lilli had set to work on the mechanical delivery of yet another idiotic pop song. The floor was packed with people, all swaying back and forth as if they wanted to dance away all their sorrows and the troubles of everyday life. They were taking time off from reality.

We went out to the men's room. The stench was beyond description. The floor was a mess. Demichev looked at himself in the mirror and didn't like what he saw. His face was white and furrowed, and his eyes were bloodshot. His thin hair looked as if it were glued to his scalp. We stood next to each other trying to avoid the puddles of urine on the floor.

"All right, Pyotr. Tell me about Vera and Sonia. With all your connections, maybe you know why they died. Apparently the whole city knows about it. You weren't surprised when I told you that Vera is dead," I said.

He tried to laugh and almost choked on the vodka that he had consumed in the course of the evening. When he had recovered, he went over to the washbowl and began to splash water onto his face. There wasn't any towel. He stood with water running down his face, looking at me. He didn't seem to care about the fact that it was dripping down upon his shirt. His necktie was askew.

"What do I know? I know nothing. But I can tell you a story. I'm in love, Jack. Do you understand that, Jack?"

"Aren't you always, my friend?"

"You don't understand Russians, and you don't understand poets. You're a businessman. You're a rational Westerner, a boring creature of reason. Try living in your emotions, instead of always controlling them. Where is your soul?" He looked at me as if he had given up beforehand trying to make me understand, but still he continued, "She's only twenty-two years old, and she is so beautiful, and she loves me. She is from Petrozavorsk. To her, Moscow is a metropolis, an empire, a glittering jewel. New York and Paris are distant planets inhabited by capitalist heathens." He was getting more and more involved as he spoke. A man whose hair stood straight up in the air came into the men's room but ignored us and, dead drunk, began to make his contribution to the mess on the floor. Demichev switched into English.

"Her name is Anna. She stayed with me for four days, but then she went home to pass an exam. She'll be back on Sunday. She came to me, and after I'd had her for the first time, I ask her: 'Annoschka, what do you want? Tell me, and I'll get it for you.' She's lying on top of me, her hair caressing my chest. Then she looks at me with those young, innocent eyes and says: 'Pyotr, give me a piece of salami. We've never had a piece of real salami in Petrozavorsk.' "

I couldn't help smiling, although there was not a suggestion of a smile on his face. On the contrary, it almost appeared contracted in pain and despair. He switched back into Russian.

"Don't laugh. I didn't laugh. I cried. There we were, warm and cozy inside, belonging to one of the greatest and most powerful nations of the world, and one of the fair daughters of this country says that never in her life has she been able to buy a piece of salami. I ran downstairs to the refrigerator, but I didn't have any. The next day we went to Moscow, because I wanted to buy the best salami for my little Anna. I was all over the city. No salami. At the moment, there is a salami deficit even in glittering Moscow. I could have gone to the Beriozka with the foreigners and used my fancy credit card to buy good Russian salami for dollars, but I didn't want my little Anna to see that. She still has the faith of her childhood. She still believes what the teacher told her about the best country in the world. She still feels sorry for those who must live on the other side of the borders of the Soviet Union. She was with me: she saw my humiliation and that of my country."

He looked at me with tears in his eyes. Like Russians in general, he was uninhibitedly emotional in moments of privacy and could switch from noisy playfulness to weeping sorrow. I felt for him in his grief.

Demichev raised his hand in a deprecating gesture when I was about to interrupt him to ask about the conclusion of the salami adventure. The drunkard had finished fouling his own shoes and the floor. He walked into the door with a hard bang, but managed to get out all right at his third attempt.

"My mother is all of Russia's mother. She won't let me provide for her. Although she is past seventy, she still opens up her small newspaper stand every morning. She is known by everyone in the neighborhood. She has been there for as long as anyone can remember. Everyone honors her and respects her, not because she has connections, but because she is pure; because no dirt clings to her. In the neighborhood they don't respect me for being me, but because I'm Mama's boy."

Demichev's face was dry now. When I realized it, I lit a cigarette and handed it to him. He took it without a word, and I lit another for myself.

"So Anna and I go to see my mother. Mama forgives me everything. Mama understands everything, so she kissed Anna and said, 'Call me Babushka. What can we do for Annoschka, my little Peter?' Mama says with her fine Siberian peasant voice. 'She would like so much to taste a piece of real salami, Mama.' 'Then buy her a piece for the money you get for writing in the papers, Petruschka.' 'There isn't any, Mama. We've looked everywhere.' 'Come with me,' Mama says, and takes us across the street to the butcher's shop. They all know her. She's been selling her newspapers for fifty years. Under Stalin and when the Fascists bombed the city, and I was sent to Siberia with the other children. In the shop we see four old bones and three pieces of lard. Mama says to the manager, who is well-dressed with foreign shoes and rings bought for all the money he makes from selling under the counter instead of to ordinary customers, 'I need a piece of salami of the best kind.' He smiles his false predatory smile and fawns: 'Of course, Babushka. It'll only be a minute.' Then he goes out in the back and returns a moment later with the finest salami, as good as or better than you can buy in the foreign-currency shop. He gives it to Mama and won't accept any money. Mama gives it to Anna. Anna kisses Mama on the cheek and breaks off a small piece and eats it with an expression that I would give five years of my life to be able to bring to her face when we make love. I stand there like one forlorn and feel like a nobody, more humiliated than at any other time of my life."

I said nothing, but dropped my cigarette among all the other stinking butts in the bowl. Demichev was swaying, and sweat was trickling down his forehead, but he actually seemed rather sober when he continued.

"You won't find those who let Vera and Sonia die. I knew them both. What harm did they do? None. You're looking for the culprits. Don't. You can't catch a whole system. It's a many-headed monster. You can find them everywhere. But they don't just eat salami, Jack. They eat people. They eat human dignity. And they've eaten our little Vera."

10

It was close to midnight, and the dollar bar of the National was crammed with businessmen, Soviet black marketeers, and easy virtues. The Hotel National is like a portly, but imposing old lady scowling at the Kremlin on the opposite side of Revolution Square. While the Party bosses mark out the Communist future, true human nature flourishes in the National bar around brown mahogany tables sloshed with liquor, in a semi-darkness that helps the heavy makeup hide the blemishes of prematurely aged faces. Between the heaps of ice outside the massive reddish brown walls of the hotel, long lines of black Volgas were waiting. The chauffeurs were leaning against the official cars, talking and smoking, while their bosses were stuffing themselves in the many small *chambres separées* that make up the restaurant of the National. For five rubles they would use the state cars as taxicabs.

The National reminded me of the society around it, a monstrosity in decay, divided and stratified according to class, privilege, and rank. If you had dollars, you could have a room with a view of Red Square. For rubles, a hole with a view of a concrete air shaft. In order to get inside at all, you had to be well connected or have enough money to bribe the manager, the headwaiter, and the doorman who was blocking our entrance.

That was understandable. We had definitely dined well. Even the flawless Caroline was glowing and had become amorous from champagne and vodka. She had a firm grip on my arm and was pressing her breasts against me. I was the most sober member of our group. Demichev lurched, and Peter wasn't walking quite straight, either. This time Demichev wanted to show that he, too, had what it takes to get past a doorman. He knew the specimen that stood just inside the revolving door, a heavyset man with a red, glowing face and a black uniform with shiny buttons. He looked Demichev up and down, but let him pass. I let Caroline step into the revolving door before me, but she laughed and pulled me along, so that we were squeezed up against each other. With amazement I felt how she took my hand and pressed it against her sex underneath her coat.

"Don't get too drunk, Jack," she said as we stepped out of the revolving door and were hit in our faces by a current of warm air. I hadn't been with a woman for a long time, so I chose to be the last one to check my coat. There were enough scandals in the air, and I had no desire to create one myself. A broad carpeted staircase led up to the second floor and the dollar bar from where the sound of voices and the smell of liquor was pouring at us.

The room was jam-packed, but four drunk Swedish businessmen were just leaving with two girls as we entered, and Peter rescued the table for us. The brown, heavy mahogany tables and chairs stood closely together. There was red plush and posters with advertisements for American cigarettes. In a corner above the bar was a flickering television set showing an ice hockey game. The sound was turned up rather loud. An advertisement for Aeroflot lied shamelessly, proclaiming that Aeroflot was internationally renowned for its outstanding service. The advertisement showed a young, smiling stewardess in a blue, unattractive uniform.

The bartender was a muscular man with sober, watchful eyes. He looked like one of the KGB goons, which is probably what he was, too. An old, fat woman with a kerchief and a flowered apron walked about muttering to herself and sweeping a little now and then with a besom. It didn't help much. She removed some empty glasses and emptied an ashtray. Exhausted from the effort, she then sat down to watch television with an exasperated expression on her face.

Peter pushed through the crowd in front of the bar. I took a seat and thought of Sonia and Vera, who might have sat at this very table sometime. Caroline was talking to Demichev, who was listening, but looked tired and aged. At the same time, I felt Caroline's foot rubbing against my shin. Around me, I could hear many different languages spoken. One table by the entrance was occupied by two prostitutes. Three others sat with a group of Japanese businessmen. I could hear or maybe just feel through the din how they were negotiating the price. The girls wanted dollars; but rubles, too, to cover the bribes for the doormen and the police. They also bribed the headwaiter to give them a table in the restaurant, preferably in the proximity of potential customers. Solitary businessmen were their preferred target: they had an easy job with men who were spending days in Moscow just waiting for a preliminary agreement about a possible meeting.

Peter returned with four large glasses of Scotch on the rocks, holding two in each hand as if he had done nothing but carry drinks his entire life.

"That's all they had, if you don't want brandy," he said. We touched glasses and drank. Peter looked around. He spotted the two prostitutes by the door. Seen at a distance through the heavy tobacco smoke, they looked young. They were smoking cigarettes. Their blouses had not been bought in GUM, but for dollars. One of them gave him a slight smile, and he raised his glass.

"It's one of Vera's friends. Her name is Tatyana. They had the same stud for a while," Peter said.

"Stud?"

"You know, pimp. Most of the girls have a stud. He protects them and is around if the customers become too wild. Of course, he also beats them up sometimes if they don't do what he tells them to or just to show them that he still cares."

"A real man of the world," I said.

"The stud is also the one who settles things with the taxi driver and gives a helping hand if the police get too greedy with the girls. It's a complex system, and strictly illegal, of course."

"You're a gold mine of information." He gave me his cocky grin and took another gulp of his whisky. I only sipped from mine, having enough excitement around me. I needed no stimulants. Caroline's stockinged foot was still caressing my leg. She was discussing exile literature with Demichev, who wasn't listening, but she didn't notice. There were fine wrinkles on her neck and by her eyes, but she was beautiful. She turned her face toward me and let her tongue flicker between her lips for a second. I didn't expect that—it wasn't her style to be so vulgar—so I looked away, ill at ease. She laughed loudly and turned to Demichev again. He looked as if he were falling asleep. He was pale and sweaty. Life was getting to be too much for him, but he still wasn't ready to face the fact that age was getting the upper hand, and that death was no longer a distant cousin.

Peter stared intently at the girls by the door. The one he had called Tatyana jerked her head imperceptibly. I only noticed it because I was looking straight at her. She then turned her head to her girlfriend again.

"I'll be right back," Peter said, and got up. He left the bar.

A moment later Tatyana got up and followed him out. I took a sip of my whisky. The muscular KGB bartender was pouring drinks generously and figuring out the exchange amounts, first on a pocket calculator, then on an abacus.

Peter returned. I could smell the cold night air as he bent over me and whispered into my ear. "Tatyana and her stud would like to talk with you."

"What about?"

"They say that they want to tell you about Vera and the red-haired Danish girl. They say that the police won't do anything about the case, because some big shot is involved. Tatyana says that even someone like Vera has a right to proper treatment."

"That sounds mysterious."

"Are you coming?" he continued in his stage whisper. Caroline was looking at me inquiringly.

"Now?" I asked.

"Yes. Tatyana has a customer later on. A rich Japanese, she says. You just have to go down into the underground walkway."

"I'll be back in a short while," I said to Caroline. "Peter will look after you."

She smiled. "Don't you dare dump me here. I can't drive."

"Not to worry," I said, and kissed her on the cheek.

The weather was changing. Sometimes it does so very quickly in Moscow; the temperature can go up or down thirty degrees in a few hours. It had become less cold, but it was still freezing. I went down the stairway into the system of tunnels underneath Revolution Square. People were hurrying by, their steps resounding hollowly in the dimly lit passage with its dirty gray tiles. I followed the signs leading to Red Square. I hadn't walked far before Tatyana appeared and took my arm. She was now wearing a cap and a long Russian coat.

"Come," she said. "You speak Russian, right?"

"Why do you want to see me?" I said in the same language.

"Vera talked about you a couple of times; and Sonia once said that you were the only decent person at her embassy. She also said that you were a real man," she continued in a flirtatious voice, clutching my upper arm hard. "I can see what she meant."

"Save the charm for your customers," I said. She pulled away from me somewhat, but still held on to my arm. We walked on the right side, attracting no attention. A couple among many others on their way home, perhaps from the theater or a movie. She led me up the stairs, and we surfaced next to the brown Lenin Museum that encloses Red Square on one side. The cobblestones of the square were covered with a fine layer of snow crystals, and a floodlight illuminated the red flag over the Kremlin. People were crossing the vast space of the square like silent and fleeting shadows. The clock of the tower showed five minutes to midnight. There were breaks in the cloud cover, and a pale, yellowish moon hung low above the power plant on the other side of the river. Thick white smoke was pouring out of its chimneys.

She held firmly on to my arm, and we walked on the cobblestones in the direction of Lenin's mausoleum. There were quite a few tourists on the square. I could hear their enthusiastic voices talking in French, Danish, German, and English about how beautiful the night was. They were right. I tried to see it through their eyes. The silence, the moon, the massive façade of the GUM department store. The onion domes of St. Basil's Cathedral, the heavy red wall of the Kremlin, and behind it, the yellow buildings and golden cupolas of the ancient churches inside. The cobblestones under my feet. The red stars on the spires of the towers. For a moment I felt an intense joy at being privileged enough to get paid to be in a country that fascinated me so deeply. On Red Square I always felt the great rush of the wings of history. A cliché, but it was true. For a short moment I had the feeling of being lifted out of myself. I wasn't walking with a Russian prostitute on my arm, but with Susanne, like when we had just moved to Moscow and went for long walks at night while I told her about Moscow and about Russian history. About Ivan the Terrible who poured molten lead in the eyes of his enemies on Red Square. About Stalin watching the soldiers arrive with German banners that they threw at his feet. About Bukharin and the other revolutionaries who were sentenced to execution during the show trials in the beautiful green House of the Labor Unions, where Brezhnev had lain in state surrounded by all his medals and decorations, as pathetic in death as he had been in life. About Lillian Hellman and the others in the restaurant of the Hotel Metropole, where Nordahl Grieg wrote most of "The World Must Still Be Young."

As we walked toward Lenin's embalmed body, I missed Susanne seriously for the first time, and I realized that I had hoped till the very end that we would be able to stay together, have children together, and become the family that I myself had never had. And which I knew at that very moment I would never get.

Tatyana dragged me along, and I tried to shake off my feelings of fear and despair. About twenty people were waiting for the change of the guard. I looked in the direction of the Spassky Tower. The three soldiers were approaching in slow goose steps. The steaming air poured out of their mouths and drifted behind their shoulders as they banged their long-black-booted, stretched-out legs into the concrete in a slow rhythm. By the entrance to Lenin's tomb the two guards stood motionless in their gray uniforms with empty eyes directed at each other. Their faces were so white from the frost that they looked like death masks.

The three relieving soldiers turned around right in front of me and walked like one person up the steps to the entrance. Then they waited.

"*Priviet,*" a deep voice said right behind me. Before I could turn around, he was next to me. We were standing in the middle of a group of elderly German tourists.

"My name is Dima," he said. He was dressed in a full-length coat and an expensive fur cap. His collar was turned up around his face, which was square with small eyes and a large mustache. The bells of the Kremlin sounded sharply, and in a quickly accomplished, coordinated movement, four of the soldiers veered around, and the two new guards were in place.

"You wanted to tell me something about Sonia?" I said.

"Do you want a cigarette?" he said, and held out a pack of Winston. I shook my head. The soldiers slowly stretched their right legs straight forward and slammed them into the frozen concrete with a hollow thud. It had to hurt all the way up in their heads—they had stood motionless for an hour—but they didn't bat an eyelid. Then they turned on their heels again and continued with slow goose steps toward the Spassky Tower and the tea that awaited them there.

"Come, let's walk a little," Dima said. It seemed quite natural. The other people who had watched the changing of the guard were also beginning to drift out on the square in small groups of couples. Dima walked downhill toward St. Basil's Cathedral and continued along the river, speaking in a low voice as we walked. He had an accent. My guess was that he was Armenian. I felt certain of one thing: his name wasn't Dima. Tatyana walked by his side.

"Vera was my girl. She was a good girl and an honest girl," he said, puffing deeply at his cigarette. He lit a second one with the butt of the first. "Some months ago she wanted to quit. I told her that I was sorry to hear that, but I didn't want to force her. I'm not like certain other guys. That's why I have the best girls."

"I'm moved to tears by your concern," I said.

He ignored me and continued, "She said that she had met a man who wanted to marry her. 'A foreigner?' I asked. 'No,'

Vera answered. He was Russian, but a great man. I didn't believe her. Where would someone like Vera meet a great man? I asked myself. But I'm a democratic person. Everybody is allowed to live his or her life the way they want to. So I kissed Vera good-bye and wished her good luck and good health."

"You do everything out of the goodness of your heart," I said.

He stopped. We were standing by the river, leaning up against the stone embankment. He stood with his back to the frozen river, puffing at his cigarette. He wasn't very tall, but his compact little body seemed full of strength. The lower part of his face was almost hidden. Tatyana gave herself a shake. She was cold. She had been drinking, and the false warmth of the alcohol had lost its effect.

"Listen. If all you want to do is to offend me, we may as well stop here. I'm doing this because Tatyana is unhappy. She can't sleep, and when she doesn't sleep, she gets ugly. And when she's ugly, she can't work. It's as simple as that."

"So we got that much straight. It's business. Not philanthropy."

"I'm not making myself any better than I am. A man's got to live as best he can. I try to be fair. I don't demand the impossible. My girls do what they want to do. I don't force them to go with blackasses, even though there's a lot of money in that."

He looked at me coldly, as if he expected me to react to his racist remark.

"You really move me," I said.

"I don't have to put up with you," he said.

"Just go on," I said.

"That happened in August," he said in a monotonous voice that I had to strain to hear whenever a car drove past us. "So at the beginning of December I met Vera in the bar of the

National together with a red-headed woman whom she said was a Danish diplomat girl. I warned Vera and said that it was all right to go with foreigners, but smartest to stay away from the residents. Vera was really out of it. So I asked her how the marriage was coming along. Then she looked like a little kid who can't have her teddy bear. Apparently it didn't go so well. The man was already married. But he wanted a divorce. Only not right now. She needed money. A lot of money."

"What did Sonia say?" I asked.

He gave me an irritated look, as if he didn't like to be interrupted in his tale.

"Come, let's walk," he said, and Tatyana and I obediently followed. Dima walked with firm, long strides in his good Western boots.

"Sonia said nothing. Sonia sat there smiling and was a little tipsy, and she was in love with Vera. I'm not big on morals. Sex is a private matter. Sex is a commodity. But I didn't know that Vera had those tendencies. Sonia didn't understand Russian. 'What's that, my angel, have you betrayed us men?' I said. Vera said no. She seemed annoyed. 'He likes the two of us together,' she just said. And then there was the money matter again. She needed four thousand rubles, and she needed them now. I'm not complaining. I'm not a poor man, but I have many expenses. After Andropov, palm oil is getting more and more expensive. But darling Vera had a plan. She could get cassettes of pornographic movies. Could I distribute them?"

He paused again and leaned against the stone embankment. I waited, but he didn't say more. It was a story with no end.

"Did you accept?" I asked after a while.

"That's my business. That has nothing to do with the case. But I did get an arrangement with Vera and the beautiful Danish girl. There wasn't enough money in it right away. It's a long-term investment. You have to spend a lot of money on bribes at first, until you develop a network of video salons where the films can be shown. But it's a good business. It's just that it's long term. I couldn't lend Vera the four thousand rubles. I suggested that she could start working again, but she didn't really want to do that."

He lit a new cigarette and took a bottle from his coat pocket. It was vodka. He handed it to me. I took a pull. He did likewise and passed it on to Tatyana. She took a deep draft, and Dima had to take the bottle away from her. There was a light wind, and the clouds were drifting hastily past the yellowish white moon. A police car drove slowly past us, but they weren't about to get outside in the cold.

Tatyana took over. She couldn't be much older than twenty-two. She had a round, childish face with a small pointed mouth and badly plucked eyebrows.

"It was her sister. It was Lilli. She had just got married, but her husband was to be drafted and sent to Afghanistan. He was a musician. A puny and soft fellow. Lilli was convinced that it would kill him. Either the Dusmanians in Afghanistan or life in the army. He would die in any case, of that Lilli was certain. She is very superstitious. If you have the right connections, they let you off; but it costs four thousand rubles."

"Nobody who's somebody is sent to Afghanistan," Dima said.

Tatyana stamped her feet on the concrete, which was covered with a fine layer of ice mixed with gravel. A little farther down, two men came staggering. They could hardly stand, but held on to each other for support. Then they began to argue and push each other, till finally one of them fell and stayed down. Cursing, the other staggered on. Dima looked up, but otherwise he ignored them. Not far behind them, I noticed a blue Lada. It had been there all the time, I suddenly realized. Apparently it was observing us. Either it belonged to Dima, or else Dima was far from what he pretended to be. I grew rather nervous. I was definitely involved with something here that TASS would call "incompatible with the duties of a diplomat."

"So I talked with Lilli. She is a pretty girl, but honest." Tatyana's voice was shaking, but whether it was with emotion or from the cold, I couldn't tell. "I said that I could only see one way out. She had to go with some foreigners, then I would get . . . Dima . . . to change the money, and with a loan we could scrape together the four thousand. Lilli was going to think about it, but her condition was that her older sister wasn't to know that she did it."

Dima moved his feet to stay warm.

"I didn't like the idea." He looked at me. "You won't believe me, but I have a weak spot for Lilli. She's pure. She has lived surrounded by dirt all her life, but it never stuck to her. Vera drank in her life with her mother's milk, but it's hard to believe that the two of them had nursed at the same breast."

"Get to the point," I said. Even the criminals in the Soviet Union were incapable of being brief.

"Vera cried," Tatyana said. "She had managed to get away from it. Now she was going back. She hated going with strange men. Dima was a shit. He didn't tell Vera that he would arrange something for Lilli. When she found out, she got mad as hell. She told Dima to stop Lilli. She was going to get that money herself."

The man who called himself Dima didn't bat an eyelid at this.

Tatyana continued, "Of course, it didn't work. Lilli wasn't any good at it. She tried twice and cried afterward each time. But she looks so sweet and young. She doesn't look like that kind of girl at all. She didn't use any makeup then. She found a couple of Americans, older men who paid well and who were heartbroken afterward when she cried. Then they gave her more money. But it didn't work out at all. She couldn't take it. Vera went back to Dima, and he arranged something for her, and Vera was scared as hell that her future husband might suspect something."

Tatyana stopped. I looked at my watch. I had to get back.

I couldn't make sense of what they were saying. There seemed to be a purpose that they didn't want to express directly.

"Did they get the money?" I asked. The cold was biting into my legs. I looked over at the Kremlin. A short distance away I could see the cars crossing Gorky Bridge.

"It was too late," Tatyana said. "Much too late." She began to weep. Tears were running down her cheeks, but she wept without a sound. Dima flicked his cigarette out over the river, making the sparks fly as it hit the ice.

"Lilli's a sentimental fool," he said with his dark voice. "She just had to go and tell her husband what she had done and why, and that she would never do it again. He was a weak man. He felt that it was his fault. So he hung himself that same night."

I stared at him. Now the story suddenly took on meaning. It was a Russian tragedy. I had difficulty believing it, but it was absurd enough to be true. It had all the aspects of mendacity and double standards that form the moral foundation of the society in which the characters lived.

"Come, let's go," he said again, and we began to walk back in the direction of Red Square.

"Lilli hardly reacted at all. She shut herself up, even more than before. It seemed unnatural. It wasn't human. She began to paint her face as if she were a Red Indian on the warpath," Tatyana said.

"But Vera reacted. She wanted the four thousand rubles back. So did I. I had lent her one thousand. I was a softhearted fool," Dima said as he continued walking with long strides, his black coat sweeping around his ankles.

Dima was speaking faster now, as if I were a patient in a doctor's office whose consultation time was up and who wasn't entitled to more for the fee.

"On December thirtieth Vera was very agitated. She called me. She said that she was going to get the money that day. With interest. She had a hold on the man who had taken the money. He was very fond of her and Sonia; so much so that he had promised to produce the entire amount and add interest. 'Sonia and I can get him to do anything. He's a real pig,' she said to me on the phone. 'I thought that he was just a stooge, and then it was him all along. That big cocksucker.' That's what she said."

He spoke in spurts. The sentences were coming so fast that I had to strain to understand his Russian. In between, he took long pauses. We were back in the underground passage again. He remained silent until we got out on the other side. I saw Caroline standing by the entrance of the National. She waved her hand at me, but I shook my head. Demichev was being helped into one of the black Volgas. He didn't see me, but pulled himself together sufficiently to blow Caroline a kiss.

I grabbed Dima by his upper arm and squeezed it, leaning over him. He was strong, but not strong enough to tear himself free. I could feel my blood pumping harder.

"Let me tell you something, you little shit," I said. "I think you've been paid to fill me with a lot of nonsense. You're setting up a smart little trap, but it's not going to work."

"I don't care what you think," he said, without fear in his voice. I let go of him.

"He isn't lying," Tatyana said as she grasped my hand and looked into my eyes. "He's telling the truth. Why won't anybody do something? Vera was a human being, too. And Sonia was from your country. Why do you let them get away with it?" She almost shouted the last words. Dima grabbed her by the arm and shoved her away from me.

"Now I've said it. I've kept my promise. Now get the hell back to work. You've been on vacation long enough." His voice had changed completely. It had turned into a brutal snarl. Tatyana looked at him with fearful eyes, but stayed. Dima opened his mouth as if to threaten her, but checked himself. Instead he scowled at her in a way that made Tatyana cower, but she stayed.

I offered him a cigarette, and he lit both his and mine.

"Has it occurred to you," I said, "that Vera's future husband and the man whom she paid so well might be one and the same person?"

He laughed for the first time. I could understand why he rarely smiled. His mouth was full of gold teeth.

"I've thought of that. I don't know him. I don't know his name. But I know that Vera talked about having to learn to live with the smell of long boots. She never had the chance. She and Sonia didn't get away alive from their meeting with the long boots."

Dima turned around and disappeared into the tunnel, and Tatyana walked away in the direction of the National. Caroline stuck her arm under mine and placed her head on my shoulder.

"Who was that?" she asked in a husky voice.

"He wanted a light," I said.

"Then why were you talking about long boots?" she said, and tugged at me.

"Were we?" I asked.

She looked at me with her cool diplomatic gaze, stepping out of her seductress role for a moment. "In Russian 'long boots' means a military person, doesn't it, Jackie?"

"You're a clever girl."

"And a tired girl. Take me home to bed, Jack."

"Why not?" I said.

11

I called Basov from Caroline's place. She was still asleep when I got up in her state-furnished apartment at the Swedish embassy. She had left her mark on the room with light blue colors and beautiful paintings of cool Swedish summer landscapes on the walls. There were mysterious jars in front of the toilet mirror: ammunition for the battle against age. I stood stark naked looking out at an iced-over tennis court and a couple of buried cars. It had been snowing again. Just as I was lifting the receiver, she woke up and looked at me with surprise, then she stretched herself like a warm cat and the bedcover slipped down to reveal her breasts. She was doing very well in the fight against decay.

"Morning, loverboy," she said softly.

"Morning. May I use the phone?"

"You look rested."

"You know what they say. A good fuck is just as good as five hours of sleep."

"Do they say that? Then you won't have to sleep for a while."

I turned around and began to dial Basov's private number—there were no public phone directories in Moscow, and I considered it a privilege to have been given it—but I couldn't remember it. I found my jacket by the door and fished out my notebook. Caroline was looking at me.

"Where did you get all those muscles?"

"Hard work," I said. "Is there a phone in the living room?"

I also found the rest of my clothes scattered on the floor like a trail, leading to the treasure we had found in the bed. It had been a good night. We had clung to each other like a couple of shipwrecked people. I found Basov's number and dialed while trying to zip my pants. I could hear Caroline turn on the shower.

Basov answered the phone himself.

"Hello," he said, without introducing himself. In the background I could hear a woman's voice calling Tolya, and a child's loud, happy laughter. It sounded damned cozy. I felt quite envious of Basov and his domestic happiness.

"It's me," I said in Russian.

"Yes," he said. Tolya stamped around the phone, shrieking with delight as, apparently, he was caught by his mother. I could hear her voice. It sounded clear and happy, full of laughter and summer.

"Could we meet before work?"

"If we can make it short."

"It's important. Nine o'clock at Pushkin."

"OK," he said, and hung up. The last thing I heard was Tolya's happy laughter once more. Imagine being in such a good mood at seven o'clock in the morning.

But our morning wasn't so bad, either. Caroline pulled me back into bed, and although she claimed that my unshaved cheeks scratched her, she put up with it. Afterward we lay in bed smoking for a while, until Caroline got up and took another shower. I borrowed a towel and showered, too, while

Caroline fixed breakfast. It had been a long time since anyone had made breakfast for me. We talked in a civilized manner about this and that. She was an intelligent and attractive woman, and with her clothes on she again became the slightly cool, professional colleague, but of course there was something more between us now, and when I left, she kissed me lightly on the cheek.

"Are we going to see each other again?" she asked. "Or should I leave it to you to ask?"

"It would be difficult to avoid that in this village," I said.

"Get out of here, you asshole," she said without anger.

"You may fix breakfast for me some other time," I said.

"Don't feel too sure, in spite of all your muscles," she said, and she closed the door.

It was cold again, and the clouds hung low, threatening more snow. I drove home through the city, where people hurried along with closed, chilled faces or tried to look out through the iced-over windows of red streetcars rattling over knotty, frozen switches. In one place a trolley bus had lost the connection to the electric wire above it. A heavy woman stood on the roof of the bus, struggling with the rods. She wore thick leather gloves. With surprising agility she jumped down onto the street and managed to tip the rods back in place by pulling two ropes. Then she took off again, and the traffic moved slowly on. I made it home in time to find a clean shirt and shave. The morning was still good. I found a parking space right in front of the large editorial building of *Izvestia,* and Basov emerged from the subway exit a little before nine. There was a throng of people on Pushkin Square. I could see all the bobbing fur caps of the pedestrians who were pushing down Gorky Street. More and more people kept appearing all the time from the various subway exits, all on their way to work. They formed the spine of the society, the ones who made it function in spite of all.

The traffic moved slowly. Pushkin was contemplating the dense flow from his pedestal, his back turned to the gray concrete of the Rossiya Cinema.

Basov looked rested and freshly shaved, as if he had brought along a part of his happy family life. We walked in the direction of the cinema along the empty flowerbeds, a profusion of brilliant colors in the summer. I told him about the conversation of the night before, but without mentioning any names. We walked all the way up to the terrace in front of the Rossiya. They were showing a film about World War II. On the terrace an icy wind was blowing. Basov sniffed the wind as if he felt a change in the weather. He said nothing, but began to walk back toward Gorky Street. Then he stopped and took my arm.

"Your sources are doubtful. I'm not going to ask you where you got this information, but is there any reason to pursue the matter?" he said.

"You could call it justice."

"That's a fancy notion nowadays," he said with bitterness.

"Yes, but maybe you could pass this on to the colonel?"

"You know how complicated the situation is, Jack. I don't have to pretend in front of you. If nothing happens soon, Russia is finished."

"That's not what we're talking about," I said.

"You saw the investigation documents yourself. They're clear enough. There's no sign of violence. There's no sign that there was anyone present other than the two women," he said and he began walking again.

"The whole affair reeks of mafia or corruption in high places. I know you're honest, I know that you love your country, and I know that you're sickened by what's happening." I stopped, and he turned halfway around, but his eyes looked straight past me over my shoulder.

"Vladimir," I continued, "justice begins with the small people. If we don't care about small people and small things, then everything collapses."

He smiled. "I didn't know that you were a crusader. You talk like an old Bolshevik."

"I'd rather be talking like an old Bolshevik than like a modern Communist," I cut him short.

He looked straight at me, then he slapped my shoulder and laughed loudly. I had never quite learned to understand the sudden changes of mood of the Russians.

"The day will come when once again we can be proud to say: I'm a member of the Communist Party of the Soviet Union. The day will come."

"When hell freezes over," I said, switching into English. I was angry and didn't hide it.

Basov stopped laughing. He slapped my shoulder again, but more gently this time, almost like a shy caress.

"I'll go tell it on the mountain. Have a nice day, crusader," he said, and slipped into the crowd. I followed him with my eyes until he was eaten by the darkness of the subway entrance.

CW and Castesen weren't enthusiastic, either.

We were having coffee in CW's office.

"It's an idiotic theory. It serves no purpose to pursue the matter," was Castesen's irritated comment.

"You could call it justice," I said.

"Justice! For whom? A tart. I don't see the purpose. It's not in the interest of the nation."

"OK. But then we're accomplices."

"Stop talking like a boy scout," Castesen said.

CW cleared his throat. "Jack. Is this something you think we should pursue officially?"

"For Heaven's sake, CW!" Castesen said.

"I don't think it'll be of any use. Most people seem to think like Castesen," I said.

"Have you talked to someone about it already? Don't you know what the instructions were from back home? The case is dead, Jack," Castesen said.

"I haven't talked to anyone officially," I said. It wasn't a good morning anymore. I tried to recall Caroline in the bed and at the breakfast table, but I saw only Castesen's haughty face with the cigarette between the narrow lips.

CW cleared his throat again. "I suggest that we mention your information in a subordinate clause when we write the conclusive report to the ministry today after the meeting with Kamarassov."

Both Castesen and I noticed CW's word: conclusive.

Castesen looked relieved. He said, "Do we have other and perhaps more important matters to discuss this morning?" He already behaved like an ambassador. Actually, he always had.

"Only a couple of trifles. I would like to hear your opinions on yesterday's *Pravda* article about Mongolia. Is it possible to read a Chernenko angle into it?" CW said.

After the meeting I went out in the garden. It was cold, but there was no wind. I took a couple of deep breaths and tried to clear my head. Castesen came outside and placed himself next to me. We stood there for a while.

"I'm going away soon," he said needlessly. "I managed to sell my car yesterday. To an Egyptian."

"I'll be willing to take some rubles," I said.

"That was all that I wanted to know," he said. "It's cold, I'm going inside." He hesitated for a moment, but then he left.

I guess it was just the matter of the rubles that he wanted to settle. He probably hadn't wanted to talk about it inside. Selling cars was very lucrative for Western diplomats. You bought a good Western car, a Volvo for instance, for six thousand dollars out of bond in the West. Then you sold it for rubles to an Arab or African diplomat, who had plenty of rubles that they received from the Soviet state. They were prepared to pay 25,000 rubles for the same car. Cash. The plates were changed in Finland. The Arab diplomat got a Western car. The Western diplomat got cheap rubles. The loser was the Soviet state, whose rubles weren't sold at the official exchange rate. I didn't care. Like everything else in the Soviet Union, the ruble was strongly overestimated. Now I was getting cold, too, and I went into my office and began to go through the piles of papers.

I wanted to write my political report, but first I looked at some visa applications. There was a delegation from the Soviet labor union, Trud, that was going to visit Denmark. They had been invited by the Danish Trades Union Congress. I carefully went over the names and checked them against a list of KGB agents. I found two official agents right away, and approved their visas. We knew who they were. Their job was not infiltration and espionage. They came along to make sure that no member of the Trud delegation would feel tempted by the pleasures of capitalism and defect.

One name bothered me. I had seen it before, or heard it during a classified briefing. The grayish white passport photo seemed familiar, too. It showed a heavy, gray-haired man with fat cheeks and large glasses. I have a good memory for names, but I couldn't place his. Finally I gave up and coded an inquiry, which I sent home via telex. I asked for a quick answer. While I waited, I began to go through the papers. They were dismally boring, but there was one interesting article on corruption in the Ukraine. It was a badly disguised attack on Chernenko and his group. There was more scheming going on than ever.

John came in with the telex answer. It was in code. He stayed by the door, looking rather nervous.

"Give it to me," I said.

"Any news?" he said.

"What do you mean?" I said, although I knew very well what he was referring to.

"Well, about Sonia?"

"No. There's nothing new. You needn't worry."

"OK. I just wanted to ask," he said.

"I'm busy," I said.

For a second he looked at me as if he felt like hitting me, but then he just closed the door a little too hard.

We changed our codes every week, but never felt quite certain that the KGB didn't break them as fast as we changed them. When I decoded the message, I saw that I had been right: they did have the KGB agent in the computer. The man was listed as a journalist at the newspaper, *Trud,* but he had been expelled from Portugal in 1974. He had been caught red-handed. An agent for the third department of the First Directorate, which also covers Scandinavia. I went into CW's office and placed the telex on his desk.

CW looked at it for a short while, then he scribbled, "Give him a visa."

I looked at him inquiringly, and he added, "Let's see whom he meets in Denmark."

"You old schemer," I said, and left a content CW. I coded a new telex with the name: Valentin Alexandrovich Seriyogin, formerly second economic attaché at the Soviet embassy in Lisbon, now journalist at *Trud.* Purpose of visit to Denmark: to promote international understanding. Real purpose: probably industrial espionage or selection and recruitment of possible agents.

I wrote for most of the day, and when I had finished my report, I handed it over to Jette for her to code and send to Copenhagen. CW trusted me. Many ambassadors would have asked to see the report before it was sent, but CW harbored a healthy skepticism about bureaucratic procedures. Jette was miffed.

"I've got a hangover, and you bring me more work," she said.

"Tough," I replied.

"You might show a little compassion."

"It's self-inflicted, so I don't feel sorry for you."

"You're a jerk, but that doesn't keep you from looking good. Single life seems to agree with you."

"I'm not complaining."

"Who's the lucky girl? A little twenty-year-old Finnish nanny or an old bag like me?"

"Just mind your work."

"My door is open, too."

"Relax, Jette."

"I miss Sonia. It's idiotic, don't you think?" she said.

"I don't know."

"I've asked for a transfer."

"I'm sorry to hear that."

"You are? I'm *glad* to hear that."

I turned around to leave.

"Any news?" she said.

"We'll bury the case officially in an hour," I said.

"Ashes to ashes. From dust to a dusty pile of papers on a shelf," Jette said.

"I wish you'd stop quoting. You always miss the mark."

"It's better to miss the mark than not to shoot at all, Jackie boy," she said.

Jette was right, of course. Sonia and Vera became a dossier on a shelf in the foreign ministry. As the chief of the Scandinavia department, Kamarassov conducted the meeting. CW acted as our spokesman. Castesen cheeped along, and, as the junior staff member, I kept quiet. It all took place as if it had been written in a thoroughly prepared script. As a matter of routine, we were reprimanded for the aggressive intentions of NATO. We ought to make our influence felt and stop the preparations for war. The island of Bornholm was being transformed into a springboard for aggression against Socialist countries. The clichés were pouring out of him while I looked outside at the beginning darkness, and Castesen looked indignant. Kamarassov was a small, agile man in his seventies, who had spread his poison about the Scandinavian countries since the days of Stalin. Over the years, he had alternately threatened and fawned on us. Basov was present at the meeting, but, like me, he knew his place and kept quiet. It was difficult to take Kamarassov seriously, hearing the small country of Denmark described as an armed giant meditating war against Socialist countries. If it had not been so tragic because of his sincerity, it would have been comical.

CW answered diplomatically and reciprocated by touching on the SS-20 missiles, Afghanistan, and atomic submarines in the Baltic Sea. When he began to inquire sharply about Chernenko's health, the ritual dance came to an end.

Then we expressed our thanks for the excellent investigative work. CW said that the Danish state considered the case closed, and regretted that there had been certain irregularities in the life-style of the deceased. The atmosphere changed noticeably for the better. There was reconciliation and mutual understanding in the air. Kamarassov generously regretted in return that not all Soviet citizens led a moral and socialistically correct life. The meeting was concluded in the most positive manner when Kamarassov said, "I have been authorized to say that the Soviet state has decided to place the order for four container ships with a Danish shipyard."

It was going to save jobs for Danish workers at the expense of Yugoslavian ones. As we drove back to the embassy, CW was as happy as a schoolboy who has gotten an A.

He invited us to a glass of whisky to celebrate the outcome.

"That was that," Castesen said.

"Yes," CW sighed. "I could have done without this affair coming just a couple of years before my retirement, but now it seems to be buried, and, of course, the ships were a surprising bonus."

"Four ships for Sonia. Not a bad price," I said.

Castesen gave me an exasperated look.

CW got up from his chair and walked over to his desk. He looked out at the garden, which lay shrouded in darkness.

From the residence we could hear Mozart. It was Mrs. W playing her favorite music. The sound streamed into the semi-obscurity of the office. CW had lit only a single lamp, and had probably got up to turn on more light; but, like Castesen and myself, he was captured by the crisp sound. For a while we didn't say anything. CW sighed once more. He looked tired in the soft light. It occurred to me for the first time that he might not get to enjoy his retirement for long. Life had left its mark on his face, his belly, his ruddy, clean-shaven cheeks, his clean nails, and his thick gray hair. Under the surface I imagined that his body was about to give up after so many years of cigarettes and social drinking. I sat there listening to Mozart and thinking of CW and how much I cared for this old amiable fool. CW was the first to tear himself out of the mood, and he turned on the light with a quick movement.

"That'll be the last we'll hear of her," Castesen said. "The case is dead and soon it will be forgotten."

We were tired, and I was beginning to share CW's relief that it was over—apparently without any lasting damage to Danish-Soviet relations. And yet, I had a gnawing feeling that something was wrong, and that Sonia and Vera would prove difficult to bury.

I went straight home. Exhausted, I found an old videotape on the shelf and began to watch *The Dirty Dozen*. That would keep me from thinking. Halfway into the film, I could hardly keep my eyes open. I listened to the news on the BBC, and finding that the world was in its usual catastrophic state, I decided to go to bed. Then the phone rang. I could hear that it was Basov, even though he didn't introduce himself.

"You ought to go skiing on Saturday if you have nothing else to do," he said.

"When?" I said, thinking of Demichev's party.

"In the morning. They are promising snow, so the Silver Wood will show itself in its most favorable light, I'm sure," he said, and hung up.

12

Saturday finally became one of those beautiful days that are used by Intourist in their attempts to make foreigners spend their winter vacations in Moscow. I woke up early, feeling refreshed after a good night's sleep, although the remains of a stupid dream still rattled about somewhere in my mind. I had gone to bed early and stayed away from liquor. I looked down at the Sadovaya. There were hardly any cars at all. It had been snowing heavily when I went to bed, but apparently it must have stopped sometime during the night. It had been a fine and frosty snow that had settled softly and gently over everything. The snow had given the city a face-lift, making things look so much better. The roofs were covered with the same fine snow. The city appeared all white, and the dawning light promised that for once the sky would be blue. The thermometer outside my window showed 10 degrees Fahrenheit.

The city was quiet as I drove toward the Silver Wood in the early morning. It was only eight-thirty, but there were already some people in the streets, on the hunt for goods with their perpetual shopping bags. Large snowplows were clearing the streets. We had received quite a few inches overnight; it covered up the normal sooty blackness of Moscow. Fat women dressed in several layers of clothing and orange vests were scraping and shoveling away. A strange contraption that the Russians call a *kapitalisty* was sucking up snow into a snaillike nozzle and pumping it onto the platform of a short truck. There was a man sitting in the driver's cab, and I could hear that he was playing Dylan on the tape recorder inside. I laughed at the thought of the name. Capitalist. Because it was so greedy and could swallow unsuspected amounts of snow.

I drove across 1905 Square past the cemetery where Vysotsky is buried, crossed the railroad bridge, and continued in the direction of the Silver Wood. The trolley buses were already half filled with people headed there. I could see how carefully they held on to their Russian wooden skis. The Silver Wood is a small island in the middle of the Moscow River, a recreational area where you can swim in the muddy water in summer and go skiing in winter. A policeman stood in the middle of the road right after the bridge that leads to the island. He stopped all the cars with Russian license plates. I ignored him completely and continued past him into the wood with its snow-powdered birches and pines. Several of the large embassies have weekend cottages in the Silver Wood. I drove all the way to the end of the road past a no-entry sign. Living in a system of privileges has certain advantages . . . when you're the one who has the privileges.

The sun shone from a beautiful, picture-postcard blue sky. It glinted in the golden domes of a dilapidated, closed church and was reflected in the windows of the large apartment buildings on the other side of the river. A bridge had been laid out on the ice, making it easier for the people from the apartment buildings to walk across to the wood. It wasn't there in the summer, I remembered. It was prohibited to swim across. In summer the police would race up and down the river in speedboats, exposing all the bathers to great danger and shouting at people to stay near the shore. Fortunately you rarely saw them in winter.

There were quite a few people on the island already, most of them skiing along the bank or in the middle of the frozen river. They wore thick caps and sweatpants. There were children and old women, but every now and then young muscular men spurted by with naked upper bodies in the biting frost. It was supposed to be good for you and keep you from catching cold. I stood out from everybody else with my colorful Danish ski suit, and my fine Finnish langlauf skis on the roof of the Volvo. In the distance, on the river, I could see little black spots sitting patiently like freckles on white skin. They were men who sat there fishing, each by his own little hole in the ice.

I put my skis on and began running in the direction of the main reach of the river. I ran at an easy pace and with every stroke I felt better. I forgot all about Sonia, CW, the colonel, and Castesen. I forgot all about Susanne, in spite of the fact that I had dreamed of her the night before. She had been a distant plasmatic shadow in a room filled with people that I couldn't contact. It was an animated party, where the Russian singer poured wine for the colonel and Basov, who laughed at everything she said. Nobody as much as looked at me. They all pretended that I didn't exist. I tried again and again to get in contact with Susanne. "Come home!" I wanted to shout, but I couldn't make a sound. I pushed through the crowd of festive people and kept getting entangled in their arms. Susanne looked at me through the dense tobacco haze. Her eyes were quite empty and black. When I got near her, she disappeared into the wall just as I reached out for her. She turned into a blotch, and I was pawing the dirty yellow wallpaper. Then I woke up.

I remembered the dream as I ran. I could hear nothing but the rhythmic, hissing sound of the skis on the new, frosty

snow. Some magpies flashed by the dilapidated church, probably a storage place for a lot of useless stuff. They screeched and
circled back around the golden domes as if something had
alarmed them. I ran upon the river close to the shore. At this
early hour there was still plenty of room, but others had been
there before me, and there was already a track. Occasionally I
met a skier who was headed in the opposite direction, and a
couple of times I was overtaken by young men who were using
skating technique and advanced with amazing speed. I proceeded with classic calm. There was no wind, and the sun
began to warm the air. The cold prickled pleasantly in my
cheeks. After half an hour I began to sweat. I had reached the
part of the island that curves more strongly and from which
you have a long view of the river. I leaned against my ski poles
and took out a cigarette. From the city I could hear the murmur of the traffic, but everyday life felt far away.

Behind me, a voice suddenly said, "Sports and smoking
don't go together."

"Basov, goddamnit. You nearly scared the hell out of me,"
I exclaimed angrily.

"Good morning, Jack. What a day. On a day like this there's
no better place in the whole world than Russia."

"I could mention a few," I said crossly.

He laughed loudly. It was only now that I noticed that his
upper body was naked. His skin was steaming in the cold. He
had been running very fast. He looked absolutely ridiculous
with the naked torso and a knitted cap, a scarf, and ski mittens.
He was very muscular. He had real Finnish skis and real ski
pants. Like me, he hadn't shaved.

"You'll get pneumonia."

"It's good for you if you keep moving. That's what the
experts say."

"That must be the Russian experts. The same ones that
planned your consumer sector."

His face froze, but then he laughed again.

"The day is too good for quarreling. I'm sorry that I startled you."

"That's OK. Do you want a cigarette?"

"Why not?"

But first he put on his clothes, which he carried in a small bag that was tied around his waist: a T-shirt, a sweater, and a sports jacket, which didn't seem particularly warm. We stood smoking in silence for a while. On the side of the island we had a view of naked trees and brown timber houses. On the Moscow side, massive apartment buildings. The light was very sharp and blue.

"Come," he said. "Someone wants to speak with you."

"Who?" I asked, although I already knew.

"You'll see in a moment. What he has to say is only for your ears."

"In any case I'm glad you got me out of bed on such a great morning," I said.

"I'm not sure I feel the same way," he said, and set off with violent thrusts of his poles. I watched him for a moment, before I got started myself at a much slower speed. My thighs were already aching. I had been standing still in the cold for too long.

Basov was an excellent skier and ran with steady, economical strokes. It looked effortless and elegant. I refused to compete and stuck to my own speed. He looked back when he had got quite a distance ahead, and slowed down. We crossed out upon the river, and I stayed right behind him in the trail that he had created.

We continued for maybe ten minutes out into the middle of the Moscow River. It was completely frozen, but I wasn't comfortable about being so far from the shore. There had been a thaw around Christmas. In the middle of the river was a man sitting on a small folding chair; a pair of Russian wooden skis lay beside him. He sat quite still in his heavy, unbecoming winter coat and his thick fur cap, the flaps of which he had pulled down. He wore a glove on one hand only. His other hand carefully held a small fishing rod, not much longer than six inches, which he was slowly moving up and down. The thin line disappeared into a small hole in the ice, with lumps floating on the surface, that he had bored with a heavy iron drill that lay next to his bag, which looked like an old-fashioned midwifery bag. Between his legs stood a bottle wrapped in that day's *Pravda*. Basov stopped for a second, then he turned around with a quick movement of his skis and hastened back in the direction of the Silver Wood.

"How about a drink, Mr. Andersen?" Colonel Gavrilin asked.

I reached down and took the chipped cup that he was offering me, one-quarter full of vodka. Gavrilin poured a spot in another cup for himself. His face was reddish white in the cold, and he hadn't shaved for a couple of days, but his eyes were clear.

"*Davai!*" he said, and emptied his cup. I did likewise and took off my skis. I placed the poles next to his and squatted down.

"Are you catching anything?" I asked.

"Only small fish," he said. "You had something to tell me. Take the time you need. I've got plenty of time now."

We had another spot of vodka while I told him about my night on Red Square and my suspicion of murder. He listened and interrupted only to ask me to describe the details of a coat or a face and to make me elaborate on a mood and analyze my feelings and evaluations when I had heard the story. Before I had finished, I began to feel somewhat cold. He never stopped calmly moving the fishing rod up and down. Observed from a distance, the situation must have appeared quite ordinary for a weekend by the Moscow River.

I got up and tried to get some life back in my feet.

"Is this of any use to you? Are you going to do anything about it?" I said, and squatted down again.

"No. I can't. They pensioned me off three days ago," he said.

I must have looked surprised, for he continued, "Your press would probably write 'purged,' if ever they got to know about it."

"Why?"

"Because, like you, I have an old-fashioned idea of justice and thought that there was more to this case than was apparent in the official report."

"So they tampered with the report?" I said.

"Andropov placed me in the police along with others who could have been more useful where they were. But only we would have been able to clean out the corrupt gang. Damn it, their commanding chief, the minister of the interior, took bribes quite openly!" he shouted.

He was admitting his affiliation with the KGB as if it were the most natural thing in the world. I suddenly began to suspect Basov. I wondered if his loyalty was somewhere other than at the building on Smolensk Square?

"I didn't think that the KGB let themselves be kicked in the ass," I said.

"Comrade Andropov did the right thing," he continued, as if he hadn't heard me, but I saw his eyes contract at the insult. "But Comrade Andropov died too soon, and those incompetent faggots who are at the Kremlin now are only interested in living comfortably in their fancy dachas."

"That's built into your system. You lived with Stalin until he died. You lived with Khrushchev until he was overthrown. Brezhnev was so senile when he died that he didn't know what day it was, and now you have Chernenko, who has never done anything but carry a briefcase and make boring speeches," I said.

"There's no reason to discuss politics."

"We're not discussing politics. I'm talking about the difference between democracy and dictatorial inbreeding. You had to live with whatever czar Russia gave you. Now you have to live with whatever general secretary the Party gives you."

"That's anti-Soviet propaganda."

"The truth often is," I said, and got up to stretch my legs.

He looked up at me. Then he carefully put down the short fishing rod and produced a crumpled pack of cigarettes. They were the cheapest Russian brand that you could get in Moscow, but I understood his gesture of peace, so I accepted one. He lit it with an old gas lighter. We smoked for a while, then he said, "I found this lighter in the pocket of a German soldier just outside Berlin. He must have been about seventeen years old, I think. I was twenty and already a captain in the Red Army. I strangled him with my bare hands. It was a small village. I can't remember what it was called. We had blown it to pieces with our artillery. It was a day in April, and it was raining a little. Then the infantry moved in. There was a pocket of resistance in one of the shattered houses. One of my friends and I lay behind the gable. Then my comrade threw a hand grenade through the door. We waited for a while. Then we went inside and found four young Germans lying there in uniforms that were much too big for them. They were dead. Except for one. He fired one more shot with one of those long-nosed German pistols and smashed the face of my friend. Then I strangled him, even though he was already half dead and only seventeen years old. I was with the army the rest of the way to Berlin, but I never knowingly killed another human being after that, and since then I've found that the taking of another person's life is the most abominable crime there is. I can still see him. He didn't have even a suggestion of a beard. His eyes bulged, cried for help, but I was cold as ice and strangled him."

I reached down between his legs and took the bottle and poured a spot for him and for myself, and we drank.

He continued, "I was seventeen when I went to war. I started in Stalingrad and ended in Berlin, and all the way through the counteroffensive I thought of only one thing: when we won, I wanted to help rebuild this country, and I wanted to decide how that was going to be done. I could only do that if I became a member of the Party. So I joined. It was no problem. Stalin had murdered most of the old members, and I had been decorated so many times that I was an obvious choice."

He hesitated for a moment. I said nothing. His eyes were still clear. He didn't touch the fishing rod. We were all alone in the middle of the frozen river. Around us there was white stillness.

"One thing that it has been difficult for me to live with is the German whom I killed with my bare hands. Not the others. Prisoners of war that we shot. Hand grenades thrown into bunkers. Flamethrowers. SS officers whom we lined up in the Ukraine together with traitors and mowed down, and afterward we ate their meager rations sitting on the corpses. But that young German. Since then I haven't killed. Since then I have hunted those who kill. And ever since then I have contributed to the attempt to secure a better life for our people. There are people today in many parts of the society who talk about preserving. Of memories. *Pamyat,*" he said in Russian. "They keep themselves covered: who doesn't want to support such a noble cause as the restoration of the edifices of lost generations? Who isn't ready to commemorate and re-create the great Russian culture? But look underneath the surface, Mr. Andersen, then you'll see worms feeding on corpses."

We finished our cigarettes. I got up and stretched my legs, but squatted down again in order not to spoil our intimacy. I'm not a particularly sensitive person, according to my former wife, so I said, "How the hell can you still believe in this society? How can you still be a Communist?"

Noticing that I had used the familiar form of address, he said, "So I guess we're friends now, Jack. Let's drink to our friendship. A toast to the two of us, who both think we know what justice is. To we who think we're the last righteous men in a sinful world."

"I love the way atheists always quote the Good Book."

"Even if it's full of lies, it's still a good book. Dostoyevsky is fiction, too; but still he wrote the truth."

"To literature," I said, being rather inebriated at this point.

He raised his cup and threw the vodka out on the ice.

"Communism is not a religion, my friend. It's truth. It may take another hundred years, but in the end the whole planet will become Communist."

"It's a good thing we don't live that long," I said. "So I won't be around to stand in line when that happens."

He laughed. Then he picked up his fishing rod and resumed his ritual wrist movement.

"If you guys are so strong, then why can't you do something about the case? Something concrete instead of fantasies of the future and old man's talk about a war that you and all other veterans miss like old whores miss their virginity and their youth."

He looked at me and patted my arm in a fatherly way.

"I suppose we all dream of the solidarity and the common strength that comes from common suffering." He took a pull at the bottle without offering me any and continued, "But right now I've been pensioned off."

"Couldn't the KGB pull a couple of strings? Or have all your teeth been pulled?"

"We're wasting time," he said.

"Then tell me how they have tampered with the report."

"They have removed a page."

"What did it say on that page?"

"That there was sperm in Vera's and Sonia's vaginas, and that there was sperm on the sheet."

I sat down on the ice. Gavrilin looked as unruffled as before, but the movements of his wrist had become faster, making the rod almost whiz in the air.

"Then have the medical examiner arrested, goddamnit. Surely the KGB still has the power to do that?"

"He's dead. Someone pushed him out in front of a metro train. They scraped him up with a coal shovel."

"But he called you?"

"No, I paid him a visit, and he let himself be persuaded to tell the truth. He had been stupid enough to keep the original autopsy statement."

"Why are you telling me this?" I asked.

"Because one good turn deserves another."

"But then all you have to do is to go to the Central Committee and have them reopen the case."

"I didn't get the time to do that. I was pensioned off first, and everybody refuses to speak with me. That idiot of a medical examiner didn't keep his mouth shut."

"But you're not afraid of fishing here by yourself?"

"I still have friends, and it won't be long before the situation changes. Other people will get into power. In the meantime I spend my time fishing. More vodka?"

We had another. My head was spinning, but whether it was from the liquor or because of what the colonel had told me, I didn't know.

"Can I have a copy of the document?"

"No, but you can promise me to testify and tell everything you know when the occasion arises, hopefully soon."

"I'll do that gladly," I said without hesitation, and thought of Sonia in the coagulated blood of the bathtub and Vera's silent scream through her hair and her obscenely exposed sex that I had covered with a blouse.

"I figured that," he said.

"I hope you've hidden the report well," I said.

"It rests safely in the hands of God," he answered.

"I suppose God has given you a suspect as well?" I said as ironically as I could in Russian.

"No, he hasn't. I've found him myself. And when Chernenko and his mafia are gone, then we'll get him, be he ever so much a general."

I whistled.

"You're playing with fire," I said.

"No, I've been pensioned off," he said. "I'll be seeing you."

He said nothing while I buckled on my skis and stuck my hands into the straps of the poles. But the moment I was about to start running, he tugged hard at his fishing rod and pulled a fish out through the lumps of ice.

"As you see, I catch only the small fish," he said.

The small, gray fish was the size of a sardine. The timing of the whole thing was so perfect that I felt certain that he had planned it all and probably had put the fish on the hook himself before I had arrived. That is, if it weren't just the bait.

"Enjoy your retirement," I said, and took off. He didn't answer. I looked back a couple of times and saw only an old man who sat stooping over a hole in the ice, a black dot that grew smaller and smaller and finally looked like all the other black dots.

I didn't run back along the river. When I reached the island, I cut across between the white birches. There weren't any people, and I had to make my own trail. I ran as fast as I could until sweat began pouring down my armpits and my breathing made my chest feel so tight that it hurt. Then I continued at a more sedate speed and quietly slid down a small hill. There they stood. Three men of strong build who looked like soldiers in civilian clothes. They were amazingly alike, in tight blue ski suits and blue caps, and all three of them had thick mustaches. They didn't waste any time talking. I barely had time to stop before the one in the middle stepped forward and placed a ski pole against my chest. I toppled over in the snow like a nine-pin.

"You speak Russian well, so let's not waste any time," he said. "I want to know what the old man on the ice said to you, and I want to know it now, or else I'll run this ski pole through your Finnish faggot clothes right through your balls so that it comes out through your asshole." As a nation, Russians tend to swear a lot, but still I was amazed at the elegance that he put into his threat. Not that I wasn't afraid. I was. But I had the advantage of being able to see Basov come rushing at us behind them. He banged his ski pole into the back of the head of one, making him tumble into the others and tip them over. I was grateful to the Finnish ski manufacturer for having made bindings that could be opened in a jiffy, so that I was on my feet again when the largest of them had recovered his balance and came at me with slow, circling, karate arm movements. I jabbed my left twice into his nose, crossing him with my right, and, as he was going down, I showed the bad taste of hooking him with my left so hard that it hurt all the way to the back of my neck.

Basov was the karate type as well, but not of the subtle kind. When the guy who had threatened me was getting up, Basov kicked him in the groin without hesitation, and a few seconds later he kicked the face of the man he had hit with his ski pole. The man's face was covered with blood as he collapsed in the snow, which turned red underneath him. On film, fights like that take several minutes; in the Silver Wood the whole thing lasted maybe twenty seconds. Only people who have tried boxing know how long a three-minute round feels.

I was scared to death, so I said, "It's not nice to kick someone who's lying down."

"Shut up," Basov hissed.

"Thank you, Vladimir," I said.

"Let's get the hell out of here," he said.

I ran with my skis and poles under my arms until I reached Basov's skis, which lay in the snow fifty feet away. Then we both buckled on our skis. We could hear two of the men moaning in pain. The third one lay quite still with his crushed face. Basov's Finnish boots were the kind that have steel braces on the toes. He started running through the birch wood, and I followed with my heart pounding like after three good rounds.

At the Volvo Basov shuffled impatiently while I fastened my skis onto the roof of the car.

"You know a few tricks for a subordinate junior diplomat," I said.

"Get the hell into that car and go home," he said. He was pale and flushed at the same time.

"Are we going to make a case of it? Danish diplomat attacked by military-looking thugs after conversation with retired KGB officer," I said.

"Can't you just get your ass into that goddamned car, Jack?"

"They looked like soldiers," I said.

"Go, Jack!"

I got into the Volvo, but kept the door open.

"You know what strikes me, Volody?" I said. "They all had mustaches. And you know they say in Moscow that mustaches are kind of a tribal sign that all Afghanistan veterans wear."

"People go crazy in Afghanistan—now get out of here!"

Basov looked so miserable that I didn't want to torture him any longer, so I drove off. I proceeded for about a quarter of a mile, then I had to stop. When I had finished throwing up, I drove home very slowly while constantly looking into the rearview mirror. It was only when I was in the hot shower that I stopped shaking. Before I got dressed, I wrote down the conversation with Gavrilin and put it in an envelope that I addressed to myself, care of the Danish Ministry of Foreign Affairs.

13

I got to the subway station at Mayakovsky Square a little early and slowly circled the square a couple of times. Both sidewalks were swarming with people as far down Gorky Street as I could see. Practically everyone carried a shopping net. Each person was surrounded by a whirl of fine mist in the dry frost. The sun was now shining palely through a thin layer of clouds.

At half past one I stopped the car and waited. I was thinking about how much I should tell CW about my talk with the colonel. I felt rather convinced that it would serve no purpose to pass it on. I couldn't make up my mind and was far away when I heard the tapping on the window. She got inside on the front seat next to me.

Lilli looked lovely. Her face was radiantly young and pretty. She wore no makeup except for a little eye shadow, a shining green. She pulled off her knitted bonnet and shook her short curly hair.

"You look very beautiful today," I said in Russian, using the formal address. I had an inexplicable sinking feeling.

She smiled. Her teeth were strong and regular.

"Why don't we say *ti*?" she said. She switched into English: "If we speak English, we won't have to think about *vui i ti* at all."

"Your English is good," I said inanely. The motor was running at idle speed. It was warm inside the car. She unbuttoned her coat and fastened the seat belt.

"Thank you," she said in Russian.

"I'm glad you came," I continued in the same language.

"I'm glad to be here in your car," she said, and smiled again.

I got on the ring road and continued along Kutusovsky Prospect, which is the best road in Moscow. It has fewer holes, because Kutusovsky is the exit leading to the enclosed and guarded dachas of the elite. We drove past the complex of apartment buildings for foreigners, where Sonia and Vera had been found, and past the triumphal arch that commemorates the first great national war against Napoleon. To the left of the grayish-white arch, workers were leveling out a small mound, making it as flat as a pancake. The biggest war memorial in the world was to be built here in memory of the second great national war. The one against Hitler. We had about half an hour's drive to the writers' town, Peredelkino. We talked pleasantly and easily about this and that. I felt comfortable with her, as if I'd known her for a long time. She seemed to feel the same way.

When we had driven for a while, she asked if I had any cassette tapes. I told her to look in the glove compartment. She let out a small scream of joy when she saw Bruce Springsteen's new *Born in the USA*. I was mainly into the music of the sixties and seventies, but Springsteen had some of that spontaneous rock about him that I remembered from my youth. Both Castesen and CW found it rather amazing that a grown man could be interested in rock music. Youth music. They were into classical music, of course: they were cultured people.

She fumbled a little with the tape before she managed to insert it into the tape recorder. I let her find out on her own, and eventually she succeeded in getting the cassette in place and turning it on. The tape hadn't been rewound, and it started in the middle of a song. She sang along. Her voice was clear and melodious. "You can't start a fire without a spark," she sang, and smiled at me warmly, but without flirtation. Just happy. I let her sing as we left the city and reached the country-side, where the road was lined with small houses that were painted blue and brown and seemed to crouch in the white snow. Along the road there were birch trees. Then more houses. Everything was flat. A little farther away from Moscow, many of the houses didn't have running water. Smoke from the wood burning in the kitchen stoves rose from the roofs. An old woman walked along the road with a yoke on her shoulders. She had been fetching water at the common village well. That was what the landscape and the road looked like all the six hundred miles to the Finnish border north of Leningrad.

"Where do you know Springsteen from?" I asked when she stopped singing. "This record only just came out."

"From the radio," she said.

"Have they played Springsteen on Mayak?" I asked. Mayak is Moscow's so-called popular channel. They play a steady flow of folk music and noncontroversial classical composers.

She gave a loud, but pleasant laugh.

"No, you fool," she said. "I've listened to Springsteen on foreign radio, Voice of America, BBC, and others. And I have a friend who tapes the music programs. He has a cassette tape recorder," she said, as if it were a great rarity.

"Of course," I said.

"Maybe you think we listen to Voice of America to hear news from the world and get to know all the things they don't tell us? Maybe we do that, too. But I mainly listen because of the music. They have good rock programs."

"With a lot of crackling and noise," I said.

"It's better than nothing. But I'm surprised that someone like you likes Springsteen."

"Someone as old as me, you mean."

"You're not old, and you know it. You're an extremely attractive man, and you know that, too," she said matter-of-factly.

I laughed with embarrassment and surprise.

"You're very direct. Especially for a Russian."

"I'm not Russian. I'm Estonian. I live in a society that's full of lies. That's why I try to speak the truth as much as possible. Or at least to say what I mean."

"Then thank you," I said.

We drove on. The music filled the car. I turned down a byroad between two houses, and we jolted along a bumpy road that was covered with grayish black lumps of ice. We crossed a small bridge and were in Peredelkino, a group of wooden houses, where the Writers' Society provides authors with a place to live and work for life. It was quiet and wintrily pretty with snow covering the birches and the roofs of the timber houses. Demichev's house was situated down another byroad. A couple of Ladas were parked outside the house, which was a big, brown box with two floors. I stopped the car and was about to get out when his housekeeper came outside. She wiped her fingers on her apron and arranged a wisp of hair underneath her kerchief.

"How are you, Mr. Andersen. They're at Pasternak's grave. They'll be back soon."

"We'll drive over there and join them," I said, and turned the large Volvo around with some difficulty.

Pasternak is beloved as a poet in Russia, but he died in disgrace, and *Dr. Zhivago* had never been published in his own homeland. Yet another Russian tragedy. The road meandered through the hilly landscape. I parked the car at the top of a small hill with a view of Peredelkino. To the right, the cupolas

of a church were shining golden in the wintry sun. We could
hear a train in the distance. We walked down the hill through
the frosty snow. Lilli was about to stumble, so I caught her by
the arm. Then she took my arm and kept it, as we walked the
short distance to the cemetery. Our hips bumped softly against
each other with every step.

The cemetery stretched into the birch forest as far as the eye
could see. Tombstone after tombstone, many of them with
pictures of the deceased. By many of the graves there was a
small table with two benches, where you could sit on Easter
Sunday or on the anniversary of the death, eating your lunch
and commemorating the dead. Lilli stopped and pointed, but
she kept her arm under mine.

"I've never seen that before," I said.

"Me neither," she said.

There was a sign on the frozen ground: "Here we will place
an obelisk for our son, who fell in international service. The
family."

"Afghanistan, probably," I said.

"Where else?" she said, and gave herself a shake.

"Does it hurt?" I asked.

"Not today. Maybe it's because I'm with you," she said,
looking at me questioningly.

She freed herself of my arm and walked in between the
graves. I followed her. Pasternak's grave had a stone with the
writer's features in relief. There were fresh flowers, as usual.
Demichev stood with a handful of people in a half-circle
around the tombstone. There was a small bench. I sat down on
it, and Lilli sat down next to me. People stood with thick wax
candles in their hands. Nobody spoke. It was like a religious
ceremony. More people arrived. I was beginning to feel cold.
Demichev placed himself in the middle of the semicircle. He
looked serious. Then he recited one of Pasternak's poems in his
deep, strong voice. In any other place than Russia, the scene

would have appeared pathetic, but here the emotions around the small ritual seemed real. They did the same thing with Vysotsky. They learned his poetry by heart. I wasn't very interested in poetry, but I enjoyed the quiet, the snow, the birches, and Lilli sitting next to me, her hip touching mine. When Demichev had finished, those who had arrived last placed their flowers by the stone, and the others put their candles next to the flowers. People whispered to each other. When we left the cemetery, we met others on their way to the grave. It appeared to be a Saturday ritual. As always, I was impressed by the efficiency of the Moscow grapevine. There was nowhere one could obtain information on where Pasternak lay buried, but still people came to his grave in silent protest against the unjust condemnation on the part of the Party bosses of a man whom the people loved. As we walked up the hill to the car, Lilli took my hand. Demichev smiled when he looked over his shoulder, but he didn't say anything.

The lunch turned out to be very nice. Demichev had invited about twenty people. There were several from Lilli's band; a couple of poets, whom I knew superficially, and their wives; some actors from the Taganka Theater; and a single diplomat from the American embassy and his wife, who spoke a stiff, but very correct Russian. I also said hello to the correspondent of *The New York Times* as we kicked the snow off our boots and dropped our coats on benches and chairs in the hall. The house exhaled the smell of food and heat. In the dining room a solid oak table was set for lunch. On the walls there were abstract paintings, several of which had been painted by Pasternak. Demichev's books were sold abroad, so he had traveled widely and had acquired that rarity, a video, which stood in one corner. Against one wall was a small piano. Through the windows we could see the snow and the birches outside.

Demichev poured a yellowish liquid into small glasses. He

smiled broadly, happy about his arrangement, his guests, and the table, where caviar, sturgeon, and sausages gave battle to pancakes, salty cucumbers, meat, and sharp spring onions.

"It's Samogen. From Georgia. Real vodka, not the dishwater the factories produce these days," Demichev said, and everyone stood silently with a glass in their hand. Lilli stood right next to me. She was dressed very simply in a long black skirt and a white blouse, the three top buttons of which were undone. Her green eyes sparkled. A little behind Demichev stood a very young girl with long blond hair and a shy expression. She had to be Demichev's new love interest.

"I'm not going to give a long speech, and I will only propose one or two toasts, although you probably don't believe me," Demichev said, and we all stamped our feet and booed. He looked happy and content.

"First, let's drink to peace. For without peace, nothing else can exist. Peace is the basis of life. To peace!" He raised his glass and emptied it at a single draft. So did I. The Georgian home brew was very strong, but soft and warm at the same time. It warmed every part of the body and made your head spin. Lilli had just taken a sip of hers: women are permitted to do that.

"Then I propose a toast to friendship. And to love. I could also drink to freedom; but isn't that an abstract notion? For what do we mean by freedom? Like the word 'democracy' it's a concept that everyone uses positively, but interprets in his own way. It has lost its meaning as a common concept. It only has meaning as a fire in the soul of each individual."

"Amen," I said.

Demichev laughed, but for a second his eyes flashed.

"To friendship!" I said, and emptied my glass.

Demichev filled everybody's glasses a third time.

"My last toast will be to the demolition of boundaries. Boundaries between countries and boundaries between people.

I drink to the unbounded human soul and to a world without boundaries. One true, united, and free world."

We downed the third glass, and everyone's faces turned a deep red.

We fell to, and Demichev's housekeeper saw to it that the dishes were constantly replenished. She brought in a roast veal filled with garlic. It was tender and fine. Either Demichev had very good connections or a good contact at the local farmer's market. Lilli sat next to me and ate with delicate movements. In front of us sat a poet and the guitarist from her band, who scowled at me every now and then, but thawed as the vodka disappeared. Everywhere around us there was an eager, very Russian discussion about soul and literature. The correspondent of *The New York Times* was trying to make a severe-looking man talk about Chernenko, but the man didn't seem interested. He was the literary critic at *Pravda*, I believe, and the only one wearing a suit. The rest of us were dressed in sweaters and sports pants.

The room filled with conversation and smoke as it slowly grew dark outside the small windows. I needed some fresh air. People were beginning to break up from the table to have tea in smaller groups. The conversation was still lively and loud. Russians love to talk.

Lilli sat next to me on the bench holding the hot tea glass with both hands as if she wanted to absorb its heat. Her face was half turned toward me, and her green eyes were sparkling.

"I feel like telling you something, Jack. About me and Vera. Mostly about Vera, I think." She was speaking very softly, but I could hear her clearly over the din of the conversation around us.

"We were very different, but I loved her. She was my pretty big sister. My father would do anything for her. From when she was a little girl, she could always twist him around her little finger. My father was the manager of a *produkty*. You know, the kind of shop where you buy all the most common things, and where there is never any merchandise. Vera was always in the shop, from when she was a little girl with ribbons in her hair. She got to know about evil and corruption from the very start. My father was a rich man in Tallinn, because he was the manager of a provision shop. He kept the good stuff under the counter and accepted bribes. He cheated with the scales, too, like everyone else. One gram here. Five grams there. Otherwise he couldn't fulfill the plan. It was really very simple, even with the fixed state prices. For instance, he would receive a shipment of caramels. The state said that they were caramels of bad quality. They were to cost one ruble and forty kopecks. But Papa said that they were caramels of prime quality, so he sold them at one ruble and eighty kopecks, which is what the state says good caramels should cost. People can't tell the difference. Always remember to weigh the paper as well. Always take off ten grams on every kilo of rice. That gives you a profit, Papa said. Vera learned from him that everything and everyone in the Soviet Union is for sale. When she grew up, she thought that it was all right to sell herself to get the things she wanted, now that Papa couldn't get them for her any longer."

She cautiously took a sip of her tea.

"What happened to Papa?" I asked.

"They put him in prison in the end," she said flatly. "He probably forgot to pay some small bureaucrat, for all I know."

"Everything is for sale," I said to get her to continue.

"Yes, everything and everyone. My father had a list. I don't know if I can remember them all. Every month he paid the local policeman to look the other way. He paid the fire inspector so that there wouldn't be any problems with fire protection. Every day the two thugs from the Public Control Office of the Party came by and had to be paid. The district secretary expected a gift at regular intervals, and his wife had to have meat under the counter. Papa had to pay extra to the purveyors to get any merchandise at all. He had to pay under the counter to get cleaning materials. He had to pay one thousand rubles to the man in the Party who got him the job as manager with seventeen employees under him. He had to bribe the local Komsomol committee. The union. The Ministry of Commerce of the state."

She counted on her fingers and smiled at the same time. "That was his greatest expenditure. Every day there was one inspector or other that came in order to line their pockets. And then, of course, he had to pay the bookkeeper of the Soviet to get him to falsify the accounts so that it looked as if the plan had been fulfilled. Papa always said that if he didn't have to bribe all these people every day, then there wouldn't be any reason to cheat the customers so much."

"Did he really talk about all that?"

"It's common knowledge. And he did talk. It was in the papers after the trial. Papa was stupid and naive. He kept strict accounts of all the money that he received and paid under the counter. He thought of it as a safety precaution, but he got all the blame plus fifteen years in a prison camp, and he didn't survive that. And you know what he was convicted of? Not corruption; not of offering bribes; but of giving short weight. But he gave short weight only to get money so that he could run the business and fulfill the plan."

"Couldn't he just have resigned?"

"Yes, but he earned a good salary and was an important man in Tallinn. He also admitted that he found it exciting having to deal with all that money. It became second nature to him. And he made a very good living for himself. Making money became second nature to Vera as well," she said.

"Catch-22," I said.

"I don't know that one. But if we have it here, you can be assured that it prohibits something."

Her green eyes became distant for a moment, then she went

on, "But Papa had the last word, before they came to get him. He wrote the official prices on all his wares and then next to them he wrote in parentheses how much that particular piece of merchandise cost him in bribes. It was a great scandal. He knew that it was over. Vera's world fell apart, and she immediately married a guy with a residence permit in Moscow. She had to pay him, but to Vera that was just natural. She had found an easy way of making money herself—but you know about that."

"Why didn't you become like Vera?"

"I don't know. I'm more like my mother. Besides, I'm afraid. I've tried. I couldn't." She looked at me with eyes full of hurt and fear. I bent forward and softly kissed her mouth while holding her face between my hands.

"I know," I said.

"How do you know that?" she asked.

I told her of Dima on Red Square.

"And yet you don't hate me? Or despise me?" she said when I had finished.

"On the contrary. Knowing how you feel, I think it was brave of you."

Her smile made those amazing green eyes sparkle and glitter.

Our intimacy was interrupted by Demichev, who stood with the Samogen bottle in his hand, looking at us.

"How about a song, Lilli?" he asked in a friendly voice. He looked the very image of a happy host who is relieved that his party is going well.

"In a while. First I want some fresh air," she said.

Demichev proceeded with his bottle, on the lookout for empty glasses.

"Would you like to go for a walk?" I said.

We found our coats and walked along the road and down a path that disappeared into the wood. The small windows of the houses in Peredelkino emitted a soft and yellow light, but even as we walked farther away, it didn't really become dark. It was a starry night, and a half moon threw a white light down among the trunks of the birch trees, where it was reflected in the white snow. It was cold, but not very cold. Hand in hand, without talking, we walked into the wood, and I pulled her up against me and kissed her hard. She clung to me like a frightened child, but it was a grown woman who returned my kiss and began feverishly to unbutton her coat and mine. She dropped hers on the snow, and we used mine as a blanket. She eagerly pulled off her pantyhose. I only had time to get my pants down around my heels and feel the cold before she sat down on top of me and made love to me, quickly and violently. She screamed when we came, and her eyes filled with tears as she looked at me with her face quite close to mine, white in the light that fell among the tree trunks.

"That's nothing to cry about," I said.

"That's from happiness, you fool," she said.

They applauded when we entered the room with burning cheeks. The piano was opened, and two men were tuning their guitars.

Later that night we lay in bed, and Lilli asked, "Do we have time for more?"

"We have plenty of time. No one can find us here," I said.

But they gave us only three weeks.

14

During those three weeks we spent as much time together as we could. They became three of the best weeks of my life. I enjoyed her youth. Her body, of course, but also her childishness, her lack of deceit and suspicion. She was at the same time desperate and calm. She loved music and threw herself on my tapes and records with the same childish joy as a scientist who keeps making exotic new discoveries. She told me about her childhood and her life. She heard about my alcoholic father who had left us, and my mother whom I hated, without analyzing my situation to pieces. She studied my books. Her curiosity toward life outside the Soviet Union knew no bounds. I remember her sitting on my sofa with a cup of tea in her hands, young, lovely, and pure, with those radiant, clear eyes. Again and again she wanted to hear about a supermarket, a newsstand, the streets of New York, the alleys of Copenhagen, the boulevards of Paris. I had to tell her about everything. Give details and start over again. She had a burning desire to travel, to experience the world that she was cut off from. I would stop in the middle of a sentence and just look at her and be happy.

Maybe it was a reaction to several years of bitter trench warfare with Susanne, but Lilli and I never reached the point of having skirmishes or wielding the long knives of a failed marriage. I told her of my cheap rubles. It took some time to explain to her that she could divide the prices at the private farmers' market by ten and buy whatever she wanted. She kept calling my rubles "funny money" and would meet me at the door when I came home from work with remarks like: "Look what I have bought with your Russian funny money!" She refused to go into the dollar shops with me or to accept a gift.

There were two occasions when she became frightened and assumed her sullen and reserved mask for a couple of hours, the mask that she had been wearing when I first met her in Sonia's apartment. A shell. An armor. A defense. You could tell her fear from the fact that the sparkle of her green eyes died away, and they became cold and distant.

The first time was Monday morning. My housekeeper arrived at half past nine. She rang the bell. I opened the door, and as usual she swept right past me into the hall and was about to take her coat off when she saw Lilli, who came out whistling, wearing one of my shirts. Lilli stiffened for a second, turned on her heels, and disappeared into the bedroom.

"You've just been given two weeks' vacation," I said.

She buttoned her coat and looked at me angrily: "Madame isn't going to like this," she said.

"Make that a permanent vacation. You're fired," I said, and felt relieved. She had been driving me crazy for months.

She looked at me for a second, then she left. I should have known then that she would report it. All Russian staff do—otherwise they're not permitted to work for foreigners.

"You can come out now. The witch is gone," I shouted. Lilli came out. She looked scared and exhausted.

"Has she gone?" she asked.

"Yes."

"She's evil."

"No, she's just stupid."

"She doesn't wish us well."

I put my arms around her.

"She's nothing. Forget her," I said.

Lilli gave herself a shake.

"That's easy for you to say. You're not going to live with her," she said.

The second time was the following morning. Lilli insisted on going out to get fresh bread at the baker's. I was sleepy and turned over on my other side. She called one hour later with a voice that was like ice, but underneath the coldness I could sense tears vibrating. She had bought bread, but she couldn't get back inside the courtyard. The policeman would not let her in. I got furious with myself. I should have known. She was calling from a pay phone and only had two kopecks on her. Would I come and fetch her, or should she just go home? It was as if the absurdities of her own system were to be taken out on me.

"I'll be there in five minutes," I said, and hung up.

She stood at the foot of the small hill leading up to the entrance, looking small and fragile in her coat and her white knitted bonnet. The policeman stood heavy and mighty in his black uniform and wide boots. He saluted politely when I came rushing out of the courtyard so fast that I almost fell. I gave him an angry stare and went down to Lilli, took her by the arm, and pulled her up the stairs.

"What did he want?" I asked, although I knew very well.

"He wanted to see my papers," she said.

"Did you show him your passport?"

"No."

The policeman looked at us, but he knew better than to try to stop us. He had no right to stop people, but did so if Soviet citizens whom he didn't know came alone.

"Go inside the courtyard," I said to Lilli. I was filled with cold rage. An impotent rage that seizes, from time to time, all thinking people who live in Moscow. A rage against the strength and arrogance of the controlling power.

"May I have your name? You've just violated the Vienna Convention," I said. He stared at me without answering. He was sweating a little in spite of the cold; there was a border of moisture on his upper lip. His square face was trying to conceal any emotion whatsoever. My Russian friends always maintained that only the most stupid become policemen, but I had a suspicion that those who were given the task of watching over foreigners were more than ordinary storm troopers. They reported to the KGB. He stared at me with vapid eyes. Then a devil got into me, and I took one step forward and stuck my face all the way up against his and said, "Listen, you little faggot. If you stop her again, or others who say they're here to see me, I'm going to tear your balls off. You understand?" Demichev had taught me many good expressions in Russian.

He grew pale. But only for a second. Then he waddled into his sentry box and lifted the receiver of his squealer's phone off the hook. I felt fine.

When I had to drive to work, one of the tires of my car was flat. A knife had been stuck into it.

It took her an hour to recover from this experience. I never found out what had frightened her so much. She was never stopped again, for in those three weeks we developed our own little rhythm.

I went to work later than usual and came home earlier, so that we had a couple of hours together before she had to sing at the Praga. Then I went back to work or took care of my representative duties. Around midnight I picked her up. I would wait for her in my car at the Arbat with the motor running. She would arrive with light and dancing steps and get into the car. When we got home she would take a bath and remove the heavy stage makeup while I cooked a meal for her.

She only worked four times a week. One weekend we spent in bed. I kept her away from my official life, just as she didn't bring me into her circle. She never invited me to her home, but sometimes she had to go there to get clean clothes. CW noticed that my working hours changed, but he didn't comment on it. Saturday morning the phone rang. I was in the bath tub and shouted to Lilli to answer it. She came into the bathroom.

"It's a woman. She wants to talk with you," she said.

I picked up the phone in the hall. It was Caroline. I was dripping, making a small puddle on the floor. First we talked rather stiffly about this and that. Asked each other how we were. Talked about politics. Polite diplomatic small talk. Then Caroline got to the point.

"Are you doing something tonight?" she asked with her correct, but melodious voice. "I've promised you breakfast."

"I'm sorry, but I'm busy," I said. Lilli was drying my back and the backs of my legs. Afterward she rubbed the towel down my chest and took my cock in her hand and dabbed it carefully before she took it in her mouth, sending jets of fire through my entire body.

"That's a pity," Caroline said. "Is that a young Russian maid you've got?" she said.

I said nothing. I had difficulty keeping my mind on the conversation.

"And she works on Saturday, too. How lucky for you," Caroline said.

"Maybe we can find another day," I said.

"I don't usually offer to make breakfast more than once," the cold Swedish voice replied, and she hung up.

Lilli softly pressed me down on the chair and placed herself on top of me. Her breasts stood out clearly through one of my thin T-shirts. That was all she was wearing. Afterward was the only time we talked about a future.

"I don't think I can do without you," I said. She kissed my neck and pressed her body against mine.

"I'm here."

"But I won't always be living in Moscow," I said.

"Don't think about tomorrow."

"Don't you think about the future and us two at all?" I said.

"I have you now and I don't dare to think of any more than that."

"Lilli . . ." I began.

"Isn't it enough that I love you now?" she said, and placed her finger over my lips. "I'm hungry," she continued, and gently got up, making me slide out of her.

One evening after dropping her off at the Praga, I had arranged to meet with Carl Sorensen on Pushkin. It had turned cold again, and a dense frosty mist hung over the city and mixed with the heavy smog, making all asthmatics gasp for breath. Carl came up to me with his resilient boxer's gait and shook my hand.

"You look good, old pal. What's her name?"

"None of your business," I said good-naturedly.

"You're the one who's getting burned, not Uncle Joe here," he said. "What did you want to talk about? I have a boring dinner party. Chernenko?"

"No. Is there anything new?"

"He's dying. He won't last long."

"That's not new."

"And you can put your money on that guy Gorbachev. He's taken over more or less already."

"Then I guess we'll have to study him some more, right?"

We began walking slowly up toward the large cinema. Not that long ago, I had been standing here with Basov. How many conversations had I had in Moscow among the many Russian faces beneath the thick fur caps? To be private you had to get out among as many people as possible. As we walked, I told Carl about the colonel and the attack. I didn't tell him that it was the colonel, just a source. I also told him that the case was dead, and that I just wanted to hear his opinion.

"Forget it," Carl said. "Don't get mixed up in an internal Russian power struggle or get in the way of some big shot who's protecting himself. You'll only end up at the bottom of the river."

"This isn't Detroit, Carl."

"No, but it's close."

"OK," I said, disappointed. I had been hoping that he might have wanted to discuss the whole affair, but he appeared unresponsive. I regretted having told him anything at all.

He knew me well enough to be able to tell that I was angry, so he grabbed me by the upper arm.

"Jackie. Maybe some other day."

"Why not?" I said. He let go of my arm and slipped into the crowd and was gone.

One evening Peter came over. He got along with Lilli very well, and had taught her to play backgammon. I could feel my age when I saw them together. It was Lilli's night off, so he stayed till long past midnight.

I rented a house in Savidova, the small vacation colony on the bank of the Volga River that the Russians have reserved for the use of foreign diplomats. It's surrounded by a barbed-wire fence and guarded by policemen. There are small timber houses, a sauna, and a restaurant. Russians are not admitted, with the exception of servants and guards. Savidova is about one hundred miles from Moscow, so I wasn't allowed to go there without permission from the Soviet Ministry of Foreign Affairs. I sent Basov a telex. I said nothing about Lilli, but I was decidedly on the borderline of what could be considered legal.

We went for long walks in the great white silence along the river, where Gromyko went hunting in summer. We ate, talked, and made love. I remember most vividly how Lilli laughingly asked me to go faster on the snowmobile that we had rented. Several diplomats that I knew were staying in the area. I didn't try to hide Lilli. I knew very well what I was doing: I was showing her off in order to make our relationship official when we returned to Moscow. And I was surprised myself at how fast things were going. It wasn't like me, but I was enjoying her too much to allow myself to think too deeply about the possible consequences.

Sunday afternoon it was over.

We were sitting on the bed, each with a blanket wrapped around our naked bodies, when they barged through the unlocked door. Tooth glasses with red wine were balancing on the sheet. Between us was a backgammon board: Lilli had just beaten me. Her happy laughter stopped abruptly, and she let go of my neck. There were two heavy, uniformed policemen and Basov. Basov produced a sheet of paper and read:

"Mr. Jack Andersen, you have offended against the laws of the Soviet Union and committed acts that are inconsistent with the duties of a diplomat. You have circulated propaganda hostile to the Soviet Union and stayed overnight at a public hotel with a Soviet citizen without permission. You are unwanted in the Union of Socialist Soviet Republics and must leave the country within seven days at the latest."

His face was rigid. Lilli was biting her hand. I said nothing, but felt my diaphragm contract.

Basov stood there like a general leading his troops as he said, "Comrade Smuul, you can pack your things and leave. Your mission is completed. Mr. Andersen will be escorted to Moscow."

I was caught by a violent anger against Lilli and Basov. Her glass of red wine turned over and colored the sheet red as blood.

Lilli looked at me. There were tears in her beautiful, green eyes.

"Jack," she said imploringly. "Jack, I didn't know—"

I cut her off. "Get the fuck out of here. You heard the man!"

She let the blanket drop down around her shoulders, got up

naked, and walked with undulating breasts and buttocks closely past Basov and the policemen. They didn't stir a muscle. She gathered her clothes on her way out. She locked the bathroom door. We could hear her cry as she got dressed, although she tried to suppress it. I remained sitting on the bed with the blanket wrapped around me. I felt so cold that I was almost shaking. Basov avoided looking at me. The two policemen stood in the military at-ease position. Lilli came back with swollen eyes and walked past Basov between the policemen, who made way for her so that she could get out. In the doorway she turned around.

"Jack. I have nothing to do with it. Jack, believe me!" she begged.

"Go to hell!" I said in English.

"Now it's your turn, Mr. Andersen," Basov said.

I kept speaking English. "Maybe your little cunt likes prancing about naked in front of a couple of goons, but I don't, so get outside, goddamnit, while I get dressed, Basov!"

Basov sent the men outside with a toss of his head. Like Lilli, he turned around in the doorway.

"You probably don't understand it, but I'm sorry. It can't be any different," he said in English.

"Fuck you, Basov!" I said.

In the bathroom it took me several minutes to stop shaking all over.

I drove the Volvo between the two patrol cars all the way to Moscow like a robot, full of self-pity at the deceit that had been perpetrated against me. I was furious with myself for having been naive enough to fall into the world's most common trap.

CW was cold as ice in his anger. He called me into his office Monday afternoon. He sat like a massive bear behind his massive desk and didn't ask me to sit. His face was rigid and without emotion, but his voice trembled slightly.

"You have disappointed me enormously. You have offended against the most common rules of conduct. You've made an unforgiveable blunder, you've disgraced Denmark and our embassy here. There are no excuses . . ."

"I'm not making any," I said.

He continued as if he hadn't heard me. "I've been informed from back home that Denmark will not reciprocate. I've told them that here. A new man will be accredited without any problems."

"Then everything is fine," I said.

CW's face lost some of its composure.

"Jack, I had seen you in my chair."

"No risk of that now," I said.

"No. And you have yourself to thank for that. Couldn't you have chosen another mistress? Or have been more discreet, darn it?" he said.

I said nothing. I didn't want to make it easier for him, even though I could see that he was hurting. I was full of self-contempt. "Self-contempt is a serpent at your chest," I thought. Even that wasn't original: it was a quote from Karl Marx.

CW continued in his cold voice, "I have been assured that TASS will not make the affair public. You won't get in *Pravda*. In return, we won't retaliate. I demand that you clear your office today and leave us as soon as possible. I no longer consider you a member of my embassy staff."

"I thank you, too, CW," I said. I had meant it to be a tough remark, but my voice broke.

"Good-bye, Jack," he said, and looked down demonstratively at the papers before him.

In the course of the week I found out that I had three friends and many enemies. The enemies, and Castesen more than anyone else, had difficulty hiding their pleasure. I had so much pride in me that I went to a reception at the West German embassy. That was a mistake: I was treated like a leper. Although TASS had kept its promise and written nothing about the case, rumors had spread in diplomatic circles. Actually, the rumors had improved the story. Several women overcame their disgust with me for as many minutes as it took them to pump me. I also overheard several conversations. This was finally something worth gossiping about. I had alternately been caught with a Soviet prostitute and a Soviet KGB agent whom I had told of NATO's emergency plans. The most elegant versions incorporated both the prostitute angle and the espionage part. I ran into Caroline, who looked straight through me. I left after half an hour, when the painful silences and the flushed cheeks became too much for me, but Caroline stopped me in the checkroom.

"You jerk!" she said.

"Fine, thank you. And how are you doing?" I said.

She stuck her face up against mine.

"I had to take a reprimand from my ambassador. Just because you spent one night at my place. Me! Me! What the hell do you think that is going to do to my career?" she yelled. "Was she really worth it, you idiotic man?"

"She was worth every fuck," I said. Caroline looked at me with amazement. Then she took a couple of steps backward.

"I think you're insane," she said.

"And she's twenty years younger than you," I said.

"I hate you, Jack Andersen. Go to hell."

"I think that's where I'm headed," I said.

Three friends. Demichev called from Odessa, where he was on a lecturing tour. Like all Russian intellectuals, he survived by being informed of large and small events through strange, indirect channels. His voice sounded far away through the crackling noise on the line. It took courage on his part to call. He knew, like I did, that the line was quite definitely being tapped.

"You'll be back," he shouted. "Times will change. You'll be

back. Don't let the assholes get to you. I'm going to look after Lilli for you. You'll be back. I brought you together. Love conquers all, including fucking bureaucrats."

He jabbered away. I didn't have the heart to contradict him. To tell him that, for all I cared, they could send Lilli to Siberia for fifteen years.

Carl, too, was a friend. He came in the middle of the week with a bottle of whisky and a Leonard Cohen record.

"You probably need something that's even sadder," he said as an explanation, and handed me the record. I knew that it was one of his favorites, so I was grateful for his gesture. We drank the whisky and talked about boxing and other peaceful activities and listened to music. For long periods of time we said nothing. He was simply there. When he left late in the evening, he stood swaying on the doormat.

"It's when you start being afraid of becoming an old man that it gets dangerous."

"Thanks for holding on."

"We'll take a couple of rounds in Denmark," he said, and slapped me on the shoulder. We had boxed together and gotten drunk together for the fun of it, but had never touched each other with affection. He gave me a big hug and walked down the stairs.

The third friend was Peter. He came over to help me pack. He promised to finish the packing and take care of the practical arrangements with the moving company that would take my books and records. The furniture belonged to the Danish state. I couldn't concentrate on packing. Peter walked around singing. He asked no questions. Just once did he comment:

"I don't care what they say. She was a great girl," he said.

"You talk as if Lilli were dead," I said in a voice that was becoming rather husky. I was drinking from morning till night.

"Well, in a way she is, isn't she?" Peter said.

"Do you like Springsteen?" I asked.

"He's great."

"When you do the packing, I want you to keep all the Springsteen records and tapes that you find."

"Why?"

"Just take them!"

I left early one afternoon and drove all the way to the border, seventeen hours nonstop, to get the excitement out of my system. I drove through the snow-covered landscape, and when it grew dark, black figures and houses emerged in front of my headlights. There was hardly any traffic. The road was narrow and full of potholes. In the Soviet Union there is a police post every twenty miles. The police keep an eye on the traffic and check papers: if they don't have your license number on their lists, they don't let you by. I broke most of the speed regulations on the way and was stopped at every other post, but I refused to pay speeding fines, invoking my diplomatic immunity. I don't know if it covers that kind of offense, but apparently they didn't know, either. In Leningrad I slept for two hours in the car; at night the city closes its bridges between one and three o'clock, and everyone has to wait. I had a thermos filled with hot coffee. Peter had made me a large food packet and added mineral water and a couple of beers. He had emptied out the last whisky in the sink. I was hung over and had withdrawal symptoms, tired and wide awake at the same time. When the bridges were lowered, I found a gas station that actually had some gas—the others on the road hadn't had any. I drove along the meandering roads of the old Finnish territory and arrived at Vyborg. That's the border town, but there's still a thirty-mile drive before you get to the Finnish-Russian border.

The town lay sad and gloomy in the early morning light. People were badly dressed. The paint was peeling off the houses, the roads were full of potholes, and the cars and buses were covered with dirt. I crossed a long bridge. In the distance I could see a railroad bridge across the fjord, which lay white and unapproachable. Then came the first frontier gate. The KGB frontier guards looked at my license plates and went inside to make a phone call. Then a very young guy with childishly blushing cheeks opened the gate. He had a machine gun strapped across his chest. I drove through an empty landscape with no signs of life. Thirty miles farther along the desolate road there was another gate. In the distance I could see the watchtowers and a gray building through the frosty mist. Next to the gate was a sentry box. A soldier came out and looked at my car. Then they phoned again. Five minutes later they raised the gate, and I drove up to the frontier station.

I was the only one on the way out, but three Finnish tourists were on their way into the Soviet Union. They had been obliged to take all their things out, and two mechanics were methodically taking their car apart. The dashboard was dangling by a couple of loose wires. An Italian journalist on his way out behind me got the same treatment. I sat for an hour watching the scenery. They had taken my passport and insisted on my opening the hood and the trunk of the Volvo. I had refused—I was still a diplomat with diplomatic status. Now we were fighting a war of position. I took a paperback, poured the last of my coffee, and lit a cigarette. The KGB guards were looking at me furiously. Finally the senior officer came toward the car, and I rolled down the side window just enough for him to hand me the red diplomatic passport.

"You are unwanted in the Soviet Union. I hope I'll never see you again," he said.

"Never say never," I said, although I knew that he was probably right.

I started the car and drove down a small hill. To my left was yet another watchtower with an armed frontier guard. Then came the last gate. One hundred feet farther on the other side flew the Finnish flag. The KGB soldier stepped up to the side of the car and looked through the dirty windows, to make sure that I was still alone. Then he crossed over to the gate and opened it, and I drove into Finland. I walked into the customs building and showed my passport.

"Welcome to Finland," the female Finnish passport official said with a smile. The Finns know everything about the careful, lengthy Soviet examination before anyone is allowed to leave the fatherland of socialism, so they have reduced their own formalities to a minimum. Diplomat or no diplomat.

I drove the sixty feet to the small cafeteria and stepped into civilization. There was coffee, fresh bread, bananas, newspapers, eggs, fruit, sandwiches, and a couple of videos. I had driven more than six hundred miles from Moscow, and nowhere along the road could you be sure to get coffee or a meal. I always felt the difference between the West and the Soviet Union strongly in the little cafeteria on the border. I took a tray and a cup for my coffee. I could hear the radio. I didn't understand Finnish, but I heard the speaker mention Chernenko.

"What are they saying?" I asked the young girl in English. She had fine red cheeks and a clean uniform.

"They say that the Soviet leader Chernenko is dead. He seems to have been a very old man. Do you want me to heat your cheese bun?"

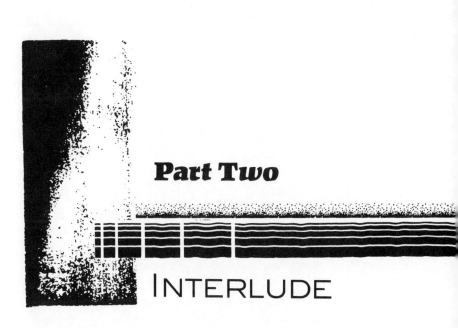

Part Two

INTERLUDE

. . . I'm ready to
grow young again and hear your sister's
voice calling us home across the open yards.
We made a promise we swore we'd always
remember
no retreat no surrender.

BRUCE SPRINGSTEEN

15

It took me more than a year to pick up the pieces of my life. I was placed in the press department, where I was profuse in sarcastic remarks and participated eagerly in the Danish national sport, which is to drink beer and knock everyone you know. The press department was a step backward in my career; from there it could only go further downhill. Of all people, Susanne became the one who helped me. We were separated, but she was full of strength and happy about her pregnancy. She grew big and beautiful to look at. We often spoke on the telephone, and one day when we were having lunch, she handed me a newspaper clipping. It was a job advertisement. A job as a teacher of Russian at a school in Jutland.

"You're a fighter, Jack. Get started. Fight!" she said.

Late that fall I traveled to a windswept little town by the North Sea and moved into a small house on the outskirts of town. The ministry was overjoyed to get rid of me. To my surprise I grew to like my life in Jutland more than I had expected. The locals accepted me, once they had got used to all the Russian newspapers that I received. I began to look forward to the lessons at the school. So many things were happening in the Soviet Union under Gorbachev that it stimulated the students' interest. I took up running again and relieved the pain inside by working on my house. It was old and needed work and tender care. I followed how Gorbachev's Soviet Union began a painful self-reassessment and a process of readjustment, and I began to write about it to the newspapers. They were interested. My private life got better. Lena was a colleague at the school, divorced with two young sons. It wasn't a passionate relationship, but based on rationality and security. I didn't quite know who was most important to me, her or her boys of eight and ten. We didn't live together, but the boys came and went in my house, and they continued to do so when, without pain, Lena and I stopped being lovers. We remained good colleagues and friends and still spent time together. Probably I was happiest in the club. It was a small, languishing boxing club that was run by an old opponent of mine. We met in the street, and he could still remember that once in our early youth I had beaten him on points. He suggested that I take over the training of the youth team.

I was getting established in my new life. I was becoming a whole person again, but I wasn't happy and had a hole inside that I closed off. But I was far from isolated, and people from my circles in Copenhagen began to visit me as my articles were published. When my rage at the betrayal committed against me grew inside and threatened to make me lose control, I used the sandbag in the gym as an outlet. At first the town felt like a straitjacket, and I had to go to Aarhus or Aalborg to booze until my nerves calmed down and my body couldn't take any more; but I needed to run away less and less often. I had a responsibility to Lena's boys and the young toughs whose violent tendencies I tried to get them to control and use in the ring instead of in the street. I had a good way with them. Sometimes the chief of police sent me some young guys who had been nabbed for the first time. Unfortunately, most of them didn't stick around, but I was very proud of the few who stayed and found in the comradeship of the club the strength to stop a criminal career at the outset. I had always talked deprecatingly of teachers. Now I was making teaching my calling. The most surprising thing about it was that I liked it better and better. There were far less lies in my existence in Jutland than there had been in my diplomatic life.

I lived in my own small universe most of the time, but stayed in touch. Old colleagues and scientists from Copenhagen and Aarhus came to visit. I had several visits from a young sovietologist, Mikael Petersen, who was preparing himself for service at the embassy in Moscow. He was straight out of university, spoke Russian, and couldn't care less about my past. We got along well together, and I recognized in him the same eagerness and interest that I myself had had when I was in my late twenties. We sat up till late at night discussing Gorbachev and his intentions. I told Mikael in broad outline why I had been expelled, and of Sonia and Vera.

My old friend from the Danish Military Intelligence Service also came from time to time, and we good-humoredly pumped each other. During one visit he asked me some questions about Castesen. He wasn't very direct, but circled around the subject without mentioning the letter that I had once sent him. I answered evasively. I was following Castesen's career with interest, but without ulterior motives. When I got drunk, I wished him to hell. They said that he was doing very well in Poland. When I had been in Jutland for almost three years, the newspaper *Politiken* asked me to go to the Soviet Union for them, but I refused point-blank. I wasn't ready to risk the reopening of my newly healed wounds. It had taken me over a year before I could listen to Russian singers on long wave from Moscow without being on the verge of tears.

The fourth summer the past caught up with me. Just before

the exams I was sitting in the garden one morning, reading. Like the previous years, and for no reason at all, I was terribly nervous on behalf of my students. A dark blue Volvo drove up in front of my house, and out stepped CW. Behind him came Mrs. W, carrying a basket. A slender white-wine bottle stuck out of it. I could hardly recognize CW. He was dressed in an old pair of slacks and a shirt that was open at the neck, around which he had tied a sweater. The sun was shining. It had finally turned into something that you might call summer. I put my glasses down on the book and remained sitting. They came walking toward me, CW first with his impressive belly, but he looked strange. Then I realized that I had never seen him wear anything but double-breasted, dark suits. And then that fateful night, when he had worn a dressing gown that made him look like Noël Coward. Now he looked like one of those rich German tourists who were already filling the vacation houses in the dunes.

I got up from my deck chair and looked at CW, who looked back at me.

"Hello, my boy," he said.

"Hello, CW," I said. "How are you, Mrs. W."

"The name is Mogens," CW said.

I began to laugh.

"I'm retired," he said. "Since six months ago."

"Is that why you're decked out like that?"

"I promised myself that I would never wear a dark suit again after I retired." He was silent for a moment. "Except when Her Majesty gives me the Cross of Knighthood, of course."

"You old rascal, welcome to my house," I said, and offered him my hand.

"And I've told him that I'll never arrange a dinner for more than four people. I've served food for forty all my life. No more," Mrs. W said. "But I've prepared a basket." She triumphantly held up the basket so that the sun was reflected in the neck of the bottle.

We drove down to the beach in my old Volvo, which, like myself, still carried the scratches from Moscow in its paint. There was a mild breeze coming in from the North Sea, which lay calm in front of us, blue and inviting. I carried a heavy cooler, which Mrs. W had produced from the trunk of their car, in one hand and the basket in the other. CW was ahead of us, carrying his shoes and socks in his hands. I had bare feet and enjoyed feeling the wind and the sun on my naked legs and arms. Mrs. W walked by my side, a little out of breath as we walked uphill. She was saying, "He's fine now. He had a minor heart attack six months ago. He could have stayed till he was seventy, but I said stop. I want to keep him a little longer. The fool refuses to give up the cigarettes, but he stays away from too much liquor, and the pressure is gone. He is enjoying his freedom."

I looked over at CW. I couldn't make myself call him Mogens. It didn't suit the man I remembered. He walked with his head up and screwed up his eyes against the strong light.

Mrs. W said, "He has thought of you a lot. It keeps troubling him that you parted the way you did."

"It was his job," I said.

"I've listened to that excuse my entire life," she said.

"Did you persuade him to come and visit me?"

"I didn't have to. He wanted to himself. And after the Castesen affair there was occasion to apologize. To get reconciled. You were the only one he ever really liked. He has always respected you."

"What was that about Castesen?"

"He'd better tell you that himself," she said.

We finally found a hollow where there was both sun and shade, and where German tourists hadn't already built an unapproachable fortress.

"Why don't you two men go down to the water and cool off while I prepare our lunch?" It was meant to sound like an invitation, but it was an order.

CW rolled up the legs of his pants and let the waves wash over his ankles. I could see the tired blue veins. We stood at the water's edge. To our right, two seventeen-year-old boys were playing violently to attract the attention of a couple of girls.

"They say you're a boxing trainer," he said.

"I earn my salary as a high school teacher."

"And a well-informed writer of commentaries on the situation in the USSR. I've read your articles with interest."

"Why did you come, CW?" I said.

"I've never understood your interest in such a bloody sport."

"Do you see those two guys?" I said, pointing. "One of them is Brian. Two years ago he was headed for a criminal career. He got into fights and committed a couple of thefts. He cut his classes. Now he's on my boxing team. He'll never become world famous. He's not good enough for that; but he thinks he is, and that's what's most important. Nobody had ever told him that he could be good at anything, and he had never experienced being taken seriously by an adult. Now he doesn't drink beer. He attends to his school and his training and has got a job as an apprentice. And you know why? Because I've told him that if not, he'd be off the team. I can't use boxers who don't have any self-discipline. He also knows that if he gets into trouble with the police or is involved in a fight, he'll lose his boxer's license. And that's very dear to him."

The two boys continued their antics. The sun made the drops of water on their muscular bodies gleam in all the colors of the rainbow. The two topless German girls were getting interested.

"I came to give you an apology," CW said. "An apology for having contributed to ruining your career. For not standing by you when it really counted. For having behaved like a coward." He looked away as he said this.

Brian caught sight of me and waved. Then he dived under and came up a moment later with his head between the legs of one of the German girls. He stood up with a jerk, making her fall backward into the water as she shrieked joyfully.

"To be young again," CW said.

"No, thank you. I feel sorry for them. No work. Even fucking is dangerous now with AIDS and whatnot."

"You've always had a coarse tongue, Jack."

"You don't owe me an apology, but I'm glad you came."

"When I see you now and hear about Brian, it seems as if I almost did you a favor. You appear to be in harmony with yourself. You're doing something more useful than lying for your country."

"Brian's is a successful existence in a long line of tragedies. Now tell me about Castesen."

"Over lunch, Jack. Castesen is our dear Sonia's most recent victim. I know that you couldn't stand him, but he does deserve a small funeral feast."

Mrs. W had brought good things in her basket. Cold chicken, paté, homemade bread, good sausage, and a cold Chablis. We sat in the sun, enjoying life, while CW told the pathetic tale with his eyes screwed up against the light beneath a faded sun hat. Ice-covered Moscow in the grasp of cold winter seemed light-years away, but as he talked, the past came closer.

"It's a filthy story, but rather simple. Do you remember John? The tall, lanky guard. He was involved with Sonia, like everyone else apparently. Sonia told him that she had seduced Castesen. John persuaded her to film one of their meetings. It was a ménage à trois, very advanced, I understand. Then they began to extort money from him. Large amounts, and John continued even after Sonia was dead."

"Then Castesen killed the two of them?"

"Unfortunately it's not that simple," CW said, and poured

more wine into our glasses. Mrs. W sent him a warning glance.

"You see, Castesen was an easy victim. He was willing to pay for his ambassador's post, but John kept raising the price. In the end, the poor man couldn't pay. And John was stupid. He talked too much, and someone you know in Vedbaek, if I may put it that way, heard of this guy who boasted of milking a Danish ambassador in a Communist country. He thought that when he heard about it, chances were that the Russian embassy might also hear about it, and voilà: there we have a security risk. Then he remembered that you had once written him about your suspicion that Castesen might be involved with a Soviet prostitute and exposed to Soviet pressure."

"I was told that I was irresponsible," I said.

CW's face twitched slightly. His nose was beginning to get red.

"Your acquaintance put the police on the case. Not directly, but he made them look into extortion cases. As it did concern national security they also took a look at Castesen's bank accounts. He was spending a lot of money, but his life-style didn't show it. John was greedy. He tried the same routine with a well-known actor, but he didn't care. He suggested that John sell the pictures to a magazine—it would be good for the rumors about his sexual powers, I believe he said—and then he went to the police. The police got hold of John; and John told them everything."

"That's right, he wasn't worth a lot under pressure," I said.

"They called Castesen home and confronted him with the allegations. He denied everything completely, but one month ago he was found in a wood. He had taken pills. He had written a letter and admitted that it was all true, but he swore that he hadn't killed Vera and Sonia and that he hadn't damaged Denmark's security interests, which was something that he put great emphasis on. It's a sad and beastly affair. It's dirty and humiliating for everyone. But I don't think that a man who is going to take his own life would lie on his deathbed. When you're alone with your God, you speak the truth," CW said.

"Then who killed them?" I asked.

"Maybe you and the others were wrong. Maybe it was only an accident."

"I still don't believe that."

"Then the answer lies in Moscow. And you probably aren't welcome there in spite of the new style and all that. I guess you don't feel like going, either, after what happened," he said.

"Poor Marie," I said.

"She's happy," Mrs. W said, joining the conversation for the first time. "Marie gets the pension and the life insurance. If Castesen hadn't been a man in the end, what would she have had then? They would have kicked him out of the service. There would have been a public scandal. You know, they look after their own. He died of a heart attack."

"Unless John feels like selling the story."

"No one would believe him. He was fired himself as soon as his time in Moscow was up. He's scraping through. He's a criminal. The brotherhood of the ruling classes would prevent a scandal like that any time," CW said.

"You sound quite revolutionary," I said.

"Maybe I just realize that stability in a country must necessarily have some costs," he said.

"Exit Castesen," I said.

"Yes. Sonia has quite a bit on her conscience. So many rotten fruits in our little basket in Moscow."

"Perhaps the circumstances turned them into what they became," I said.

"Moscow?" he said, wonderingly.

"No. The possibilities offered to them by Moscow combined with normal human traits such as envy, sex, and greed."

"Well, I think that it was rather much at once. After all, I have been in the profession for a lifetime."

"That all sounds very well, CW," I said, "but there is something you have misunderstood. I didn't write to my friend in the Military Intelligence Service that Castesen was under pressure from the KGB. I wrote that he was a CIA agent. They always knew everything about us at the American embassy, but that's not all."

CW looked at me, surprised and hurt. In spite of his retirement, he didn't like it when you spoke directly. The diplomatic evasions and paraphrases had become part of him.

"Why on earth did you—and do you—think so?" he asked.

"Do you remember Carl? Well. He lied to me at first. But he was my friend. He got into a conflict of loyalties. In order not to have to lie, he stopped telling me anything at all. And he has never visited me here in Denmark, either. I think that Castesen worked as an agent for the CIA long before he came to Moscow. Carl was told to protect him when things started heating up."

"That's pure speculation," CW said with little conviction.

"But is it true?" I said.

"I can't tell you everything. I have my vow of secrecy, and besides, I don't know everything. But there may be something to what you're saying. Castesen was never what they call a controlled agent. He never received money. He didn't feel like an agent for a foreign power. The only thing I can say is that he probably sometimes went too far in his interpretation of the loyalty that must necessarily exist between allies. That is, as I possibly understand the situation."

"CW!" I said.

"A couple of times he may have informed a little too specifically and unnecessarily about internal deliberations on security policy in the government before they were publicly known, but we have been assured that it wasn't a controlled situation."

"A spy is a spy," I said.

"It's not as simple as that. And we're talking about our most important ally. If what we're hypothetically discussing were true, it could hardly be called treason. Besides, it would be such a sensitive matter that neither we nor our American friends would find it to our advantage to dig into it. We all have dirt under the carpet, once you take a close look. It's one of the loose ends that life leaves you with, Jack. Castesen is dead. It's over."

"OK, CW," I said. He had begun to sweat and was wiping his forehead with his handkerchief. I remembered his bad heart and felt rather angry with myself.

"That ought to be enough shop talk for now, I think," Mrs. W said in her firm, angelic voice. "You gentlemen can smoke a cigar or go swimming, but now I want a nap here in the shade of the lyme grass."

We stayed in the hollow till it began to get chilly and our skin looked like boiled lobster. I went for a swim and the two of them took a nap. Time stood still, and the light vibrated drowsily over the white dunes and the blue sea. We drank coffee at home in the garden, and then they left. We were going to see each other again.

Mrs. W said through the window of the car, "What about your Russian girlfriend, Jack? Or is one not allowed to ask?"

It still hurt when I thought of Lilli. I tried to keep her out of my thoughts and was fairly successful doing so in the day-to-day, but I couldn't control my dreams, where she appeared alternately as a witch and as a saint. I often dreamed that I was having sex with her in the most bizarre places, but she slipped through my hands just before we got to the actual intercourse.

"You may ask. I don't know," I said.

"Well, it's probably best to leave it alone," she said blandly.

I tended to agree with her, but one week later Basov stepped into my life again and wanted me to go to Moscow.

16

I finished off with a couple of training rounds with Brian. They were going to their first real out-of-town meet and were excited and nervous. Brian was quick and strong, but had a problem with his temper. We were both sweating. Every time he punched with his left, he lowered his right, and I carefully planted my left on top of his boxing helmet. Finally he lost his temper and began to strike without concentration. I locked him.

"Temper, Brian. Don't get angry, and keep that right hand up." We stood in a tight embrace, panting. Then I noticed a figure down by the entrance to the gym. It was a stocky, muscular man with dark hair, dressed in faded jeans and an open, short-sleeved shirt with button-down collar, a leather jacket casually draped over one shoulder.

"That was fine, Brian. Take a shower now and don't forget your run tomorrow morning," I said. Brian smiled happily and jumped out between the makeshift ropes that we extended in the school gym, which we were permitted to use twice a week. The only way I was active in local politics was that I tried to get them to give us a clubhouse.

Brian threw a glance at Basov as they passed each other. Basov's new sneakers squeaked a little. He looked like an American businessman who stayed fit and was now on vacation.

"How do you do, Jack," he said formally in Russian.

"You deserve a beating. Are you going to join me in the ring?" I said.

He stood six feet away from me and smiled. "There's no reason for you and me to fight. I did you a favor," he said.

I crawled down and went across to the corner, where a large sandbag was suspended. First I hit it with my left, then with all the force that I could put into my right, and I finished with a series of combinations that made pain shoot up through my shoulder. I embraced the sandbag and leaned my head against it as if it were a woman.

"You ruined my life, you asshole," I said.

"I couldn't vouch for your safety. I wanted you out of the country. I couldn't think of anything better on such short notice."

"Go to hell, Volody. Leave me alone."

"I can tell you one thing. Lilli knew nothing. I used her . . ." he said, but I sneered.

"And the flight of the crows shows what the weather will be like; Russian grannies say that, too."

"I swear on the Holy Bible that she knew nothing, Jack," he said. His face was very serious. He hadn't aged very much, although his hair had grown thinner.

"You're getting so goddamn religious over there. Gorbachev also quotes the Bible every other day," I said, and let go of the sandbag. I took off my boxing helmet, found a towel, and wiped off the sweat.

Basov waited patiently, before he said, "I would like you to come to Moscow. We're asking you to. We would consider it a favor. It goes without saying that the old score would be erased."

"Why would I do you a favor?"

Basov continued without answering. "We would like to hear what Colonel Gavrilin said to you on the ice. Whether together we could find out where he has hidden his papers. We can't find them."

"Ask the colonel himself."

"He's dead. He was found drowned in a hole in the ice the day before I arrested you in Savidova. They tried to make it look like an accident, but he had been strangled before he entered the water. I couldn't have you walking about in Moscow, Jack. First Sonia and Vera, then the medical examiner, and then Gavrilin. And think of the attack on you in the Silver Wood. I had to get you out: I used Lilli; I had no choice."

I sat down on the floor and felt the wall bar against my back. Basov sat down next to me. He helped me pull off my boxing gloves. He produced a crumpled pack of cigarettes and offered me one. I looked around, but I couldn't see the boys. I could hear them laughing and talking in the showers, a loud and warm sound, so I took one.

"Why have you come now?" I asked.

"Times have changed. We can do something about the case now. We couldn't then."

"Did you ever find out who the three thugs were?"

"Come to Moscow, Jack. The answers are in Moscow. I'm not allowed to tell you more." He paused for a moment. "You might see Lilli again. She's still there."

All the old feelings welled up in me, making my chest so tight that I felt as if I couldn't breathe.

"Why should I see that KGB whore again?" I whispered.

"She knew nothing, Jack. She wasn't an agent."

I knocked the ash off my cigarette into my hand, but Basov tore some tinfoil off his pack of American cigarettes, and we used that as an ashtray. We finished smoking, before I said, "I'm not promising anything, but I'll invite you for dinner, now that you've come so far, and to thank you for your help in the Silver Wood."

"I don't want to inconvenience you."

"You already have," I said. "But this isn't Russia. Here we shop at the supermarket on our way home, and that's that. It'll take ten minutes. Your perestroika probably hasn't got that far yet."

"Unfortunately I can't pretend that it has, but it will come someday."

"We'll be long dead by then, Volody."

"OK, I accept, then," he said, and reached out his hand. It was dry and strong when I grabbed it. My own was sweaty and greasy, and not only because of the physical exertion.

"But I promise nothing," I said. He got up and kept my hand in his and pulled me up from the floor.

"Dinner sounds good enough for a start," he said. "Better than your first offer. You're still in good shape. I wouldn't have lasted long."

"Don't give me that shit, Basov," I said good-naturedly, and smiled at him for the first time.

We shopped at the supermarket. Basov was a sophisticated and widely traveled man who belonged to the elite, and still his eyes opened wide. He tried to hide it, but I knew that he had to compare the abundance on the shelves in our little town with the empty, dirty, and dreary shops in Russian provincial towns. If a supermarket like this one could become common and commonly accessible, I knew that Basov would see it as the final victory of communism in his lifetime. It wasn't his fault, but I couldn't help teasing him. He pushed the cart, and we quarreled amicably like in the old days while I bought food and wine.

I made a salad, broiled lamb chops, boiled ears of corn and fresh green beans, and opened a bottle of good Rioja. I handed him a drink and placed him on the kitchen bench. At first he looked at me with the amazed expression of most Russian men when they see a man occupied with feminine pursuits. He didn't say anything, just complimented me on my house. We talked politics. He suggested that I could write about the political developments in the Soviet Union when I came to Moscow. He talked with warmth and enthusiasm about glasnost and perestroika. We ate in the kitchen. I answered his questions about my life in the last couple of years and asked him about his family and his own life. He answered somewhat evasively and seemed to prefer to talk about the new era into which he thought his country was on its way. A new revolution. He said that Gorbachev was a man for whom his generation had been waiting a long time.

We had coffee in the garden. It had become cooler, but I lent Basov a sweater. My birches and pines were swaying softly in the west wind. The scent of the roses was strong enough to make you think it had been produced at a perfume factory, and the birds were singing in the light summer evening as if they had their own demanding five-year plan to fulfill. We were sitting in the sheltered corner of the terrace, and it struck me how fond I had grown of my provincial life. But I had made up my mind. I would go back to Russia.

"I can understand it if you're angry, hurt, and feel betrayed. But you're a fighter, Jack. If I hadn't denounced her in a way that made you hate her on the spot, would you then have accepted that we took her away? That we separated you?" Basov said.

"I don't know."

"The times were not for pity."

"That's not a quality that I find to be prevalent in the KGB, either," I said harshly.

He laughed. "Why do you think I'm KGB?"

"Why shouldn't I think so? You were hand in glove with Gavrilin, for one thing."

"Gavrilin was my father-in-law," he said.

"I'm sorry, Volody," I said.

"In many ways he was an old-fashioned, stubborn man, but I was very fond of him. I respected him. He was incorruptible. As you know, that's a rare quality in my country," he said.

"He was your father-in-law, but he didn't tell you what we talked about on the ice?"

"No. I don't know why. Maybe he wanted to protect me. Maybe he figured that it would take years before he could get to the bottom of it. And he didn't want to damage my career. Gorbachev has many enemies," he continued without transition, "and they're powerful. Nobody lets go of his privileges voluntarily. The fight against corruption affects many people painfully. It touches deep chords and creates unrest. We're walking a narrow mountain path, and there are dangers lurking both right and left."

"Then it's a good thing that you're so good at tightrope walking. In the circus, at any rate," I said, and made him laugh.

"Unfortunately we're going to need stronger forces than circus performers if we're to succeed," he said.

"Are you still a diplomat?"

"Yes and no. I work directly under the general secretary. I'm on his personal staff."

"You've got ahead in the world, my friend," I said.

He laughed again. "Does that mean you're coming?"

"I suppose it does."

He reached into the interior pocket of his jacket and produced a visa. It was lavender, the color of the Ministry of Foreign Affairs. He handed it to me.

"You must have been rather sure of yourself," I said. He shrugged. I continued, "But you'll have to change it. I'm not going in a couple of days. I have a class to take through an exam in Pushkin, and a couple of days later a bunch of very nervous and very proud young men are going to box in another town for the first time. I don't intend to let them down."

"It's important that you come as soon as possible, Jack. There's little time."

"I can come in a little less than a week. You have to change my visa."

He looked at me with some irritation, as if he were deliberating with himself whether it was worth trying to press me. He chose to give it a try.

"Jack, listen. I'm not authorized to say much. But it's highly important that you come as soon as possible."

I looked straight at him. "Vladimir. I'm no longer a diplomat. I don't have to accept double talk and abstract notions. I don't have to live according to them. My students and my boys at the club have confidence in me and trust me not to let them down. That's concrete. Those are fixed points in my life and make it meaningful. So you can shove your politics and your major considerations to the interests of power. I'm coming in a week or not at all."

"OK, Jack. I understand."

"The hell you do, but never mind. Come, let's go inside where it's warmer and see if I have any Russian vodka, so that we can drink to our reconciliation, regardless of whether you are KGB or something quite new that means the same thing under Gorbachev."

He gave me a forced smile, but followed me inside like a powerful little circus bear.

Part Three

SUMMER

I loved you for a long long time. I know this love
is real. It don't matter how it all went wrong. That
don't change the way I feel. And I can't believe
that time's gonna heal this wound that I'm speaking
of. There ain't no cure for love.

LEONARD COHEN

17

All my students passed the exam, and most of my boxers lost, but with honor, so they were happy, and I landed in summerly, hot and sunny Moscow, where the air was so full of poplar pollen that at times it looked like snow in June. Nobody was at the airport to meet me. I was to stay at the Hotel National. I would be contacted. The passport control was just as painstaking as I remembered it. Customs was slow and lengthy. I was entitled to a car from Intourist, but found a yellow cab, and we rumbled toward the city on roads that were as bumpy and full of holes as they'd always been. The city looked the same. There were large banners; all the slogans had to do with perestroika and glasnost. The tires of the cars stirred up the brown dust. They still took off the windshield wipers when it didn't rain to make sure they weren't stolen: like all other spare parts they were impossible to procure. The city had a southerly air in the summer. On every spot of dirt grew a green tree. The low rays of the sun played on the beautiful pastel colors of the houses in the center. Moscow was like a dinosaur, too big and too mighty. A dying monster, but beautiful in its decay.

The cab driver drove fast with one hand on the wheel, while he smoked stinking cigarettes with black perfumed tobacco and listened to folk music on the Mayak station.

"I guess you laugh a lot in your country at all our talk about glasnost and perestroika," he said. He was of heavy build and had a thick mustache.

"No. We actually take it very seriously," I said.

He gave an irritated snort. "It makes room for a lot of blackasses, Jews, and bandits. There's no order anymore. Criminals run around freely in the streets. The whores stick out their tits as if they owned the world. What we need isn't glasnost, it's steel." He said Stalin, but in such a way that it could mean both steel and refer to the dictator's name. He probably meant the latter. Uncle Stalin's likeness was dangling from the rearview mirror framed by an oval ring of metal that looked as if it had been cut out of the bottom of a mortar grenade.

"Are you *afgantsy*?" I asked.

"Twice by the heathens. May they rot in hell," he said. "Wounded both times. Decorated four times, but I have thrown my medals in the garbage can. Now they're pulling us out. What the hell were we fighting for then? And what do we come back to? Shit and contempt. Criminals and whores make the decisions. Corrupt Party bosses get rich at our expense. Newspapers and television that are run by long-nosed Jews. Young people who don't want to work, but who think only of buying jeans and listening to rock music and taking drugs. Comrades who've lost a leg and must wait several years to get an apartment because the local boss needs it for his mistress. Prices that go up all the time and salaries that go down. Where the hell is Russia headed? Not for socialism, that's for sure."

"Still, Gorbachev has tried to clean up, hasn't he?" I said.

He turned his head toward me as he blinked his lights angrily in order to make the car in front of him pull to the right.

"Gorbachev is good enough. But he isn't hard enough. All that talk about democracy. What does it lead to? The Russian people have always loved the strong hand. It's best that people tremble a little when they hear the boss's steps across the floor. Things are going badly when they think of abolishing the death penalty and letting the criminals have the last say."

He drove aggressively and full of anger toward other drivers. Just before we passed Belorussia Station, he exclaimed irritatedly, "Was that necessary before, maybe?"

He waved his hand, making the blue tobacco smoke undulate around us. In front of us was a brown vehicle with darkened windows and a blue blinking light on the roof. I had never before seen an armored car like that in Moscow. An armed guard sat in the passenger's seat.

"In the old days they transported money in a taxi. Now all the money has to go to the bank in a car like that. The young men were beginning to rob the taxis. They attacked them with pistols, as if this were Chicago. Where the hell are we headed?"

I heard similar sentiments several times during the following three days, while Moscow was panting in the heat. I looked up old contacts and listened to the hopes and fears of the intellectuals, but first I went to my old apartment, where Mikael Petersen now lived. It looked the same. The same rooms, the same furniture, the same courtyard, and the same sullen policeman still carefully guarding his little square.

Mikael received me warmly. We had a very nice first evening. He was very nervous, because he had just had a daughter. He was very preoccupied with the fact that he had been present at her birth. But we mostly talked about the reasons for my return. I told him in rough outline what it was all about, and that I would like to have a backstop in case complications arose. Late in the evening he asked me if I would do him a favor.

"Tell me," I said.

He had just sold his first car, every new diplomat's small
baptism of fire. But now the problem was that he had spent all
his vacation days on being home for the birth. Could I drive
the car out of the country for him?

"I can't spare the days. I simply don't have them," he said,
and nervously sucked the frame of his glasses. He was almost
new and very eager to do his bit. I remembered very well how
the Ministry of Foreign Affairs counted days off like a miser
counts money.

"If you take care of all the paperwork and get permission
from the foreign ministry then it's all right," I said. "But I
don't want any trouble."

"You won't have any," he said, relieved. "You know the
whole business. You know where to hand it over. It's a Libyan
who has bought my car." The idea appealed to me. I would like
to drive out of Russia once more instead of just getting on an
SAS plane and being home the minute I stepped into the blue,
friendly cabin.

I rediscovered Moscow on foot.

The Arbat pedestrian street was swarming with people.
There were long-haired hippies, punks dressed in black and
with safety pins in their lilac-colored hair, protest singers, and
people who could draw a portrait in charcoal for fifteen rubles.
Stands selling shish kebab and others offering pancakes. Young
people in badly fitting leather clothes with bristling metal
spikes who called themselves *metalista*. But there were also
many things that hadn't changed: the police in their light blue
summer uniforms on every street corner; the usual line in front
of the shoe store on Mira Prospect, waiting patiently for East
German footwear. I nosed around in food stores and found
only dirty-looking fresh lard. I saw for myself and heard people
say that the food supplies had never been worse. There had
never been so few articles. Even the foreign correspondents I
met complained that their dollar shop was as empty as the

Soviet coffers. I walked into the small back streets that tourists never see. In the backyards nothing had changed. There were piles of rusty old iron and dried mud. Paint and plaster were peeling off the walls of all the houses, and the staircases of the apartment buildings were still dark with footworn or cracked steps. The sidewalks were so full of holes that they were dangerous. Everywhere the decay of the city had continued, and it seemed even more run-down now than when I had lived in it. The lines in front of the few liquor stores reached far down the sidewalks. In the lines I sensed a smoldering discontent, and abusive language was flourishing. The city vibrated in the heat, and there was an undercurrent of confusion and a readiness for confrontation. In the newspapers there were stories of street fights between youth gangs and of riots in Azerbaijan, where many had been killed or injured when Muslims and Armenians decided to settle their centuries-old score. Curfews had been imposed in cities both in Azerbaijan and in Estonia, where there had also been demonstrations and riots.

I went into the Praga on the second day, but Lilli didn't sing there anymore. No, they didn't know where she was. Pyotr Demichev's answering machine stated only that the poet could not be reached. I left a message. Basov's old number had been taken over by someone else; of course, he had a new and better apartment now that he had been promoted. I couldn't sleep. I was restless, and I wandered through the city in the summer twilight, hoping that I would soon be contacted. One noticeable change was that I no longer met drunk people everywhere. I didn't see that typical group of three men sharing a bottle of vodka. It occured to me that I didn't have Lilli's telephone number or exact address. And Moscow still had no telephone directories.

Early in the evening, as I came out from the Hotel National, a great crowd of several thousand people came marching across Revolution Square. The traffic came to a halt. The policemen were unable to stop them and didn't seem to want to, either. In the lead twenty young men walked arm-in-arm with a banner stretched out behind them, saying: "Justice for the Soviet heroes from Afghanistan!" The crowd following them was a mixture of all generations. Many carried posters with just one word: "Pamyat." Others carried slogans like "Jews and Freemasons are destroying socialism," "Death penalty for criminals," and "Stalin lives." The crowd was buzzing angrily, and there was trouble and violence in the air. At Gorky Street they turned and began to move in the direction of the Mos-soviet. The mayor and the Party leader were going to receive a visit. I followed the demonstration. People on the sidewalk stopped and stared at the surprising sight. The vibrating heat was like a blanket over the city, and I was sweating, although I was wearing only jeans and a short-sleeved shirt. On the other side of Revolution Square, by the rise leading up to Red Square, I could see the Kremlin guard begin to bar the square. Armed soldiers were lining up and starting to clear the square of tourists. More people were joining the demonstration. The Afghanistan veterans were leading the way with closed, stiff, and decisive faces.

"A wonderful gang, don't you think?"

I turned around. "Pyotr!" I exclaimed, and we gave each other a big, Russian embrace.

"I got your message," he said. "What do you think of this?"

"Pamyat?" I said. "A bunch of madmen. They see Jewish conspiracies everywhere."

"That's only the surface. They're a dangerous gang. They can't get used to the fact that they have to learn to think for themselves, and that democracy will have some costs. Their leader is a fool. He firmly believes that the Kremlin adds narcotics to the drinking water in order to turn young Russians into drug addicts. But he's only a figurehead: others are pulling the strings behind him. They're reactionary, Russian nationalists. They're dangerous, Jack. And how are you doing? Tell me everything," he continued without transition.

I didn't have time to answer. Like so often before it was one of the old babushkas who had the courage. She wore a kerchief around her head in spite of the heat and brown, unbecoming stockings. She had no teeth and was carrying two big bags. She pulled a small cart filled with empty bottles and old cardboard that she collected in order to earn a little to live on. She left her cart and walked straight through the crowd up to the man who carried a placard with Stalin's picture. He was a large man, but she reached up and grabbed the stick and pulled. He was so surprised that he let go, and she trampled vehemently on Stalin's face while she shouted, "Sons of whores! He murdered my whole family in the camps. Don't let him out of the grave!"

I don't know if they pushed her on purpose or if it was the pressure from the people behind, but the old woman was knocked over, and a young man in white jeans and a light-colored leather jacket kicked her in the stomach, without mercy. Then the fight began. A group of young men in leather jackets with spikes started hitting the demonstrators, and hefty young men with sticks appeared, striking out indiscriminately at anyone within reach. In the distance we heard the howling sirens and saw buses filled with helmeted riot patrols entering Revolution Square. Panic broke out, and together with others we ran up Gorky Street, moving with difficulty among the many people. Children were crying. An old man was trampled down, and every time he tried to get up, he was knocked over. Right in front of us a television crew tried to film the panic, but three young men in blue denim jackets tore the camera from the shoulder of the photographer and banged it against the wall, so that it opened up and all the expensive electronics poured out onto the concrete slabs of the sidewalk.

Demichev grabbed me by the sleeve and pulled me into an

alley leading to a backyard. He was heading for a hole in the row of houses, but a young man blocked our way, his face twisted with rage.

"You traitor and Jew lover," he shouted when he recognized Demichev. He hit Pyotr hard in the stomach, making him fall forward, and then kicked him twice in the side. Demichev hunched himself into a fetal position, trying to protect himself.

"Come here, you asshole," I yelled in Danish. He saw me coming at him and kicked with his right leg against my knee, but hit the shinbone instead. He was wearing jogging shoes, so the pain wasn't so bad. I jumped aside and took his next kick with my hip, then I was close enough and hit him hard in the chest with my left, making him stagger back. I sent him up against the wall with my left again and crossed him with my right, so that my knuckles began to bleed. He tumbled against the wall, but came back and hit me on the mouth with such force that I felt my head clatter and could taste the blood from my lip. But he was too slow in following up, so I caught him again with a left-right combination and drove him up against the wall once more. There was no reason to be nice, so I stuck my knee in his crotch, and, holding him by the throat with my left hand, banged his head into the wall and pumped blow after blow into his face. When I let go of him, he collapsed.

Demichev held his hand against his stomach as we ran on. We then slowed down and stepped out onto a street where everything breathed peace. We could hear both police sirens and ambulances as we leaned against a yellow wall and caught our breath.

"Let's walk away from here," Demichev said.

We walked slowly, Demichev holding his stomach and me licking the blood off my split lip. We reached the inner boulevard and sat down on a wooden bench. The paint was peeling off. People with anxious faces stopped to listen to the wailing sirens. A bus filled with policemen drove up and deposited eight officers. They were placing them by all the entrances to the boulevard. We sat in the narrow park between the two traffic arteries, bordered by tall poplars. The evening light was soft and pleasant, as if we were in a green tunnel. I handed Pyotr a cigarette and lit it for him. He pulled a bottle out of a pocket in his jacket and took a swig before passing it on to me. I also took a good pull and felt the taste of Russia spreading in my stomach. Pyotr was holding his hand by his right kidney.

"Is it bad?" I asked.

He shook his head. "No, it's just that I'm getting old. I can't take so much anymore. I'm not like you."

"I've reached the wrong side of forty."

"I can't remember when I was fifty," he said, and winced, pulling his face into a grimace of pain. We smoked in silence for a while. Then I brushed him clean, and he dabbed my lip with a clean handkerchief. The police looked at us, but left us alone. They probably recognized Demichev. Now that was an advantage—before, it had nearly cost him his health.

"I have read of fights and riots both in Danish and in Soviet newspapers," I said, "but I would never have thought that it could happen so close to the Kremlin."

"They've gone too far this time," he said. "Pamyat will be prohibited now. They deserve it. They're a gang of Fascists. The worst thing about it is that it will affect other organizations, from stamp collectors to discussion groups."

"You can't give people half freedom," I said. "They will always want more and more. In the end they will want full freedom."

"Don't be banal," he said irritatedly. "Two years ago this country was bubbling with optimism. People thought that heaven was just around the corner. We have taken a road of no return. But it's a long process: it will take at least twenty years. Yet most people think that it's going too fast. In the West you think that there's a critic of the system hidden in every Russian soul. Here in Moscow, in someone like me, maybe. But not in the people. They're reactionary, conservative, and immovable. If you can imagine that Gorbachev and Stalin presented themselves as candidates for presidency, who do you suppose would win? Gorbachev among the intellectuals. But he wouldn't stand a chance against Stalin out there in the big muddy country called Russia. Stalin won the war and kept his house in order. Gorbachev talks about openness and has lost in Afghanistan," he said.

"You're being too pessimistic," I said.

"I am? Maybe. Maybe I'm just tired of those in power here and everywhere else. Maybe I'm just tired of writing poems against the bureaucracy. Maybe I'm just tired of fighting idiotic censors. Maybe I just want to write another good poem about love and fuck my young wife as long as I can."

"OK, Pyotr," I said. I could see how upset and disappointed he was. He was obviously worried. I could feel his fear that the clock might be set back. Or that the violence today, the other riots, and the press revelations of corruption and power abuse would cost Gorbachev his head in the end. It was the second time that the Pamyat organization had demonstrated in the streets of Moscow. They were given a much freer rein than other so-called unofficial groups, and had been granted an interview with the Party leader of Moscow. It was said that they had connections high up in the system.

"Don't tip the boat," he said.

"What do you mean?"

"It's the phrase you hear most often in the street all over the Soviet Union. Bureaucrats and the people agree. You know what you've got and that's good enough, for you don't know that it could be any different. And we're talking about 180 million people."

I laughed, but my laughter stopped. My lip began to bleed again. I could feel with my tongue how swollen it was.

"Yes, you don't look too good," he said. "And that's too bad for the next point on our schedule. How do I get to 180 million opponents of perestroika? That I'll tell you. We have 18 million bureaucrats. Each bureaucrat has a family and a group of friends consisting of ten people. They agree with him that he should keep his privileges. That's the way it is," he said with the old intensity and eagerness in his voice.

This time I laughed even if it did hurt.

"Well, then you're in the minority."

"That I've been all my life."

"What's the next point on the schedule?" I asked.

He looked at me closely with something that seemed like a mixture of pity and curiosity. As if I were an object of research.

"We're going to listen to jazz," he just said, and winced as he got up from the bench and pulled me along.

He took me to a jazz club. It was a quarter of an hour's walk. The evening was still light and warm. People were standing in groups discussing what had happened in Gorky Street. There were policemen everywhere, but the city seemed calm, although the atmosphere was tense. The name of the jazz club was The Blue Bird. It was a cooperative. Earlier the space had been used as a boring café run by the Young Communists' League. It was Moscow's first and only jazz club, Pyotr explained. He was a friend of the man who ran it, so we walked past the short line of people waiting to get in. We got into a narrow corridor where a group of young people stood and smoked. I could hear the music clearly. It was an old Billie Holiday song. I recognized the voice immediately.

We stepped inside. Demichev's friend came up to us, and we exchanged formal handshakes. He was a small and slim Armenian with a shock of woolly hair. He introduced himself as "The Arm" and spoke excellent English as he inquired about the Montmartre in Copenhagen. His club was neat and clean with light furniture and red-and-white checkered tablecloths.

The air was clear. The authorities had requested that both smoking and the drinking of liquor be prohibited. On the walls there were good posters of Duke Ellington and other great ones from the golden age of jazz. There was a small stage. Almost all the tables were occupied. The audience was young. The Arm placed us at a small table right in front of the stage. On the table were Fanta and water and two slices of bread with sausage and caviar. Demichev took the small bottle of vodka out of his pocket and discreetly poured the last spot into our glasses. Then he filled them up with Fanta.

I was looking at Lilli. Her face had become rounder, but she was still very thin. She was very beautiful and dressed in Western clothes, as if she had a lover with access to foreign currency. She wore faded, tight jeans and a white shirt. Her breasts moved freely under the shirt. That was advanced for Moscow, but I remembered that she never used a bra. I became warm all over. Around her neck she wore a small gold chain. Her hair was longer. It was light and cut off right above the shoulder. She wore hardly any makeup at all and delivered the song with feeling and warmth. Her skin was still fine and clear, but there were little wrinkles around her eyes and the corners of her mouth. They looked good on her. She didn't appear childish anymore, but looked like what she had become: a beautiful young woman. Her green eyes sparkled. She saw me almost immediately and missed a beat, but found the rhythm again. We kept eye contact through the rest of her song. Her green eyes were filled with pain. I remembered her self-control. The audience applauded calmly. She turned around to the pianist and said something we couldn't hear. Then she sang the Beatles' song "Yesterday." The text hurt all the way into my heart.

"You knew she was here," I whispered to Pyotr. He gave me an ironical and self-satisfied smile.

"She's still fantastic," he said.

"And you're a jerk," I said without conviction.

"You know her?" The Arm asked. "Her name is Lilli Smuul. She has a great talent that she has been wasting at various restaurants. There are many things that we have missed the last twenty years. We must make up for lost time."

I was wishing that they'd be quiet. I tried to catch her eyes again, but she looked away, disappeared into her song, and was lost to me and the rest of the audience. There was only her and the pianist and a quiet drum.

When the song died away, people applauded enthusiastically. She cautiously put down the microphone and came down toward me. Her hips were swaying softly. I got up and took two steps forward. We stood facing each other.

"Have you come back to ruin my life once more, Jack Andersen?" she said in English. There were tears in her eyes, but her voice was flat and without feeling.

"No. I've come to take you home with me," I said arrogantly.

She hid her face in her hands and hissed, "I hate you, Jack Andersen. Go to hell."

She ran toward a door next to the stage and left me dumbstruck in the middle of the room.

18

Pyotr Demichev gave me a push.

"Run after her, you moron!" he shouted. "When women say they hate you, they mean they love you."

"Shut up, Pyotr," I shouted. The Arm looked at us with amazement. People by the nearest tables didn't seem to have noticed anything. They were in deep conversation over the Fanta bottles. The room was buzzing with voices. I tore myself loose and ran after Lilli. It was a naked room. There was nothing on the walls. In one corner there was a pile of Fanta boxes. There was a small window covered with a thick layer of dust. She stood with her back to the door, embracing herself. Her back was curved, and I could see her long white neck where her hair parted. I closed the door.

"Lilli . . ." I said.

"Go away."

"I love you," I said.

She turned around. Her eyes flashed.

"Now you say it! You never said it then. You ran off and left me here. You listened to them, not to me." She looked angry and hurt at the same time, defiant and furious.

"It's the greatest mistake I've made in my life. I can't ask you to forgive me. I can't even say that I'm sorry. Those words can't express what I feel."

She let go of herself for a moment, then she clasped her arms over her chest again.

"What's that I hear?" she said. "Do I hear the great Jack Andersen, the fine diplomat, crawling and begging? What's getting into him?"

"You're not making it any easier," I said. I was getting angry.

"Why the hell should I make it easier for you?" she shouted.

"Because I love you."

"Love me? Those are fancy words. What am I supposed to do? Break down and cry? Tell you that you're my prince charming? That I've waited for you faithfully? Go to bed with you? So you can play a little with me again and then go back to your rich little country?" She turned her back on me again.

"Go away, Jack. Leave me alone," she said.

"Not until I've explained to you what really happened."

She pressed her hands against her ears. I waited patiently, then she embraced herself again. I felt a fantastic urge to take the five steps forward and hold her, but I didn't dare. Instead I told her of Basov's visit. She stood with her back to me, but I could tell from her back that she was listening.

"I've never regretted anything in my entire life as much as those minutes in Savidova," I concluded.

She turned around again. "You're only making it worse," she said. "Why the hell did you have to come back? Before I could at least dream, when I was in that mood, that you had given in to pressure. Now you tell me that you trusted some official more than you trusted me. What the hell do you take me for?"

"I love you," I repeated stubbornly.

"Stop saying that all the time," she said pleadingly. Her face was in turmoil.

"I think you still love me," I said. She flew at me so swiftly that I was defenseless. She hit me in the chest again and again and finally banged her clenched fist into my face. The blows fell erratically. Then she stopped.

"You're bleeding, look what I've done," she said, frightened. My lip had burst open, and I could taste the salty blood.

"It was cracked already," I said.

She cautiously raised her hand and placed a finger on my swollen lower lip, passing it gently over my mouth, slowly and almost erotically. I raised my own hand and touched her lips, caressed them as if they were her other, hidden lips. We stood still, caressing each other without saying a word, as if we were trying to let the physical contact determine what was left between us. We let our fingers remember the good things while our minds only registered the wounds in the soul. She stood so close to me that I could feel her breasts against my shirt front. The music had begun again. It reached us as if through cotton wool. It was a slow, traditional jazz tune. I put my arms around her and pulled her up against me. She leaned against my shoulder, and once more we stood still for a while before she put her arms around my waist.

We stood like that for an eternity. It was as if neither of us wanted to break the spell and return to reality, but my lip was bleeding so much that a drop of blood fell on her shoulder. She let go of me and found a handkerchief that she handed to me. I dabbed my lip. The silence between us was awkward, and we both felt ill at ease. She squatted down, leaning her back against the wall. I sat down next to her.

"Do you have a cigarette?" she asked.

"I didn't know that you smoked," I said.

"What do you know about me?" she said with some of the aggression from before in her voice. I handed her a cigarette and lit it for her.

"Are you stationed here again?" she asked, as if we were having a polite conversation at a formal dinner party.

"I'm not a diplomat anymore. I'm a teacher," I said. "I live in a small house in the countryside now. I would like you to move into it."

"You're incredible," she said. "You come here and in five minutes you want to drag me away from my country and my life. Who do you think you are?"

"I've wasted almost four years. I don't intend to waste more. I love you."

"Jack," she said without anger. "It's impossible. You know that."

"I'm not letting go of you again."

"What do you mean by all this? Are we going to get married?"

"If you want."

She gave an angry snort. "I didn't expect to see you ever again. And now you want to get married. Can't you see how crazy that sounds?"

"I don't care. I haven't thought of anything else since Basov's visit."

"But I have," she said.

"Maybe there's someone else?" I said.

She turned around and took my face between her hands and looked straight into my eyes.

"No. There isn't someone else. There have been others, but not someone else," she said, making me jealous. "But I don't believe what you are saying. Besides, you forget I'm a Soviet citizen. I can't just travel wherever I want."

"We'll find out about that," I said.

She let go of my face and got up and walked over to the dust-covered window, where she placed herself with her back to me again. Her light blouse was covered with a fine, gray layer of dust from the wall. I took her handkerchief away from my lip and carefully probed it with the tip of my tongue. The bleeding had stopped, but the lip felt sore.

"I've applied for permission to leave," she said in a low voice.

"I did it six months after you had left. It was stupid of me, but I wanted to find you and explain to you how unjust you'd been. How wrong you were. I've applied every six months ever since. You know, we're only allowed to apply every six months. But no longer to find you. I just wanted to get away. I wanted to begin a new life in a place where there wasn't so much dirt clinging to everything."

She looked at me angrily.

"What do you think happened the first time? And all the other times? Of course they refused. First they took my job away from me and then my residence permit. The apartment was in Vera's name. The same day that I handed in my application at OVIR, the Praga fired me, and all the other places were closed to me. One week later the police came and threw me out and sent me home to Tallinn to my mother's apartment. We lived in the same rooms like two strangers. And even there I wasn't allowed to sing. I could get work in the fishing industry. The alternative was fifteen days in prison as a parasite." She was embracing herself again. I was full of anger against myself for the suffering I had contributed to cause. I couldn't make myself blame it all on the system. I had been the catalyst. I had played her into the hands of the minions of power. I also realized that Basov had lied in Denmark: he had said that Lilli was still there, as if she were leading a normal life. Basov had used her again without her knowledge, as a trump card. She had been manipulated from all sides.

"I can get you out if you want," I said. "I can impose some conditions on them. I'm in a position of being able to do them a favor. I have something that they want."

She turned around.

"There, you see," she said. "I'm going to be used again. I'm a pawn. I'm a number. If and if and if . . . then I can most graciously be permitted to leave. They decide, or you do. I don't," she said.

"If you still want to leave, I'll do everything I can to get you out, and afterward you'll be free to do what you want. But I love you and I also want to do everything in my power to make you stay with me."

"Why didn't you talk like that then?"

"I was another person, and I was probably too proud. Now I have everything to gain and nothing to lose." She walked over to me, and we again held each other carefully as if not to break something fragile.

"If you don't have *propiska* for Moscow, then where do you live?" I asked. She pulled away from me a little, but kept her arms around my waist. I knew that without a permit she could stay in Moscow for only three days. She probably broke the law like thousands of others who had been expelled from the capital.

"At the moment I'm staying at The Arm's apartment," she said. I must have looked hurt and jealous, because she continued, "I have a great desire to hurt you. I hurt you just now, and I must be a bad person, for it made me glad to see you hurt. But you needn't worry. The Arm is married to a beautiful woman. I sleep on their sofa, not in his bed."

She took my face between both of her hands like before. She rocked it back and forth.

"I can't figure it out," she said. "I feel like scratching your eyes out, but I also feel like kissing you."

"Try kissing me," I said.

"Like you, I guess I've nothing to lose," she said. It was a soft kiss, resigned and without passion. I should have felt happy, but what I felt was closer to deep unhappiness. We had a long road ahead of us, and I felt uncertain whether I could ever regain her full confidence.

"I have to sing again," she said, and placed her finger softly on my mouth. "Don't say more, Jack. Just be quiet. I don't believe in words anymore."

Lilli sang with the band for another hour. Jazz and soft rock intermingled. She had become much better, or else it was because she was singing something that she liked. She made me think of the party at Demichev's dacha. There was the same intensity and honesty in her voice now as there had been then, but it had become deeper and more secure and experienced. This was something she knew how to do. It was the element in her life that enabled her to survive. I felt in despair, but also strangely optimistic. Like me, Lilli was a survivor.

The Arm's wife arrived. She was a small, chubby Armenian woman with brown eyes. Her name was Silvi, and she was dark and alive and full of talk about political prisoners who had been released. She couldn't hide how fond she was of her husband, and she obviously shared his great happiness about the small jazz café.

The Arm closed the café at 11 P.M. as the authorities requested, and when the last guests had been let out, he produced a bottle of wine and an ashtray. We sat talking for half an hour about the events of the evening, about music and travels. The Arm had been to Denmark once on a carefully guided group trip. He gave a light and friendly portrait of Copenhagen for Lilli, but talked mostly about himself and his wife. Demichev smoked one filter cigarette after another as if he needed to make up for the time he'd lost during the last couple of hours' ban on smoking. He talked about the American jazz musicians that he'd known. The whole situation felt normal and peaceful. Lilli was sitting next to me, and we were holding hands.

"You look like a couple of idiotic sixteen-year-old kids, except for Jack's lip, which makes him look like a gangster from Chicago," Demichev said. The Arm had lowered the lights and put a tape of Ben Webster on the tape recorder in my honor. He had gotten it from the correspondent of the Danish Broadcasting Company. It was the recording of a concert at Club Montmartre in Copenhagen.

"You're just envious," I said good-naturedly.

"You should be thankful to your old uncle Pyotr. He brought you together again. Didn't I promise you to do that?"

"You might have warned us first," I said. Lilli looked ahead of her with distant, green eyes.

"No. You needed to have the shock. Your hearts needed to speak. Lilli is Estonian, and so half Western. You speak Russian, but you think like a Westerner. You would have analyzed the situation. I am a Russian artist. I know that the soul needs to scream out its pain and its longing."

"You're too much," I said.

"That's what I'm saying. You're too hopelessly rationalistic. And Lilli was right to hate you and to love you. Always deal with women on an emotional basis."

"You'll make me throw up soon, Pyotr," I said.

He sucked his filter cigarette and tipped it up and down between his narrow lips as he contemplated his creation with an air of satisfaction.

The Arm closed off his friendly and pleasant café for the night and turned off the light in a new, civilized spot in Moscow, a fragment of hope in the middle of an everyday life that was still bleak. We found a couple of taxis and went out to Demichev's place. None of the official yellow taxis were willing to go that far, but we managed to stop a couple of private Ladas. I sat with my arm around Lilli on the backseat. She sat very close to me, and the breeze from the window blew her hair back from her straight forehead. She had a small scar above her right eyebrow, I discovered. Demichev chatted with the driver, who told him that he was an engineer, but moonlighted as a cab driver to supplement his insufficient salary. He was a product of the new era and was giving a lot of thought to becoming registered and making his moonlighting job legal, but he was reluctant to pay taxes on his income. He just wanted to wait and see which way the wind blew.

The many trees of Peredelkino appeared like fine paper cuttings in silhouette, but there was already the first suggestion of a bordure of light in the horizon when we drove across the bridge and through the writers' town down to Pyotr's house. We could hear voices and laughter from many of the gardens. People didn't want to waste time sleeping in the bubbly, light night. We passed a man on an old bicycle who drove as if he were doing a slalom. In front of him, on the crossbar, was a girl with a bottle of wine in her hand. They almost toppled over when she laughingly turned around and tried to give him a sip of wine and a kiss at the same time.

"Oh, Russian night. Your light and your lavender darkness make my blood dance!" Demichev recited, pathetic and happy.

Anna was wearing a dressing gown, but didn't look surprised that Pyotr had brought guests home with him at such a late hour. She seemed young and fragile, with long blond hair and a touch of acne. She wasn't pretty like Lilli, but had an open and unfinished face. Anna kissed Lilli on both cheeks, and I understood that this was another of those places where Lilli had found illegal shelter when she had come to Moscow to visit her friends and get a chance to sing.

"You found him again," Anna said, and looked at me with something that resembled hostility.

"He found me, or Pyotr found us both, what do I know," Lilli said.

"Pyotr is good at meddling in other people's business, but maybe for once it was a good thing," Anna said.

"Perhaps it was inevitable," Lilli said. "But it makes me more afraid than happy."

I felt jealous of their apparent intimacy. It was as if the rest of us weren't there, and I felt big and awkward, as if there weren't room for me in my own body.

"Come on. We must celebrate, not cry," Demichev said. With a proud proprietary mien he grabbed Anna, who let herself be pulled into his embrace. "We'll have some food on the table. It's midsummer. We don't have time to sleep."

"First I'm going to have a talk with Lilli," Anna said. She disengaged herself and took Lilli upstairs with her. I could hear their soft voices as they went. Demichev theatrically spread his arms and had to put food on the table himself. In his small kitchen we found cheese, sausage, cold cuts, salty cucumbers, and leavened black Russian bread. I held the red salami up before him. It was from Hungary and had been bought in the dollar shop, but I could tell that he remembered nothing of our conversation in the stinking toilet of the Praga. He produced a large bottle of wine, which he said came from a monastery near Odessa. We each had a glass. It was strong and full-bodied. The Arm put on a jazz tape. The mood from the café still hadn't left us. We set the long table in the main room beneath Pasternak's paintings. The Russians were beginning to publish *Dr. Zhivago,* so something had happened, after all, since that winter when we had visited Pasternak's grave. Lilli and Anna came downstairs when Demichev and I had finished setting the table. They were holding each other round the waist. Lilli's eyes were shiny. She had touched up her lips with a light color and put some green on her eyes. Anna, too, had put on makeup, but more heavily, with rouge on the cheeks in the Russian manner. She was also dressed in jeans and a blouse. They were the same height and looked like two sisters. Maybe Lilli borrowed some of her clothes from Anna. Demichev had access to foreign currency: by Soviet standards he was rich, and could probably buy what he wanted for his young wife. Lilli smiled at me and kissed me on the mouth as she sat down next to me. The atmosphere improved by several degrees, and Demichev applauded with exaggerated movements, like a circus clown.

It became a gay and lively meal. The music was very low, and we could hear the wind in the birches outside. There was a change in the weather, and a storm was brewing. Like years earlier, I sat with Lilli next to me on the bench with her hip pressed against mine and looked at the way she held her teacup as she carefully pointed her lips and blew away the hot steam. She didn't say much, but listened, like me, mainly to The Arm's enthusiastic talk about his new jazz café and all the plans he had for it.

It struck me that the conflicts and struggles of the Soviet Union were gathered here in a small group of people. There was Demichev with his ravaged face and youthful body. He was in the news with a new novel that ran as a serial in *Novy Mir* and was sold in large editions in the West. Only it wasn't new—he had written it twenty years earlier. It was about Stalin's terror seen through the eyes of the children from the Arbat. It had been gathering dust on the censors' shelves for twenty years, but now it had been published, making Demichev a much-talked-about person once again. He had been one of the angry young poets from the sixties along with Yevtushenko and Voznesensky. He wasn't so angry anymore. He had learned to live with the inexplicable fluctuations of the system.

The Arm had written about rock and jazz in a newspaper for ten years, but he always had to make sure to write negatively about Western rock in order to be allowed to write short articles about his real love: jazz. He had taught himself to write between the lines, inventing his own coded language that could be deciphered by those who shared his interest, but which the censors were too stupid to understand. Now he had a weekly column where he wrote freely, and his own jazz café that he ran together with others who thought like him. He feared a backlash, for he saw the reactionary forces gaining momentum. He became deeply worried when Demichev told him of the violence on Gorky Street.

Silvi wove in her free time and had sold her products on the black market for years. Now she and three other Armenian women and two Russian friends had been given permission to open a small shop. They wove carpets and sewed clothes. They were very successful, but the local Party secretary was beginning to dislike the fact that they made so much money and was threatening to close down the shop. At the same time, she had thrown herself into the fight for the rights of released political prisoners and pestered foreign journalists to call their attention to those who were still in prison. She proudly called herself one of Sakharov's children. The authorities still hadn't tried to stop her, but she figured that she was living on borrowed time.

And then there was Lilli. She couldn't travel where she wanted to. She wasn't allowed to sing officially, only unofficially with The Arm and in other places where there were people of courage. They weren't permitted to pay her. They risked prison if they did. In the system Lilli was registered as a worker in the fishing industry, with a residence permit for Tallinn. She was a number without right of appeal.

At one point The Arm looked at me seriously.

"Jack. Can you see how fragile it all is? It's a house of cards. It may collapse tomorrow. And no one at this table can do anything at all. We're entirely dependent on the decisions that the bosses make between themselves in the Party. We have to hope that Gorbachev means what he says and is allowed to carry it through. What's the alternative? To leave. I would like to visit Denmark again—but I can't live anywhere but in my country."

"I admire you for having the courage to let Lilli stay with you," I said.

The Arm laughed and rumpled his woolly hair. It was a nervous habit.

"They can report me if they want. But today I wouldn't put up with it. We're learning that we actually have certain rights. In the end, of course, it makes no difference. If they really want to get you, they can always find ways of doing it. But something is happening in people's heads now. They can't erase that without a lot of problems."

"Then many of us will go into inner exile and stop working. Then they won't get us to believe in anything again," Silvi said.

"It pays to fight," The Arm said. "It took me two years to get permission to open my jazz café. I could talk for hours about the attempts that the bureaucrats made to stop the project. Now they'll have to carry me out. I'm grateful that at least the dream of my life has been fulfilled."

"It's a strange country where we are grateful when those in power do what is obviously right and just," Lilli said. "Why do we thank them for some scraps instead of getting angry about the many wasted years?"

"Do you think it's so different with them?" Silvi said, and nodded in my direction.

"I don't know. I've never been there. But Jack talked a lot about life in the West, you know, back then. Here everything is prohibited if it's not expressly permitted. There, everything is permitted if it's not expressly prohibited. That's the whole difference, I think," Lilli said.

Seriousness had crept in upon us, and we went to bed as the first tender light of morning was breaking over the horizon. Demichev had plenty of room and insisted that we all stay. He was the only one a little intoxicated, and Anna helped him up the stairs. He always looked so scarred and old when he had too much to drink. Then you could see that he was a person who was living through yet another hope, but had seen most of it before and hardly dared believe that change was possible.

Lilli showed me the bathroom and pointed to a door at the end of the narrow hallway. It was a small room with a low window through which you could see the trunks of the birches outside. There was a narrow bed and a small table. In a corner hung, in the traditional Russian manner, an icon with a candle beneath a severe-looking saint, who held up three admonishing fingers. The window was open. I walked over to it. The birds had already begun to sing, and the birches were changing from dark to light tones. I looked out at the dense wood. I could hear her take off her clothes. I didn't dare turn around.

"Look, Jack," she said.

She stood naked. Even though it was warm, she had goose pimples. Her nipples were tense and hard. I walked toward her, but she was faster than me, and we held each other desperately and hard. She began to unbutton my shirt, but I couldn't wait any longer and pulled it over my head myself, and I frantically got the rest of my clothes off. She pushed me softly down upon the windowsill, and she was soft and warm when I entered her and came right away.

We collapsed on the bed, choking with laughter.

"I love you," she said.

"The next thousand times it'll be better," I said.

"It's good enough the way it is," she said, and began to cry.

19

The storm broke in the morning, and we heard the pouring rain in the trees. We made love again, slowly and tenderly this time, and afterward we talked and tried to make up for some of the lost time and to fill the large void before we could finally sleep in a close embrace under the icon's watchful eyes. Anna woke us up. It was still raining. She stuck her head through the door and smiled slyly.

"Telephone, Jack. A certain Basov. He says it's important."

I felt Lilli stiffen next to me. She pulled the blanket up around her.

"Everything is OK," I said, and kissed her. Anna withdrew from the doorway so that I could pull on the wet jeans and the damp shirt.

"Good morning, Jack," Basov said. He sounded fresh and rested, but his voice was tense. "The meeting has been scheduled for today at eleven A.M. Do you want me to pick you up?"

"How did you know where I was?" I said.

"We've been keeping an eye on you. There'll be a car at Demichev's in a quarter of an hour. It's on its way," he said.

"I'll be ready in half an hour," I said. "Meet me at the hotel."

"The car will be there in a quarter of an hour," Basov repeated.

"And I'll be ready in half an hour," I said, and hung up. Lilli still lay on the bed.

"Lilli," I said. "It will be all right. We've talked about everything. You'll get the letter from your mother and go to OVIR. It'll all work out," I repeated, trying desperately to fill my voice with an optimism that I didn't feel. Lilli was a grown-up woman, and still she had to produce a letter from her mother when she applied for permission to leave the country, stating that as her last living relative her mother didn't claim her and therefore permitted her to go abroad. There were also other, more bizarre formalities, the most serious of which was that the local Party committee of her district in Tallinn should give a written analysis and evaluation of her character and political attitude. The committee could take many interviews and several months to produce a paper like that. According to the rules she also had to appear for a personal interrogation by the Party committee at her place of work. And if the committee demanded it, she had to explain to all her co-workers at a grand meeting at the fish factory why she wanted to leave—even if she were only going on a vacation. One negative word was enough for the passport office, OVIR, to refuse to process her application. But I figured that we could get around that. I kissed her again. Her lips were dry and cold.

Anna had made breakfast. Demichev sat by the table, dripping wet, slurping his tea. He always went running in the morning, regardless of the weather. I explained to him that I wanted Lilli to apply for her passport today. I told him to use his name with the Estonian writers' union. I wanted Lilli's mother's letter to go by courier to Moscow that very day, or the next day at the latest. He had to find a colleague who was coming to Moscow.

"I say, you play the sergeant from early morning on," he said.

I cut him short. "You'll be helping Lilli!"

"It's your life," he said.

"What the hell do you mean?"

"Jack, my boy. You've been married before. I've been married four times. We know that being in love is the easy department. But after seven years the flowers lose their scent."

"Can't you spare me your philosophical nonsense and just help?" I said, more pleadingly than I'd intended.

"Uncle Pyotr is always at your service," he said with assumed gaity.

We heard a horn hooting impatiently outside. It was a black Volga, and as I ran through the pouring rain I could tell from the plates that it came from the fleet of the Central Committee. The chauffeur said nothing and didn't show if he was surprised to be picking up an unshaven and cold foreigner in jeans. He drove with insane speed and a blinking blue light on the roof in the marked-off section of the road that was reserved for official vehicles. On our way to the city we heard the news on the car radio. They only briefly mentioned the riots of the evening before. It was an official TASS report. It described in short, formal phrases that a group of criminal troublemakers had caused violence. There were losses. A government committee had been appointed. Order had been restored. The guilty would be severely punished. That was all.

Basov was waiting for me in the lobby of the Hotel National. He stood, with a wry smile, in his impeccable dark blue suit, on the floor between the four Greek plaster youths who supported the ceiling. They were naked except for the seemly loincloths wrapped around their waists.

"You'd better get dressed," he said, and reached out his hand.

In my room he sat down on a chair and waited while I took

a shower, shaved, and put on a dark suit. I had one of the best rooms in the hotel and was treated very respectfully—the office of the general secretary had reserved it for me. The room was large, with high ceilings and gold embroidered wallpaper. From the small balcony you looked directly at the Kremlin across the square. Through the open door we could hear the rustling of the traffic in the rain down on Revolution Square. Basov said nothing. As I tied my necktie, his silence began to get on my nerves.

"TASS says there are losses?" I said. "But there weren't any details."

"Four killed. Twenty-eight wounded, six of them seriously. There is no reason to alarm the population unnecessarily. The situation is completely under control. It won't happen again." He was like a coiled spring of tension, and he nervously lit a cigarette. His face was gray, as if he hadn't slept all night but had participated in an important crisis meeting. His freshness on the phone had been mere playacting.

He continued, "There are some costs. We have to temporarily suppress a number of unofficial organizations. A regrettable setback. Only temporary. But without discipline there's no reform. Democracy is order and authority before anything else. We can permit neither right-wing nor left-wing extremism."

"As long as the temporary doesn't get permanent," I said.

"Get ready. We have more important things to do than talk," he said with a hardness in his voice that he had never used with me before.

I turned around and faced him. He got up and took his umbrella from the small table and impatiently hit it against his thigh.

"Just one thing, Vladimir. If I am to cooperate one hundred percent, I need your promise that Lilli will be allowed to leave. Otherwise there's no deal," I said in Russian.

He looked at me angrily. "You know our rules. There are certain formalities."

"I'm sure that a call from the office of the general secretary can speed up bureaucratic procedures," I said.

He took one step forward. He was compact and strong, but reached only to right under my chin. He hissed, "You're in no position to make demands. I don't have to tell you that Lilli is illegally in Moscow. I can have her sent to Estonia with a single phone call. I can also, if necessary, put her in jail for fifteen days for refusing to work, hooliganism, and vagabondage. Am I making myself clear?"

I hardly heard the last words before I grabbed him by the throat and forced him up against the wall with a bang that made the glass clink on the large black-and-white Soviet television set in the corner.

"If you as much as touch her or bother her, then I'm not saying one word and I'll kill you. Am I making myself clear?" I shouted, out of control. Fortunately he didn't resist, so I let go of him and sat down heavily in one of the armchairs. He picked the umbrella up from the floor and wiped it demonstratively against his thigh. I grabbed the whisky bottle and looked around for a glass. I was breathing heavily. Basov seemed quite unaffected. He went out in the bathroom and came back with two glasses. We drank.

"I'm sorry, Volody. You didn't deserve that," I said.

"You have a violent streak in your character, Jack. Someday you'll get seriously hurt."

"It's what I have from my father. A strong physique and the fact that I get violent very easily. I've spent all my life trying to suppress and control that damned heritage. Other genes have given me some brains, otherwise I would have been in jail today," I said flatly.

"You don't have to threaten me, Jack. I can't promise you anything, except that I'll personally do what I can."

"That's not good enough, but I can live with it," I said.

He stuck his hand into the inside pocket of his jacket and handed me a black-and-white photograph. It was of a military person. I could tell from his badges that he was a general. He was a handsome man in his sixties with a sharply drawn mouth and his hair intact. He stared straight into the camera with narrow eyes.

"Do you know him?" Basov said.

"Should I?"

"You're a sovietologist. Think."

I dug into my memory and let the many official photographs that I'd studied in my life run past my inner eye. Basov looked at me attentively.

"Sergey Ivanovich Panyukov," I said. "General. War hero. I believe that he wrote his memoirs, and that with typical Soviet modesty he chose a title which, I think, is 'My Blood for My Country: The Glorious Road from Stalingrad to Berlin,' or something like that. Earlier: the Far Eastern theater. Then the general staff. Fired along with others when Matthias Rust landed."

"Retired, but otherwise correct. I knew you had a good memory," Basov said, and got a bit of color in his gray cheeks.

"And then what?" I asked, and reached for the bottle, but Basov moved it out of my reach as if I were a small boy.

"It's a rather long story, but this is what we have: He is a Russian nationalist fanatic. He's opposed to Gorbachev. He wants increased, unlimited means for the military. He has been a member of the Party since he was twenty. He's been decorated several times and claims that he took part in the march from Stalingrad to Berlin in the memoirs that for fifteen years were compulsory reading for all new recruits and high school students. But he is also a murderer."

"Then arrest him," I said.

"We seized the opportunity to get rid of him when the

young West German visited us, but we can't judge him without proof. Maybe we could have done that some years ago, but not today. We have enough circumstantial evidence; but we want a watertight, public trial. Panyukov has become one of the most eager partisans of Pamyat. He scrapes money together for his own gain, but others think that he's doing it for a cause that they hardly understand. The essence is that they think the Russian soul is in danger, and that he is chosen by fate to save it. In reality he is a corrupt devil who lives on the fat of Brezhnev's pickings," Basov said bitterly. He got up and began to walk about in the room.

"I'm not sure I understand what you're aiming at." I said.

Basov thought for a moment before he went on. "General Panyukov is highly respected. One of the good myths of our country. But the myth is based on a lifelong lie. We have a strong suspicion that he is behind a new kind of crime in the Soviet Union. Not directly—he's too smart for that—but indirectly. He picks up dissatisfied Afghanistan veterans and organizes them in units. He uses them for extortion and violence. But he's a sly dog. He must have learned something from the imperialists. For he approaches only corrupt Party members and others who are feathering their own nests and threatens them with violence and disclosure if they don't give him a share. I believe the American mafia calls it protection money," he said.

"You're becoming quite a modern state," I said.

He ignored me and continued, "We also suspect him of running *gontzy.*"

"I don't know that word."

"No, it was kept away from the public when you were here. It's a narcotics dealer who goes out to Central Asia and buys the opium harvest. It's a flourishing business. We can't provide enough food for the population, but we are self-sufficient in illegal heroin," he said with bitterness.

"This new honesty of yours is very becoming."

"I fail to see anything funny about this," he sneered.

"I'm sorry, but I've always had a problem with recent converts who've seen the light."

He looked at me appealingly, and when he was convinced that I wouldn't make more remarks, he continued, "No one wants to report him. He gets his share, not only from corrupt elements in the Party, but also from the underworld. More protection money. You know, an illegal video parlor with pornography. A gambling joint. Prostitutes. If they don't give his Afghanistan gorillas a percentage, they're in for broken legs and cracked jaws."

"You seem to know quite a lot. Last time I was here, no one wanted to say anything," I said.

"We've had more than a hundred of our best criminal investigators on this case and related corruption cases for more than two years. It's only now that we're beginning to be on firm ground. But it's depressing, too, Jack. Every time we peel off another layer, and we think we've reached the bottom, we find a new hollow with slimy maggots."

"You said that he claimed to have taken part in the march from Stalingrad to Berlin?" I said.

Basov looked as if he felt ill at ease about what came next. "Panyukov is one big swindle, but the public doesn't know that. He always stayed at least three hundred miles away from the front. He was a political commissar. He gave patriotic speeches about fighting to the last drop of blood, and then he went home and ate caviar. But he was born under a lucky star: he comes from the same lousy town in the Ukraine as Brezhnev, and they were friends from their youth. You know how Brezhnev rewarded his friends: lots of medals, big dachas, and fat positions. Panyukov and Brezhnev loved to drink together. Panyukov also procured women for Brezhnev. Panyukov is the epitome of the lie that we've been living. He was no war hero, but proclaimed himself one. He was no general, but became one because he knew Brezhnev. He doesn't give a damn about the future of this country, but only wants to continue living a pleasant life."

"It's a wonderful system you've got," I said.

"Shut up, Jack. Don't set yourself up as our judge," he said, and sat down heavily in front of me. "Things have changed and will change. A few rotten apples don't ruin a good harvest."

"No, but as far as I can read in *Pravda*, only Lenin and Gorbachev have been all right. The rest have been more or less regrettable mistakes, committed over a period of seventy years."

"We don't need to be taught by you or anyone else. The Soviet Union can take care of itself. Could we get back to the case?"

"Put the man in jail. Tell people about yet another lie, another myth that was nothing but a balloon filled with hot air."

He looked at me irritatedly as if he were thinking of interrupting the conversation. But then he appeared to pull himself together and took a deep breath before he said, "Proof, Jack. Proof. That's what we must have today. We want no rumors of a show trial. We want an open, public, watertight trial that places Panyukov, Pamyat, and others in such a bad light that the air goes out of the balloon. There must be no doubt. We're dealing with a Russian officer and a war hero. Besides, he still has good connections. Both old friendships and loyalties based on fear."

"It's easier with black-assed Uzbeks or cunning Armenians," I said.

"A conviction of Panyukov would create a good balance. I admit that. But I don't admit that we have been racist. Unfortunately, Brezhnev solved all problems by permitting the local bosses in our brother nations to enrich themselves as long as they saw to it that order and appearances were maintained."

"What's my part in this crusade of yours?" I said.

"I think we can take one more," Basov said, and poured us another spot. I emptied mine at once. He drank his in three small gulps.

"Panyukov has a weakness. It's women. He can't get enough of them. He prefers to have two at a time, and he is supposed to own the most extensive collection of pornographic films in Moscow."

"Now he sounds almost human," I said.

"Also when I tell you that he killed Sonia and Vera?"

"No."

"We think that Vera was a mistake. It got out of hand, and he strangled her by accident. Then he was stricken with panic and knocked Sonia out, placed her in the bathtub, and cut her wrists," Basov said.

"How do you know?" I asked.

"His chauffeur talked, but after a meeting with the general he withdrew everything and claimed that he had been brutalized by the security police. That was before Panyukov was retired. You could hear the sabers rattling from the general staff in Gorky Street all the way to Irkutsk. The long boots stick together. One more thing," he continued, as I was going to interrupt him. "My father-in-law said to me the day before he was killed that he had the final proof. He had identified Panyukov's fingerprints."

"Why wasn't that in the report?"

"That's your fault . . . and mine and my father-in-law's," Basov said. I must have looked rather amazed, and Basov continued, "Remember the whisky bottle we drank? Good. Gavrilin got so angry about our breach of discipline that he stuck the bottle in his pocket. Only some time later did he have it checked. There were the finest fingerprints on it. Yours, mine, his own, and some that the KGB identified without problem as Panyukov's."

"Why didn't he have it checked right away?"

"For one thing he was embarrassed to have removed it. But he didn't take it so seriously. What were we dealing with? A banal accident. When he began to suspect that someone high up in the system was trying to suppress evidence, he began to investigate the case further. He discovered that they had destroyed evidence and became seriously worried. He used his old contacts in the KGB to have the fingerprints on the bottle identified."

"I'm still sorry, Volody. But I can't really see the problem. Other people are in power today."

"We don't know where Gavrilin has hidden them . . . the original prints and the lab report. We were hoping that you might be able to help us."

"And if not?"

"Then our deal still stands. In any event we would like to have you as one of the incorruptible, internationally respected witnesses that will guarantee that no one can start a campaign saying that it's a show trial, that it's persecution. We want to have a murderer convicted, in a courtroom with the whole Soviet and foreign press present. Do you understand what I'm saying? Will you cooperate?"

"I'll be glad to cooperate," I said, and remembered Sonia and Vera the way they had lain extinct and dead in the warm apartment with the buzzing television.

The Volga with the silent chauffeur took us to the Danish embassy, where I picked up my notes from Petersen's safe. I briefly explained to him where I was going to be and promised to keep him informed. Then we drove to the building of the Central Committee next to the Kremlin, and Basov's ID card got us respectfully past the watchful police guard. The interrogation room was on the seventh floor. Like all Soviet offices,

it was rather austere. There was a small table with an uncomfortable high-backed chair in front of a longer table which was
covered with green felt. Bottles of mineral water stood arranged in groups of three. There was a microphone on the
small table and three microphones on the table with the green
felt. To the right was a man in an unbecoming brown suit
holding a shorthand pad. On the wall, Lenin watched over
everything. Two men stood in soft-spoken conversation as we
stepped into the room. They both belonged to the new efficient
type that Gorbachev had promoted: as close as you could get
to yuppies in the Soviet Union, with impeccable suits, well-
shaven cheeks, efficient eyes, and dry hands. Each was some
undefined age between thirty-five and forty-five. When I
served in Moscow, they had been as rare as fruits in March.
Now they had moved into many positions and had pushed the
old people aside with the same ruthlessness with which the
young ambitious career boys in multinational companies move
up full of contempt for those who can't keep up. They were
experts in the new power struggles on the shiny floors and in
the long corridors. A product of the university, connections,
family, and progress. Like Basov, they were Party members in
order to be part of the elite and to forward their career, but
ideology meant nothing to them. They administered and contributed to change a society that they had been born into and
therefore had learned to use.

They introduced themselves with efficient handshakes and
asked about my health and my family. The oldest, who had
close-cropped, grayish hair, was Makarenko. The younger,
with black, half-long hair that was carefully combed away from
the ears, was Grossman, and he was obviously Jewish. He said,
"I'm hoping for a fruitful collaboration. Please sit down."

He indicated the high-backed chair by the small table, and
I sat down. Makarenko sat down in the middle with Basov
and Grossman on either side with their faces turned toward

248

me and their hands resting on the green felt. It was formal from the outset. It quickly became clear why.

"I represent the Office of Public Prosecution," Makarenko said. "Basov you know. He is here as the personal representative of the general secretary. Mr. Grossman represents a special investigation committee against corruption under the Ministry of the Interior. If necessary, we will summon representatives of the Committee for State Security. Before I go on, I inform you that we are being recorded on tape and filmed on video. Is that acceptable?"

I nodded and poured myself a glass of water. I suddenly felt that I was in the chair of the accused and not there as a witness. The atmosphere was cold, efficient, excessively polite, and impersonal.

"Mr. Andersen. Please answer yes or no to our questions for the sake of the stenographer and the tape recorder," Makarenko said.

"It's acceptable that we're being taped and filmed," I said.

Then it began. Makarenko put on a pair of narrow reading glasses and looked down at the papers that he pulled out of a green file that had been brought to him without a sound by a very young man, who had then disappeared again through a door in the back of the room.

"You are Jack Andersen?"

"That's correct."

"Can you declare that you are here in front of an investigative commission of your own free will, and that you are in normal health and do not suffer from mental disturbances?"

"Yes."

"Are you prepared to listen to and answer questions in the Russian language in light of your fluent knowledge of that language and in case of doubt let an authorized Danish-Russian interpreter be summoned?"

"Yes."

"Will you, if necessary, let yourself be called to a public trial as a witness for the prosecution?"

I nodded. Makarenko looked at me over his glasses.

"Please answer yes or no, Mr. Andersen."

"Yes on both accounts," I said.

"Have you been informed that the work of the investigative commission is being recorded on video and on tape?"

"Yes," I said.

"Do you promise to treat the work of the investigative commission as confidential until further notice?"

"Yes."

"Do you declare that you will answer all questions truthfully and without reservation to the best of your ability?"

I straightened myself in the chair and took a sip of water. "As long as it doesn't harm the national interests of my country or my own personal interests," I said.

Makarenko gave me a glance over the narrow glasses. He conferred in a low voice with the two others before he said, "That's acceptable."

Over the next four days they went over the whole chain of events with me, from my arrival at Sonia's apartment to my arrest in Savidova. They were very meticulous, very polite, and very interested in details. We began at ten o'clock in the morning and ended at five in the afternoon. We had lunch for one hour in an adjacent room, a Russian meal with appetizers, soup, a warm dish, ice cream, and coffee. We drank mineral water and tomato juice. The silent chauffeur picked me up every morning and drove me home every evening. At first it was exciting, but soon it became boring. They repeated the questions again and again, constantly returning to details. I identified Dima from Red Square on a black-and-white photograph that looked as if it came from the rogues' gallery of a police station. I pointed out Tatyana, his prostitute, in an album filled with sad, young women's faces. And I confirmed that the now-retired official Kamarassov had declared the case closed in the Ministry of Foreign Affairs. I pointed out the leader of the technical investigation on a photograph. I couldn't remember his name. I only remembered his dark eyes, narrow face, and nicotine-spotted fingers. I recognized him on the photograph right away.

Every now and then I got the feeling that I was behaving like an informer. But I was thinking primarily of myself, rather than that the purpose was to convict a murderer. A bestial, sadistic murderer. If at the same time it served current political interests, that was something I could live with.

The first afternoon I had to use my notes from back then. But already on the second day I could almost go through in my sleep the conversations I had had then. Over and over they returned to my meeting with Colonel Gavrilin on the river. They were never impatient. They were never irritated. Only careful. They reminded me of children with an enormous jigsaw puzzle in front of them, looking for the one small piece that will take them further so that a clear picture can emerge out of chaos.

Every night after the interrogation, Lilli stood waiting patiently for me in Demichev's driveway with her arms crossed over her chest. Anna had persuaded Demichev to move into his small apartment in the city, so we had the big, cozy timber house to ourselves. The weather stayed warm with heavy rain in the afternoons. I came home, and we made love. It was alternately gentle and desperately violent, but never quite happy. It was as if there were an invisible wall of glass between us. We ate and went for long walks on narrow paths in the heavily fragrant wood. I tried to tell her of my life in Denmark with many details, but although she listened, her eyes grew distant as if she would not or could not understand me. She only had vague and often quite incorrect ideas of life in the West.

We stood by Pasternak's grave late one evening. As usual, there were fresh flowers on the grave. We almost had the vast cemetery to ourselves. It was still light, and the birds went on and on singing. The contorted sculptures on the graves stood gleaming in the evening light. A woman dressed in black was arranging flowers on her son's grave. There was now a stone obelisk over him; but the sign that predicted it would be placed there in memory of their dead son, fallen in international service, had been left standing, defiantly, by the family. On the tombstone there was a photograph of the fallen soldier. It showed a square, young face, awkwardly smiling at the photographer. The mother moved about cautiously inside the gray metal fence and touched the soil as if it covered a priceless treasure.

We were sitting on the bench by Pasternak's grave, and I was trying once again to press Lilli to commit herself. She rarely asked me about the interrogations. She had handed in her passport application and her mother's letter. They had been received without comment.

"You don't have to say so much," she said, and placed her hand on mine on the white bench, the paint of which was peeling off. "You have to understand that I can't believe in anything. I'd rather wait and see what happens. I'll take a day at a time. I have said yes to going away with you—but who says that I'll be allowed to?"

We walked home hand in hand past the church, with the smell from the open woodburning stoves in our nostrils. The air was calm, and the smoke rose in a straight line from the chimneys of the small village houses. Around midnight Pyotr arrived with Anna and four writer friends, and we sat for an hour drinking white wine and listening to their intense discussion on literature and its purpose in the society. They were still talking when we went to bed. Lilli fell asleep right away, but I lay awake listening to the distant voices from the garden.

Once again I went over the conversation with Gavrilin and tried to remember what the scenery had looked like. The ice. The river. The magpies. The church. The domes. His ruddy face and his words about God and a young German soldier.

The following day the interrogation was concluded at lunchtime. Makarenko gathered his huge pile of notes and thanked me formally for my irreproachable collaboration.

"Could you come by tomorrow and sign your statement? We'll have a Russian and a Danish version ready."

"Of course."

We walked into the lunch room next door. The table wasn't set for lunch, but there were four small glasses with vodka. Makarenko gave each of us one and raised his own.

"It's a little against the rules. But I think we have earned it," he said, and we all emptied our glasses. There was no second round.

Makarenko said, "You have been very cooperative. The Soviet state is grateful to you. I've been authorized to say that the matter you've discussed with Comrade Basov will be solved without complications."

"You're very friendly," I said in order not to upset the official atmosphere.

He cleared his throat and found support in putting the four glasses carefully back on the plate. He was young and ambitious, but he had all the manners.

He cleared his throat once more.

"I'm also authorized to say that your fiancée will receive a normal passport. By registering regularly at the Soviet embassy in Denmark, she will be able to retain her duties and rights as a citizen of the USSR."

"I appreciate your understanding very much," I said, and cursed my own hypocrisy.

"We don't want to separate our citizens from their families and their country," he said.

"No. You're very humane," I said.

He smiled with relief and extended his hand to me, and I shook his formally. He said, "You still have no idea or haven't been able to deduce where Colonel Gavrilin might have hidden the papers? Speaking quite informally, I mean. Sometimes memory plays strange tricks with us. In dreams hidden layers appear."

"No. I don't know," I lied.

For I did know. It had occurred to me in all its simplicity when I sat with Lilli at Pasternak's grave. But my knowledge was my security. My trump card. I wasn't about to let them know that I held it.

20

I walked from the building of the Central Committee across to the hotel. There were lots of tourists on Red Square. Large clouds loomed up above the stars of the Kremlin. The weather was hot and humid. I changed into a pair of gray pants and a shirt and a short leather jacket, and took along my shoulder bag. I left the National and walked left to the system of passages under Revolution Square, where the subway lines meet. I put five kopecks in the slot and hurried with everyone else through the barrier and let myself be carried into the depths on the escalator that moved with furious speed. I took the green line to Mayakovsky station. I got off, but didn't leave the subway and took another train back under Revolution Square to Paveletskaya. Again I didn't leave the station, but waited for only a second before a new train came rushing in and stopped with shrieking pneumatic brakes. I got on, but right before the automatic doors of the train slammed together, I got off again. I checked along the train. No other passenger had gotten off in a hurry. I didn't know if I was being followed. Actually, I didn't think so, not anymore, but I didn't want to take any chances. Then I rode around at random on several lines, still for the same five-kopeck coin, and finally got off at Smolensk Square. I took trolley bus B down the ring road for four stops. I paid another five kopecks for a ticket in a ticket machine and took a streetcar across the city. Then I got off and walked through narrow streets with only a few people. I saw nothing suspicious, so when one of the yellow state taxis rattled by, I hailed it. The driver didn't want to take me where I was going on the taximeter, but for five rubles he agreed to go there with the meter off.

He let me off right by the bridge before the Silver Wood. I stood with a small group of people waiting for the electric trolley bus. We were sweating in the heat. I had spent almost three hours on the trip, which would normally have taken half an hour directly by taxi. Finally the red trolley bus came, and we got on and each put our five kopecks in the machine and received a ticket. We were only a few people on the bus. I remembered the snow and the ice; but now the wood was dense and green, hiding the secluded dachas almost completely. I stayed on till the end station, where the last two passengers got off. It was a young woman with an eight-year-old child. She was heavy and wore a dress with a big-flowered pattern. She desperately clutched the hand of the boy, who couldn't wait to get into the water. I walked up along the river, looking behind me. I was alone. There were kayaks upon the river, and children and fat women in big bathing suits and tight-fitting bathing caps were swimming near the shore. People sat in groups on blankets or lay sleeping in the sun. They had red noses, and many had folded a *Pravda* into a hat to protect themselves. On my left I had the outskirts of Moscow, and when I looked behind me, I could see the sparkling reflections of the sun in the dilapidated Trinity Church. I walked away from it until I reached the small landing. I bought a ticket and waited patiently with others for the small, smoky ferry. On the river a speedboat passed at full throttle. A policeman in the short-sleeved blue summer uniform shouted at the bathers to stay away from the middle of the river and swim closer to the shore. In front of me there was a rusty iron sign on which it said, in admonishing letters, that it was highly dangerous and therefore prohibited to swim from one shore to the other.

The blue-and-white motor ferry came and disgorged a swarm of people. We were only a few who got on board, mostly women with small children. The ferry belched black smoke and glided out upon the river. It followed the shore for a while, before it crossed and moored on the other side. I stood by the rail, looking at the Silver Wood and remembering the violent, short fight. I also thought of Lilli and of a future with her. I was deeply worried that life in Denmark might not agree with her. When she talked about the future, she wasn't logical. She alternately dreamed of children and of becoming a singer. I didn't have the heart to tell her that both goals would be difficult to achieve. At other times she was evasive and wasn't sure that she wanted to stay in Denmark. She had begun to talk more and more about the United States, which she called the land of opportunities. She said that she knew people who had been allowed to go to America, and who were now doing very well.

I sat down in the grass and smoked a cigarette as I watched the scene: the bathers, the kayaks, the sun worshipers, and the sturdy men who were playing ball with their children. But I could see that people were beginning to pack their things. The sun was still warm, but Moscow's heavy thunderclouds were gathering threateningly on the horizon.

Then I walked up to the church. It stood at the top of a hill, decaying and closed off. The paint was peeling, and there was a heavy padlock on the door. The windows were closed and dusty. It hadn't been used for years. The apartment buildings had moved closer and closer to the church. There was a scaffold around the belfry as if the authorities hadn't yet decided if they wanted to let it fall into such disrepair that they could tear it down with a clear conscience or if they should repair it. Behind the church was a small cemetery. The graves were overgrown with weeds so tall that the tombstones were almost hidden from view. An old woman was puttering about by one of the graves. It wasn't very well kept, either. She tried, but apparently she didn't have the strength for it. She was tiny, almost as broad as she was tall, and she wore a garish, large-flowered dress that left her shriveled arms naked. Around her head she wore an old peasant kerchief of the same nut brown color as her arms. She held on to a rake and stood muttering unintelligibly to herself when I entered the cemetery. A short-handled spade stood leaning up against a weathered tombstone.

I cleared my throat softly in order not to startle her, but apparently she was hard of hearing.

"Good afternoon, babushka," I said loudly. She turned around and screwed her small eyes against the sun.

"You're not a boy," she said. I could hardly understand her. She had only three teeth left in her mouth. Her skin was dark brown from the sun, with tiny, fine wrinkles.

"I thought it was one of the nasty boys from the new houses. They like to bother an old woman. Other than them, no one comes here. They're all dead. God hasn't buried people here for many, many years, may a sinner receive His forgiveness."

"No, I'm not a boy, babushka," I said. She chuckled with pleasure.

"How interesting the way he speaks Russian. Are you from the Baltics, my son?"

"Yes. I'm from Estonia," I said. She again chuckled for no apparent reason.

"You come at the very last moment if you want to tend the dead. Soon they'll be quite gone. Do you have relatives here, or were they liquidated by Stalin, who liquidated my church,

or was it the heathen Nikita? I don't remember." She laughed
and smacked her lips. Then she eagerly began to rake the grass.

"No, babushka," I said, and she started as if she heard my
voice for the first time. "My father told me many times of the
dead Germans who lay buried here."

She again laughed idiotically.

"So you're his son. Yes, he came on a winter's day and talked
about dead Germans." She spat and quickly crossed herself as
she whispered an incomprehensible prayer. "May the Good
Lord forgive me. In death everyone is innocent, even if they
took Vassily, that fool."

"I'm his son," I said.

"I see. So it's all right, I guess. He said it was a secret. I
mustn't say anything to a living soul. Who should I tell it to?
I only talk to myself and the Lord. Who cares what an old
woman says? I said to him. He had to use a mattock. He was
terribly cold, the poor man. I've known cold, so I don't feel
cold anymore. I don't know why God doesn't say that I've
been here long enough." She crossed herself once more and
began to walk, muttering to herself. The sun was hot, and the
grasshoppers zipped through the grass. Toppled tombstones
lay covered by tall grass. Broken vodka bottles bore witness to
old drinking bouts. I grabbed her spade and followed her. She
took me to a corner of the weathered cemetery. There were
three overgrown graves with identical small crosses of disinte-
grating concrete. With difficulty I read the inscription. It had
been black once, but now there were only the dents in the cross
left: Hans Joachim Vogel. Geboren III Mai 1929. Tot II Feb-
ruar 1946.

"It was a hard winter. Hunger took many of the prisoners
of war who worked in the rubble. They were mere children
in much-too-thin coats," the old woman said.

"May I use your spade, babushka?" I said.

"Why not. He probably doesn't mind after so many years.

And it's the very last moment. Soon the big machines will come, they say. Everything must be cleared away. They want to make room for the dead from the war in the warm countries." She laughed her mad laughter and crossed herself. Then she stood for a while muttering incomprehensibly to herself before she left, still mumbling and gesticulating.

The soil was soft, and I had no difficulty digging the turf. Underneath the turf, there was a metal case. It was square and made of aluminum with fittings in the corners and a padlock. It was wrapped in clear plastic. I lifted it up and put it into my shoulder bag. It was no bigger than an LP record and about as thick as a good Russian novel. I didn't want to disturb Hans Joachim unnecessarily and filled the hole again and stamped the turf down on top. I looked around. There was no one but the old woman, who was talking in a low voice to her dead husband's tombstone. I walked over to her and placed the spade up against the stone. She looked at me with surprise.

"Who are you?" she said.

"Thanks, babushka," I said. She laughed and let me see the three gray stumps of teeth.

"What a strange Russian he speaks. It's the son, isn't it?"

"Yes, babushka. It's the son. Thank you so very much and may the Good Lord be with you."

Braying with pleasure, she crossed herself.

"He'll fetch me soon. It's taken him a long time to get around to it."

"Good-bye," I said.

She again stared at me with amazement and mumbled something. Suddenly I felt claustrophobic. I quickly left the cemetery and walked down the hill until I reached the apartment buildings. I held desperately on to my bag. The storm broke, and I had to seek shelter from the pelting rain under a large tree. I stood there for ten minutes, shaking. A younger man came rushing out from a stairway and hurried across the street

to a parked Lada. I ran up to the car and knocked on the
window. He rolled it down one or two inches.

"Are you going to town?" I said over the thunderclaps.

"What if I am?" he said.

"Can you give me a lift?"

"What if I can?"

"Then I'll give you ten rubles."

"Then it's OK," he said.

He drove me right to the door of the embassy and took only
five rubles for the trip. We were both former boxers and spent
the whole trip discussing who would have won if ever Ali and
Stevenson had boxed against each other. The police had two
metallic gray sentry boxes at the embassy. The guards came
outside in the rain when they saw me. I let them look for a
while. Then I rang the bell of the chancellery, and they went
inside as if by command to call their headquarters.

Mikael Petersen was at work. We went out to the garage and
found a heavy pair of tongs with which, in Mikael's office, we
broke open the padlock. The colonel had written a detailed
report and enclosed all the relevant documents. There was the
fingerprint report with the comparison of the various prints
and Panyukov's page in the files of the KGB. There was also
the missing autopsy statement. I read the pages and passed
them on to Mikael, who made copies of them. We carefully
held each paper by the corners and put the originals back in
the metal case with the Ballantine bottle, which was wrapped
in silk paper and thin plastic of the kind that you can wrap
around food.

"Now you're sitting on dynamite," Mikael said.

I gave him a satisfied grin.

"I'm sitting on a passport to freedom," I said.

I walked to Revolution Square and the hotel. I wanted them
to pick up my trail again. I showed my hotel card to the

doorman, who let me in with a smile. He was fat and heavy, as if all the bribes he had received during a long life as a guardian of forbidden fruits had settled around his belly. I went into the Beriozka and bought a bottle of whisky. Then I waited till a stocky young man with a stupid expression came through the revolving door to look for me. They weren't giving me very high priority. He was sweating in his open, patterned shirt and brown leather jacket. He wasn't a good actor, either. He stopped abruptly when he saw me and turned around, but I placed myself between him and the door.

"Just a minute, comrade," I said. "Tell Basov that I'll be in my room."

"I don't know what you're talking about," he said.

"Just tell him, if you don't want to be transferred to Perm as a prison guard in a gulag camp," I said. I could see the fury in his eyes, but he left without a word when I stepped aside.

Back in my room, I placed the whisky on the table and found two glasses. Then I picked up *Pravda* and sat down to wait. Basov arrived twenty minutes later. He knocked, and I let him in. He sat down before he said, "Not very original, but we only had one man on you."

"Where did he lose me, or is that a secret?" I asked.

"It's no secret. He was looking at you through the window when you got off the train. The man's a moron."

"I have something for you," I said, and handed him the envelope. He took the papers one after the other and read them without comment. He meticulously placed each sheet in front of him on the table.

"I also have the bottle," I said. "Identical to the one in front of you on the table."

He looked straight into my eyes.

"This is precisely what we need. But the court will probably ask for originals and not copies."

"You can have the originals in exchange for a passport for

Lilli," I said. His self-control was good—or else he had long since figured it out. He got up and walked over to the telephone. As in all Soviet hotels, there was no switchboard, but a direct line out. He dialed a number. I heard him introduce himself and ask for the head of OVIR. It helps when you can introduce yourself as a representative of the general secretary's office. He was put through right away. It would have taken me or others four days and a letter to get that far.

Basov said, "This is Vladimir Basov, personal assistant to Mikhail Sergeivich. You have a special application for an exit passport for Comrade Lilli Ivanova Smuul. We've discussed the matter previously . . ."

Apparently he was interrupted. He let the man speak for a few seconds before he said, "I don't give a shit that you're closed. There'll be a car with a letter on the general secretary's stationery in one hour. I expect Comrade Smuul's passport to be ready by then and without complications or annotations. Am I making myself sufficiently clear?"

Apparently he was. He cut off the connection with an angry press on the old-fashioned telephone, and then he dialed another number and gave brief instructions. He then sat down in the chair in front of me. He looked relieved, as if a weight had been taken off his shoulders.

"Where do we make the exchange?" he said.

"Come with me to the embassy. They'll probably make us a cup of coffee."

He gave me a broad grin.

"You didn't have to do it, Jack. But I would probably have done the same thing if I'd been in your shoes."

"You can't afford Western shoes," I said.

"Who wants to own that overrated shit when you can have good East German ones," he said, and wiggled his Danish Ecco shoes, which seemed to be the preferred brand of the Soviet yuppies that summer.

"What are we going to do till then?" I asked.

"You might offer me a whisky, and then we can talk about boxing or our unhappy childhoods or something sensible like that. This thing is finally over."

So we did, until they called up from the reception and respectfully told us that there was a chauffeur from the general secretary's office waiting. Would Mr. Andersen and Mr. Basov be kind enough to come down?

Yes, they would.

21

A week later we could leave.

Lilli went back to Tallinn to liquidate her life as a Soviet citizen. In spite of Basov's smoothing the path for us in the immovable bureaucracy, she had to go through a series of formalities. She had to sell and give away her belongings. She had to close her bank account and was permitted to change less than one hundred and fifty dollars. The price of a life. When I gave her the passport, she sat looking at it for a long time, turning the pages one by one as if it were a precious old book. When you've grown up with a passport and the freedom to travel as something natural, it's hard to understand what she felt. She was happy and felt uneasy at the same time. Anna asked to see it and looked at it for a long time. Demichev was free to travel more or less as he wanted, but he had never been permitted to take his Anna with him. We still slept together at Demichev's house. Lilli refused to move into the hotel with me: she said that it was against the law. She was right, of course, but I tried to explain to her that we had the right connections, and that it didn't matter. She didn't want to meet

Basov, either. Things were good in bed now, but in other areas I felt that there was still a distance between us. Seen from the outside we appeared to be very much in love and very happy together. We couldn't be together without holding hands or sitting close to each other. Demichev teased us good-naturedly until Anna made him stop. I didn't mind, but Lilli couldn't take it.

Mikael Petersen took care of all the formalities with the car, and Basov saw to it that my visa was changed so that I could get across the border to Finland.

Lilli came back from Tallinn two days before we were to leave. She never let go of her passport, but kept it on her all the time. The Arm arranged a farewell party for her in his and Silvi's apartment in a suburb. It was a small, one-bedroom apartment in a five-storied building. Next to it there were other, completely identical buildings, like gray toy bricks arranged by a meticulous child. They had been built under Khrushchev and were very dilapidated. In Denmark we would call it a slum. But The Arm and Silvi kept the apartment in very good condition. They had only a few pieces of furniture, but the walls were covered with Silvi's colorful, woven blankets. The Arm had an extensive record collection that he had acquired through those inscrutable, mysterious underground channels that exist in Moscow. People arrived in a steady flow throughout the evening, bringing bottles and food. I felt uncomfortable. It was too emotional for me. There was crying and laughter as if they were taking leave of a person whom they might never see again. They couldn't feel certain that they would be allowed to visit her, or that she would be allowed to return. The heat lay heavy and oppressive over the city, and the temperature in the apartment slowly reached past 85 degrees. The tobacco smoke drifted out through the open windows, and the stereo played loudly. In all corners people sat or stood talking. Lilli was beautiful as never before in a light-colored dress with naked arms. One moment she was radiant with joy, the next she cried bitterly when more friends turned up. It became too much with all those hugs, kisses, and embraces. I sensed former lovers and their shadows everywhere in the apartment, a life that I had not been a part of.

Anna was there and looked after Lilli (Demichev had stayed at home). I felt like an outsider. They greeted me in a friendly manner, but treated me as if I came from another planet. I worked my way across the room to Lilli. She was showing her passport to a slender, handsome young man her own age. He touched her cheek with a gentle movement as if there had been something between them, and Lilli smiled happily at him.

"I'm going to the hotel," I said, and bent down over her. Her hair smelled softly of a mild shampoo that Anna had bought for her in a dollar store. She wore green eye shadow and a bit of lipstick, but otherwise no makeup.

"You don't have to," she said. The young man looked at me with an expression that told me to get lost. Lilli placed her glass of champagne on the floor and drew my head closer and kissed me. First hard, but then more softly. She gently stuck her tongue in between my teeth and caressed my mouth. Then she let go of me. Her cheeks had turned red.

"It'll be hard to do without you," she said.

"You won't have to."

"I'll probably sleep here with The Arm and Silvi tonight, if we get any sleep at all," she said, and let go of my neck. "Why, there's Sascha!" she said without transition. It was the bearded guitarist from her old band at the Praga. He triumphantly held up two bottles of champagne in one hand and a jar half filled with caviar in the other. I understood his enthusiasm. That wasn't easy to get in Moscow.

I stroked her cheek and left. Nobody noticed.

I walked all the way back to the city in the light, warm night. The walk made me sweaty. I took a shower, but couldn't relax, so I went down to the dollar bar. It was packed with drinking business people. Six heavily painted prostitutes were about to get lucky. One of them smiled at me with something that was supposed to look like coquetry as I entered the bar. But when she saw my deprecating expression, she made a face at me and again devoted her attention to a fat, balding man, caressing the back of his head mechanically with an uninterested expression on her painted face. When he looked at her, she lit a smile that was as phony as a neon sign. I had a couple of whiskies and discussed politics with a journalist from London who was contemplating the scene with a mixture of contempt and boredom.

In my room I had one more drink and went to bed. I dreamed of ice floes on the river. The colonel was wearing a bathing suit and stood on a floe shouting something that I couldn't hear. On another floe Lilli sat in a deck chair, naked except for a pair of dark sunglasses. I tried to get in contact with her, but she disinterestedly turned the pages of a colorful magazine. The colonel suddenly had a bell in his hand; it tinkled and jingled. I woke up. The phone rang again. It was half past four.

"*Priviet*, my darling," Lilli said. "I'm just around the corner. I miss you." She sounded drunk.

I still had the dream in my system.

"What do you want?" I said crossly. "Where are you?"

"I'm at a pay phone, I'm telling you. Are you drunk or what? Well, I am. I'm calling to ask if you want to break the law with me."

"Lilli, it's late. Go to bed."

"That's what I'm saying, you fool. Come on. Come and get me!"

Finally I realized what she meant. Then I put on a pair of jeans and a shirt and a pair of sneakers. She stood outside the revolving doors between Anna and the handsome young man from The Arm's apartment.

"She's drunk," Anna said, snapping her fingers significantly

268

under her chin. "But she wanted to see you. We tried to put her to bed." Lilli stood swaying between them. The policeman was staring suspiciously at us. I took her arm and maneuvered her through the revolving door. The doorman raised a single sleepy eyebrow, but didn't stop me. They had long since given up on finding out who I was—they knew that you don't interfere with the affairs of a man who has connections to the Kremlin.

I got her up in the room, undressed her, and placed her on my bed. She threw her arms around my neck and mumbled something incomprehensible in Estonian. She reeked of alcohol and smoke.

"Make love to me, Jackie," she said in English, and fell asleep. I was wide awake and sat on a chair for an hour, drinking and looking at her. It was warm, and she kicked off the eiderdown. I looked at her for a long time and felt warm with joy and unhappy at the same time.

We drove to Leningrad. The almost-new Volvo spun along the bumpy roads. Mikael had made his housekeeper pack a large basket with food and drink for us. Along the road old women sat in front of small houses selling strawberries and carrots. Lilli had recovered completely from her horrible hangover and was in high spirits in the car, talking and making fun. She spent a lot of time putting together a nonexistent music program on the cassette recorder. We had no tapes and were reduced to the mixture of soft classical and idiotic folk music on Mayak. I had the feeling that I might be ready to listen to Bruce Springsteen again without feeling sick. We stayed two nights in Leningrad. I couldn't get out of the Soviet Union fast enough, but Lilli insisted on showing me the city. It was as if she wanted to leave and still didn't dare let go of the life she knew.

We got a large suite at the Astoria. I lay naked on the bed, smoking and watching the news. *Vremya* was just as boring as I remembered it. Lilli was singing in the bathroom, which was almost as big as The Arm's and Silvi's apartment. Over the bed there was a large mirror and a painting of two chubby naked angels in an erotic embrace. I lay there happy and content with the smell of Lilli's body on all of my limbs.

Then they broadcast the story of Panyukov's arrest. He was shown arriving between two police officers. They talked about Sonia and Vera and showed black-and-white photographs of their dead bodies in the apartment. They told of Panyukov's connection with drug traffic. The reporter described with outrage how much money and how many pornographic videocassettes and picture books had been seized in Panyukov's apartment. The reporter stated that, through his connection with important people, Panyukov had unlawfully usurped titles and positions during the period of stagnation. Then came a photograph of me, and the reporter said that the former Danish diplomat, Jack Andersen, had collaborated with competent authorities. Jack Andersen would become a principal witness at the upcoming trial. There were photographs of Dima, Tatyana, and a short sequence showing the Pamyat crowd in the center of Moscow, then the reporter came into frame and looked admonishingly into the camera.

"Not only was Panyukov a criminal. He also manipulated immature elements in the extremist Pamyat movement and stirred up emotions that gave troublemakers free play. Pamyat and Panyukov didn't understand our glasnost and perestroika, but took advantage of the new democratic spirit in our country. The courts haven't spoken yet, but there can be no doubt that the just punishment must be of the most extreme nature."

"Bang!" I said, pointing my hand in front of me like a pistol. Any Soviet citizen would know that the reporter had just announced that Panyukov would be executed.

We walked hand in hand along the canals. We found a small

new cooperative café. The owner said that if we wanted to, we could have wine, but on the bill it would say juice. He brought the sweet, heavy Groznian wine in a dark pitcher. Everyone was drinking wine. We walked back to the hotel in the white night where the light never really fades away. We walked past the equestrian statue of Peter the Great. The promenade was filled with people. The water of the river mouth was shiny and gray, and it emitted a strong smell of salt and seaweed from the Gulf of Finland. We leaned against the brick wall and looked at three metallic gray warships in silhouette and a small ferry that puffed along with a peaceful sound. Lilli breathed deeply in and out.

"I love the sea," she said. "I couldn't stand living in Tallinn, for I had all my friends in Moscow. But in Moscow I always missed the sea."

"My house is right by the sea," I said. "You can always hear it from the garden."

She turned to me and put her arms around my waist.

"I'm looking forward to living in your house. I'd like to live there for a while. Then we must see what happens. That's all I can say."

"That's good enough," I said, although I didn't mean it.

We slowly drifted back past the cathedral and arrived at the Astoria. On the sofa inside in the lobby sat two young men with big mustaches. They both wore blue denim jackets, jeans, and dirty white sneakers.

I didn't think much about it until the next day. We went to bed and tried to emulate the chubby angels in the painting. But the following day I thought I saw one or the other of the two several times. The sneakers, as I called them to myself. Lilli didn't notice anything as we strolled around the city. I remembered how a veteran had once told me that the first thing a Soviet soldier did in Afghanistan was to throw away his high, clumsy military boots and buy himself a pair of sneakers instead. I thought of calling Basov, but didn't. In the evening they again sat in the lobby. I called Moscow, but was told that Basov was out of town. I told his assistant of my observations. I couldn't wait to reach Finland the next day.

It took us a couple of hours to get to the border. We drove slowly and pleasantly along the winding, narrow roads through old Karelia. The sea appeared as we drove through a vacation area. People waddled along in the sun with *Pravda* folded into duckbills and irritatedly slapped themselves because of the many mosquitoes. When we drove through the first frontier gate, Lilli was very nervous, until she discovered that the guard only checked our license plate before he called and got the confirmation that we were in the system and let us go on.

"Is that all?" Lilli said with amazement.

"No," I laughed. "That's just the beginning."

"Don't laugh at me. I've never crossed a border before," she said, and bit her nails.

We got through the next gate and drove up to the frontier station. An older officer with a green cap took our passports. He seemed tense and nervous. With horror, Lilli saw the man take away her passport and disappear with it as he walked up the stairs and into the customs building. I knew the routine, but she didn't. So I took her with me into the building and over to the small counter. The room was cold and gray. There was dust in all corners, and uniformed men from the KGB's frontier corps walked about with expressionless faces, while customs officials in metal gray uniforms examined suitcases. I placed my registration certificate on the counter and filled out a foreign currency form for myself and for Lilli. She looked around with wonder. A busload of German tourists were getting their backs all crooked from dragging their suitcases. They had to haul all their luggage out of the bus and through the customs control. The customs official behind the counter took my registration certificate and the letter from the Danish embassy and opened a large, leatherbound book. He ran a black fingernail down the handwritten columns until he found the number of Mikael's car. Then he wrote something illegible and took my currency forms and the car certificate.

We went back to the car and waited. We could see a soldier with a machine gun in a watchtower. I pointed past the tower.

"There's Finland," I said.

"When can we leave? What is he doing with my passport?" Lilli said.

"It'll take about an hour. It's sheer routine," I said.

Lilli bit her finger again, as if she didn't really believe it. She looked like a Western girl in her jeans and blouse, feet naked in her sandals. She had pushed her sunglasses up on her forehead, but now pushed them back down over her eyes and placed herself inside the car with a nervous, surly expression. I leaned against the hood and smoked a cigarette as I watched how two young mechanics in overalls were destroying an Opel that belonged to a West German. They took it apart and poked and hammered. The German looked desperate and tried to make himself understood with confused protests, but they ignored him. His two children were crying bitterly, while their mother tried to tell them that the car would be put back together again. When they had finished the customs inspection, they pushed the dashboard back into place, but other than that they left most of it to the man himself. The German looked as if he regretted the decision to spend his vacation in the Soviet Union.

They motioned me to move the car up and asked me to take everything out of the car. I opened everything that can be opened in a Volvo, and they checked, but not with any particular zeal.

The customs official ransacked my suitcase loosely and asked me to close it again with a movement of his hand. Lilli didn't get off that easily. He took every single piece of fabric from her two suitcases and carefully checked the seams. He made great play of knocking on the lids of the suitcases and unscrewing the cap of her toothpaste with small, meticulous movements. He opened her shampoo and smelled it and screwed her lipstick apart. He carefully counted the little money that she had and gruffly asked her to pack the suitcases again. She obeyed without saying a word. When she had closed the last suitcase, he asked her to open it again. He wanted to check a book that she had received from Pyotr. It was his latest collection of poems. The official didn't look at the dedication, but examined the title page. If the book had been published before 1970, she wouldn't be allowed to take it out with her. I stood fuming with rage, but didn't interfere. The customs official smoked black cigarettes and spoke only in monosyllables. Lilli didn't answer him. They carried on a silent, but fierce power struggle. Finally they brought in a small, fat, brown dog that sniffed at everything. It didn't find anything, either.

I loaded our suitcases on the car again. Lilli didn't say a word, but sat in the car smoking cigarettes, hidden behind her black sunglasses.

They let us wait for an hour and a half. I imagined how they tried to contact Moscow to confirm that we were allowed to leave together. Lilli grew more and more nervous. I took it more calmly, although I gradually began to wonder what was wrong. I watched how every vehicle was carefully examined, both on the way in and on the way out. It struck me that it would cause a revolution in Western Europe if the same procedures were introduced there. But in the Soviet Union, everybody is guilty until proven innocent.

We heard a helicopter over the station. It sounded as if it were preparing to land.

The official came back.

"Get into the car," he said.

He took my passport and looked at the photograph and at me and again at the photograph.

He handed the passport back and walked over to the other side of the car. His movements were careful and slow. He looked at Lilli from under the front visor of his military cap.

"Comrade Smuul? Or maybe one should say Citizen Smuul now?" He looked from the passport photo to Lilli a couple of times. Beads of perspiration were running down her cheeks, and I could see how she was pressing her hands together in her lap to keep them from shaking too much.

"Take off those glasses!" he said.

"Speak properly!" I said.

He gave me a blank stare.

"Would you mind taking off your sunglasses?" he said when we had stared at each other for a couple of seconds.

Lilli took off her glasses and looked up at him.

"They're green, I see," he said, and handed her the passport. He saluted briefly.

"You may leave now."

I buckled my seat belt, but Lilli sat leaning hard against the back of her seat with her hands folded in her lap.

"What now?" she said.

"Another three hundred feet and we'll be in Finland," I said. She breathed in and out deeply a couple of times while I maneuvered the car out between two trailers that were waiting to be examined.

We drove down toward the last frontier gate and stopped sixty feet before it. I saw two guards come out from the sentry box, but instead of walking up to the side of the car as they normally did in order to check the number of passengers, the oldest of them, an officer, stepped out in the middle of the road and released the safety catch of his machine gun. The gate stayed down. I slammed into first gear the moment he raised the weapon and aimed. The other frontier guard looked bewildered and didn't know what to do. He had never been in a situation like this before.

The general's long tentacles reached all the way into the KGB's frontier corps, I realized in one absurd second, just before I stepped hard on the gas. It was like a film that ran too fast, and yet it was in slow motion. Then time stood still as I saw one half of the officer's head disappear in a cloud of blood before he was hurled along the road.

Basov came running toward the car and motioned me off with the heavy pistol in his hand.

"Go, go, go, goddamnit!" he shouted.

The young frontier guard stood frozen as I let all the horsepower of the Volvo set off with a roar, crashing through the gate into Finland. I heard a rattling sound from a machine gun, but felt nothing. It was the soldier in the watchtower who was opening fire. I drove around the Finnish frontier gate onto a lane for trucks, pulled the wheel to the left, and managed to squeeze the Volvo into a parking lot right behind the Finnish customs building. The guests of the cafeteria were sitting outside at white tables in the mild summer morning. They were like a *tableau vivant* with coffee cups frozen in the middle of a movement from the table to the mouth. The windshield of the Volvo was streaked and milky white. My shoulder hurt from the gall of the seat belt. There was a red spot on the windshield where Lilli had been hurled against it as we crashed through the barrier. She moaned and stirred agitatedly when she opened her green eyes. They were veiled and distant.

"What happened?" she said, and passed out. The radio was playing a Finnish pop song; a shrill woman's voice singing incomprehensibly on a background of many horns and a few chords.

"Nothing. Everything will be OK," I said, and got out of the car.

Two Finnish officers in dark blue uniforms with white diagonal straps came toward me. They had their hands on their pistol cases. I raised my hands.

"What happened? Who are you?" one of them asked in good English.

"Get an ambulance," I said.

"We have to send you back," the other one said. "Why the hell didn't you drive on? Then we could have forgotten all about you."

"It's OK," I said. "Call the other side. A man whose name is Vladimir Basov will tell you that it's all right. But get an ambulance, goddamnit!"

They took me into the customs building. It was clean and neat, filled with light wood and pictures of sunny Finnish lakes. They cautiously carried Lilli on a stretcher with which two men had come running. A small, stocky man from the cafeteria came in puffing, with a bag in his hand.

"I'm a doctor," he said as he tried to get his breathing under control. They placed the stretcher with Lilli on a sofa. While he examined her, they called on a direct line. It was more like a four-wire intercom. I could hear shouting and yelling on the other side. Then came Basov's voice.

"I'm listening," he said formally in Russian.

The Finnish frontier guard asked, "I have a . . ." he looked in my passport. "Jack Andersen and a woman. There was gunfire."

"I know nothing about that," Basov said. "Everything is calm here. They have left the Soviet Union legally."

The Finnish guard looked confused, and I pointed at the receiver. He hesitated and then handed it to me.

"I owe you the world, Volody. Thank you," I said in English. "And thank God you're alive."

"They have penetrated further than we thought. It's we who owe you an apology. I only got your message last night." His voice was tense and rusty, and he had difficulty controlling his breathing. I had to hold the receiver firmly to keep my hand from shaking.

"What now, Volody?" I said.

"We're counting on you for the trial."

"I'll be there, but if things work out, maybe you could come to the wedding," I said.

"Only if there's Russian vodka and champagne. I can't stand your Western dishwater."

"That's a deal," I said, and we were cut off.

"Who were you talking with?" Lilli asked. Her face was white as a sheet, and blood was seeping through the compress that the doctor was gently pressing against her forehead.

"A good friend," I said.

"Let's get her to the hospital," the Finnish doctor said in his neat English. "It will be all right," he added reassuringly when he saw my worried expression.

"What happened? Where are we?" Lilli said as she opened her eyes and closed them again, making the green light disappear.

"We're almost home. Nothing happened," I said, and took the hand that she reached out to me.

ABOUT THE AUTHOR

LEIF DAVIDSEN was born in Denmark. He graduated from the Danish School of Journalism in 1976 and worked for a year as a free-lance journalist based in Madrid, Spain. He then joined the Danish radio, covering cultural and national affairs. Later, he became a foreign correspondent reporting from South America, Europe, Asia, the U.S.S.R., and the United States.

From 1984 to 1988, he was a Danish radio and television correspondent in Moscow. Most recently he has specialized in disarmament and international security, traveling extensively in the eastern European countries. Mr. Davidsen is married, has two children, and lives in Denmark.